OUT OF
THE PAST

OUT OF THE PAST

Tales of Haunting History

edited by

AARON WORTH

This edition published 2024 by
The British Library
96 Euston Road
London NW1 2DB

Selection, introduction and notes © 2024 Aaron Worth
Volume copyright © 2024 The British Library Board

'Come, Follow!' © 1982 The Estate of Sheila Hodgson.
'The Translation of Aqbar' © 2017 Aaron Worth.
'The Theatre of Ovid' © 2018 Aaron Worth.

Cataloguing in Publication Data
A catalogue record for this publication is available from the British Library

ISBN 978 0 7123 5560 5
e-ISBN 978 0 7123 6822 3

Frontispiece illustration from *Les simulachres et historiées faces de
la mort*, Jean de Vauzelles and Hans Holbein, 1538.
Cover design by Mauricio Villamayor with illustration by Sandra Gómez
Text design and typesetting by Tetragon, London
Printed in England by CPI Group (UK) Ltd, Croydon, CR0 4YY

CONTENTS

INTRODUCTION

Horror fiction and historiography have a great deal in common.

One thinks immediately, of course, of their shared obsession with the past—a universal human fascination, no doubt, but one which both historians and traffickers in the supernatural and the macabre might be said to take rather to extremes. Both species of writer are professionally concerned, one might say, with resurrecting the dead—and it is surely no accident that so many of the hapless protagonists in the stories of M. R. James, Vernon Lee, Arthur Machen, H. P. Lovecraft, and others are historians, antiquarians, curators, archivists, and the like. Generally speaking, the tale of terror is haunted by the past, particularly the fear of its survival or return in the present. This dread can be manifested, of course, in the figure of the ghost or revenant. Or, less supernaturally, it can take the form of long-buried secrets coming to light, with baleful consequences.

At least in their modern incarnations, the practices of both historical and horror writing share something like a common origin as well: both might with justice be characterized as offspring of the Enlightenment, the cultural and intellectual movement which gave birth to what we think of as a modern historical consciousness, as well as—as it were by reaction—the darkness and terror associated with the vogue for Gothic. It is perhaps significant, then, that the first horror novels were also, at the same time, historical novels: the harrowing scenes of terror chronicled in Horace Walpole's *The Castle of Otranto* (1764), Clara Reeve's *The Old English Baron* (1778), Sophia Lee's *The Recess* (1783), and Ann Radcliffe's wildly popular novels all unfold within medieval or early modern settings. It is at this point that the respectable literary scholar who has been listening in clears his throat and murmurs condescendingly: "Come, come. Surely you know that those aren't *real* historical novels. Historical fiction was invented (as everyone knows) by Sir Walter Scott in 1814. He was a Serious Writer who grappled with real, er, structural and socio-economic conditions, not mere surface trappings, like perukes, candelabras, and sedan-chairs." And from memory our learned friend quotes, triumphantly, the influential Hungarian critic Georg Lukacs:

> [I]n the most famous "historical novel" of the eighteenth cen-
> tury, Walpole's *Castle of Otranto*, history is likewise treated as
> mere costumery: it is only the curiosities and oddities of the
> milieu that matter, not an artistically faithful image of a concrete
> historical epoch.

Well, there's no need to quibble over definitions here. (And we'll overlook the fact that Scott was himself greatly influenced by Radcliffe, whose "genius" and "fertility of imagination" he praised highly in his *Lives of the Novelists*.) We can agree that with Scott's phenomenally popular Waverley novels, whose influence quickly spread throughout both Britain and the Continent as well as across the Atlantic Ocean, historical fiction came into its own as a distinct genre—one set in the historical past, grounded in research rather than personal experience, and artistically blending fact with fiction. For most of the nineteenth century, such fiction was to be found primarily in novels—we think immediately, for instance, of such works as James Fenimore Cooper's *The Last of the Mohicans*, Charles Dickens's *A Tale of Two Cities*, and Leo Tolstoy's *War and Peace*. But the appearance of the illustrated monthly magazine in the 1890s sparked a big bang of popular short stories which also "heralded," as Michael Cox and Jack Adrian note, "the golden age of short historical fiction" (Arthur Conan Doyle's Brigadier Gerard series, set during the Napoleonic Wars, is an early example). Moreover, historical fiction blended readily, then as now, with other genres and modes—after all, you can set different *kinds* of story in the historical past—resulting in the emergence of subgenres including historical adventure, romance, mystery—and horror.

Early practitioners of what we might call the historical Weird (the truest inheritors, perhaps, of the original Gothic writers' tattered mantle) include such nineteenth-century masters of the macabre as Nathaniel Hawthorne and Sheridan Le Fanu (and it is surely significant that in both cases, a strong sense of shared ancestral guilt helped to motivate their dark tales of colonial New England and Ireland, respectively). In the wake of historical-fiction booms in the late Victorian period and the first decades of the twentieth century (largely fuelled by the success of such authors as Stanley Weyman and Rafael Sabatini), ghost and horror writers looked more and more to the historical past for their settings—and if anything, this trend has only accelerated in recent years: some of the most successful and memorable examples of late-twentieth and twenty-first-century horror fiction, film, and TV have been historical, from Susan Hill's *The Woman in Black* and Dan Simmons's *The Terror* to Robert Eggers's *The Witch*.

It is perhaps not all that difficult to see why, at its best, weird historical fiction and film can be, well, *extra* weird. In some cases, the sheer otherness of the past is itself highlighted, exploited for defamiliarizing effect ("The past," as L. P. Hartley, himself a far from negligible writer of strange stories, famously said, "is a foreign country. They do things differently there"). Conversely, we find it deeply unsettling when historical eras that are seemingly familiar, romanticized, or nostalgized are "weirded" (when, for instance, the smiling governess in Regency bonnet and gown lifts her dress to reveal writhing tentacles…). Often, too, as in many of the stories in this collection, travelling back to earlier periods in our own history gives us a front-row seat to real horrors from the past—war, plague, torture, mass hysteria—horrors which we may think we have left behind—or which, on the contrary, are, as we are only too painfully aware, still with us today (indeed, historical horror can be used to engage directly with the injustices of the past: twenty-first century re-visionings of H. P. Lovecraft's oeuvre like Matt Ruff's (and HBO's) *Lovecraft Country* and Victor LaValle's *The Ballad of Black Tom* come to mind here). And with respect to technique, well-realized historical settings, by lending authenticity and depth to the tale of terror, can add to the sense of unease it generates. Scrupulous period detail can lend a sense of eerie realism to even the weirdest narratives.

In the pages that follow you will be transported to Renaissance Italy, Revolutionary France, and Victorian London. You'll travel to Mexico in the time of the Spanish Inquisition, and to the English countryside during the Civil Wars of the 1640s and the Great Plague of the 1660s, and in the days of the dreaded witch-hunter.

Upon each of these journeys, you'll hopefully feel that special readerly *frisson* of having been transported to another time and place. That is the gift of the well-crafted historical tale.

If the writers have done their job well, you'll feel another, more disconcerting, kind of chill as well. And when you put the book down, you may find yourself concluding that the past is not only a foreign place. It can be a terrifying one as well.

AARON WORTH

A NOTE FROM THE PUBLISHER

The original short stories reprinted in the British Library Tales of the Weird series were written and published in a period ranging across the nineteenth and twentieth centuries. There are many elements of these stories which continue to entertain modern readers; however, in some cases there are also uses of language, instances of stereotyping and some attitudes expressed by narrators or characters which may not be endorsed by the publishing standards of today. We acknowledge therefore that some elements in the stories selected for reprinting may continue to make uncomfortable reading for some of our audience. With this series British Library Publishing aims to offer a new readership a chance to read some of the rare material of the British Library's collections in an affordable paperback format, to enjoy their merits and to look back into the worlds of the past two centuries as portrayed by their writers. It is not possible to separate these stories from the history of their writing and therefore the following stories are presented as they were originally published with one edit to the text, and minor edits made for consistency of style and sense. We welcome feedback from our readers, which can be sent to the following address:

British Library Publishing
The British Library
96 Euston Road
London, NW1 2DB
United Kingdom

PRIDE

Marjorie Bowen

Under the names George R. Preedy, Joseph Shearing, John Winch, Robert Paye, and (most famously) Marjorie Bowen, Gabrielle Margaret Vere Campbell Long (1885–1952) wrote both historical and weird novels and stories, often blending the two modes to fine effect. Her first novel, begun when she was around sixteen, was the historical adventure *The Viper of Milan*, and the settings of her macabre and ghost stories range widely in space and time. Arthur Conan Doyle, whose own forays into historical fiction include the novel *The White Company* and his Brigadier Gerard stories, wrote to Bowen calling one of her collections "easily the best book of historical stories and well on the top in any book of stories" (a compliment somewhat marred perhaps by the accompanying qualifier, "I don't like women's work as a rule").

The following story is taken from the scarce collection *The Seven Deadly Sins*, a volume comprising a series of tales which first appeared in *The Pall Mall Magazine* in 1913–1914, where they were "illustrated in mediaeval manner" by Bowen's sister Phyllis Vere Campbell. "Pride" centres upon the (undoubtedly maligned) historical figure Isabeau of Bavaria (*c.*1370–1435), who became Queen of France in 1385 upon marrying the young Charles VI, whose psychotic episodes, including a homicidal attack on his own escorts in 1392, earned him the soubriquet *le Fol* ("the Mad"). As with many women in history, Isabeau's reputation has been blackened along familiar, gendered lines by historians with factional or political agendas: the writer Louise-Félicité de Kéralio, for instance, in her scurrilous *Les Crimes des Reines de France* (1791), painted Isabeau as a corrupt, profligate, and sexually promiscuous villainess, a portrait which would heavily influence subsequent accounts. Bowen here draws upon these as well as, no doubt, the widespread rumours of necromancy and sorcery which swirled around Charles's court, with Isabeau, among others, being accused of having brought about the madness of the king through diabolical means.

"Pride is the first of the deadly sins and painted in the likeness of a peacock; there are few without this sin in great or small degree, and there is no sin so likely to catch a man by the heels and trip him into Hell's Mouth."

So spake the old monk, sitting by the fire, talking to the young novices on the long winter's evening; they liked to listen to the holy stories the old monk told them, for there was always a good comforting moral and some matter of interest too, for he had been in the world once, and remembered it well enough, though he was now so far on the path to heaven.

"A man without pride," he continued, "is a saint, and a man all pride is a devil, and a dangerous devil—especially if he be not a man at all, but a woman."

"Ah," said the novices wisely, and they looked into the fire and shook their heads and pursed their lips.

The monk finished his glass of Hippocras, wiped his lips and proceeded to tell the story of pride, the first deadly sin.

"When I was in Paris," he said, "learning theology at the Sorbonne, I often saw—riding in a gilt chariot—the Queen."

"The Queen!"

"As you may have heard, her name was Isabeau, and she came from the East; her clothes were a wonder, her life was a scandal; she was quite the proudest creature any man had ever seen or heard of; she boasted that she had never set her foot in the public street nor in the house of one who was of less than blood royal; there was always a body of the Scottish Archers about her car to prevent the

15

mud from touching her wheels, and the foul breath of the baser sort from reaching her.

"But she did not mind their eyes; indeed, she was always raised high on her cushions that they might see her, and if she was in a litter, the curtains were drawn, and her beauty was displayed as freely, nay, as wantonly, as that of any common creature who goes about seeking her price.

"The treasury was empty because of her vesture and her servants and her dainty meats, her silk sheets, her baths of rose-water; the soldiers were few and so were the ships; the peasants were rioting in the country; the nobles pawned their plate, but the Queen went in cloth-of-gold and wore the keep of a regiment in a single ring.

"You will have heard of the King... He was foolish in his mind, and played with clocks and cards all day long in his closet; his only company was his jester, and they were both in frayed robes and ill-nourished. He neither saw the Queen nor asked after her; they said that she had broken his heart and shattered his wits long ago.

"There were, of course, many cavaliers in her train—I have told you she was beautiful; her eyes and her hair were tawny, like a dark tiger-skin, her complexion was clear yet golden, the carnation deep in the cheeks. The whole effect of her face was golden; she sparkled and glowed without the aid of jewels.

"It was said she put dye upon her lips and cheeks, the juice of scarlet geranium petals; I do not know, nor did it matter; she was beautiful as only a proud, shameless woman can be—beautiful to strike the eye and hold the heart, to excite, to subdue, to awe, to lure...

"I often saw her ride past the Sorbonne; her head-dress three or four feet high, scarlet, sparkling with gems, and hung with a thin white gauze veil, that now floated away from her face and now obscured it... Across her shoulders the fine ermine robe, flecked here and there with black, would fall apart, disclosing the loveliness of her bosom beneath the thin cambric sewn with pearls that edged her purple velvet bodice, and then it would be drawn together by the fairest hand in all the world, aye, and on this hand there glittered the royal gems of France.

"She was always alone, always drawn by white horses, eight of them without a speck or flaw, and always followed by the most brilliant knights and nobles in the kingdom—her humble servants all of them, her lovers, some; Duke François or another of her favourites close behind her, almost as magnificent as she herself, and almost as proud. She ruled France in those days—ruled it hideously, without justice, without sense, without pity, her sole object the making of money for her own magnificence.

"Well—there was no one to gainsay her, and her splendour and her licence pleased the great nobles, I suppose—at least they supported her; in the streets and the countryside she was cursed with many oaths, for a foreign wanton, a tyrant, a creature who sucked the blood of the nation. What did she care?

"She never heard them, or, if she did, if any occasional murmur did penetrate the scented atmosphere she breathed, it made no impression on her gilded charm. She was cruel.

"She was also very like the peacock in this; there was little else but pride in that small head beneath the high crown.

"So it happened that she let her ruling vice destroy the only thing she cared for—if indeed it was possible for her to care; who knows?

"One day when she rode abroad she saw a young man looking from an upper window; his arms were folded on the sill and the sunlight was on his face.

"This was no unusual sight, nor was the admiration in his eyes.

"But the Queen looked at him a second longer than her usual wont.

"And the next time she rode that way (it was near the '*Près aux clercs*' and May, and very sunny weather) he was there again, and yet again until in all it was seven times she had seen him leaning from the window in the full sunlight looking down at her. The Duke François saw him; he saw the Queen look up and the young man look down, but he thought naught of it, so serene was he in his pride; could he imagine Isabeau would ever smile on one not of royal blood, or the greatest among nobles?

"So the Duke went his way, swaggering through Paris, and there came a day, about the beginning of June, the court being then at Vincennes, when the young man climbed the palace wall and dropped right at the feet of the Queen where she sat alone in the orchard, in the daisied grass, with her psalter on her knee.

"What followed was a miracle—you may believe what I say, though, for I had it from the young man himself: she rose to her feet—she was in silk from head to foot, with gold on her hair, and he in his ordinary garb, for he was no more than a student at the Sorbonne—and she held out her arms and came to him and they kissed without a word.

"They loved each other; from the first instant their eyes had crossed they loved each other. She had never loved before—not even Duke François; yet her pride was still the stronger, for although she was a woman utterly without shame she kept this love secret—had she loved a Prince she would have flaunted it, but this was only a poor clerk and all her wit and her power were turned to conceal her passion.

"For a while she contrived it—for she had all France at her service, and who was there to spy on her, or to dare to speak if they did, and of whom should she be afraid?

"There was one—Duke François—but in her pride and her absorption in her new love, and her great haughtiness, she disdained him.

"She had dismissed him from her favour as lightly as she would have blown a feather from her sleeve, and *his* pride was sorely hit and his ambition also. I do not know what they had ever been, the one to the other, but she had given him her confidence, and made him virtually King of France, from which he had soaring hopes and delighted in the power her favour left in his hands. But there came a time when she must needs consult him on some affairs of State that she was too idle to attend to or too ignorant to understand, and the Duke perceived in her the effect of advice not his own, and this angered him. For her personal coldness to himself he cared little enough, I think. He was as proud as she and as cruel, but neither so reckless nor so foolish. It was said he schemed to take the place of the poor silly King and would have stopped at nothing to this end, if he could have cloaked his designs beyond discovery.

"He made no complaint now of the Queen's waning favour, nor of the daily humiliations she put on him—for she was not a prudent woman, and too proud to conceal a changed feeling; he served her ever with the same graceful readiness, but his courtesies only masked the fact that he was employing all his wit and skill in finding out his rival, so that he might be revenged.

"At first he suspected the princes of the blood, the court gallants—yet he wondered at her secrecy, and his careful watching and spying convinced him that it was not one of these who had taken his place.

"For a while he was baffled, for she was most careful—cautious and secretive for the first time in her foolish life—and she had not a single confidante...

"But the young clerk was also ambitious, and the excessive fears of discovery the Queen had began to gall him; he thought that she might have brought him to court, and let him ride openly beside her in cloth-of-gold through the streets of Paris. Yet he dared not even suggest such a thing; for when once he hinted to the Queen that she might gild his obscurity she told him that did he once lift his head out of the crowd, Duke François would set his heel on that head and crush it into the dust. So he had to content himself with his secret influence on the affairs of France—he wrought diligently and skilfully on the evil little Queen, and she trusted him with the secrets of the statecraft of France, and he advised her and gave her long scrolls of parchment covered with what she must do, and she meekly obeyed him; it seemed in those days as if she would do all to please him—all and anything save own him.

"You might think that he would have been content, yet he was not, for she had made him take a great oath that never, no matter at what pass, would he disclose that the Queen had loved him.

"This oath rankled within him day and night, till he began to irk and fret at the concealment and to consider what he might have achieved had she set him beside her on the throne of France—of how he might have been bowed down to and worshipped by those people who now took him as naught and never turned their heads to look at him.

"So in all these three pride became the one thing burning up all other passions: in Duke François, angry pride had been supplanted, killing all lingering tenderness for the Queen, humbled pride in her began to dim her true ardour for her plebeian lover, and baffled pride in the clerk began to stifle the passion he felt for Isabeau.

"As the months rolled round to another summer this conflict of pride with the softer emotions of their bosoms became a thing unbearable to all three.

"The Queen had a secret door in her apartments in the Louvre, and when the nights were moonless, and her women dismissed, she would take her lantern and in some cunning disguise or other go forth, let herself out of the Palace with her own keys, hurry along the dark streets of Paris and meet her lover either at the '*Près aux clercs*' where his house stood, or in the cemetery of the Couvent des Innocents, which stood open day and night. In this ghastly place they met not only for love, for the young clerk, in defiance of God and eaten up and maddened by pride, was seeking to raise the Devil or one of his emissaries, who, as he hoped, might help him to thwart the Queen and gain the place he longed for in the councils of France.

"And Isabeau helped in these experiments—her design, which she kept as secret as her lover kept his, being to obtain the aid of the Devil in safely removing Duke François, whom at last she was growing to fear.

"Perhaps a woman's instinct warned her that under his serene air of homage he might be working her fatal mischief.

"She was only afraid of one thing in the world, and that was the discovery of her common lover, and she knew that this very weak spot was that which Duke François would most like to strike.

"About the very heat and height of summer, when the war was faring badly (the English burning and slaying close within a hundred miles of Paris), the people bent beneath taxes heavier than any taxes had been yet even in the bad Queen's time, the harvest poor and rotting on the stalk, the air filled often with storms and the echoes of riots and rebellions and fierce punishments in Picardy and Normandy and Provence, Duke François, after six months of spying and watching, saw, with his own eyes, Isabeau go forth and meet a common clerk in the graveyard of the Couvent des Innocents.

"And then Duke François began to raise the Devil, too, after his own fashion.

"The next day he was the Queen's courtier as usual, bowing and humble at her side, and she was more than ever haughty and cold with him, for his quiet presence and soft manners were becoming daily more intolerable to her and an affront to her pride—yes, an affront to her pride to look at him and imagine his laughter did he know her secret—his laughter at her, the Queen!

"But that evening she was relieved of him; he went to Acquitaine, where his estates were, on the excuse of a rebellion among his vassals, and that he must go to punish with sword and fire those who murmured against his iron government.

"But he left behind him strange rumours—it was said that Devil-worship and Devil-raising were going on in Paris, and that to these unholy dabblings in the black arts were to be traced the misfortunes and disasters overtaking France.

"The priests, who had been made desperate by the silence of the Blessed God to whom they prayed, and somewhat discomposed besides by the temper of the people, who began to complain of a scant return for all their offerings in the churches, were eager enough to catch at these rumours and to encourage and inflame with holy zeal the miserable citizens of Paris, who, in truth, between Queen Isabeau and the English required no Devil to plague them.

"In a short while the rage against Devil-worshippers and the search for them became so fierce in France, and especially in Paris, that Isabeau's lover was frightened and begged her to desist.

"But she was the Queen—she could not imagine danger and herself in the same company; she was infatuate in her study of black magic, and mad to raise the Devil and learn from him how to be rid of Duke François—and how to get money—for she had wrung almost the last mavaredi out of France and she was one who needed to be gorged on gold to live.

"She would not turn back, and so it came about that on one night in August—the fourteenth day of August—in the year '20, this scene took place in the cemetery of the Innocents.

"You may believe what I say, for I was there.

"It was a hot night, but thick, loose black clouds raced across the full yellow midsummer moon and the two figures crouched behind a gaunt tomb were sometimes in silver light and sometimes in complete darkness. One was the Queen and one the young student of the Sorbonne...

"That night she looked most beautiful; she wore a red '*cotehar-die*' and black hose (she was habited like a man) and a short purple cloak and a purple hood drawn over her ebony hair—but no poor sentences of mine could describe the flash and sparkle of her face, the delicate carnation of her cheeks and lips, the velvet sweep of her brows, the shade and softness of her throat: she was a beautiful woman—beauty itself, sirs, the pure beauty of the flesh.

"They had made a horrid brew in an iron cauldron. There were loathsome ingredients in it, that the youth shuddered to handle, but Isabeau cared not; the cauldron stood against the tomb and round it were traced pentacles and mystic signs in white chalk.

"The Queen's white hands were busy in setting fire to the sulphurous mass that she had piled beneath the cauldron, when the moon sailed languidly free of the clouds into the clear dark ocean of heaven, and glancing up, she saw she had raised the Devil indeed; he stood beside the dark wall of the tomb in the guise of Duke François.

"She raised her hand to shield her face—she thought of that even before she turned to flee; but he seized her upflung arm and dragged it down and held her fast. 'Majesty!' he said, and in that one word she heard her degradation—and realized, for the first time perhaps, the utter depths of her fall.

"For the moment sheer terror was uppermost; she appealed to his manhood—the weaker to the stronger—an ancient instinct that had long lain dormant in her imperious soul. But it did not soften him to see her abasement; his pride was mounting as hers sank. He remembered how she had flouted him, and that this was his vengeance.

"He called up his men; they came, hurrying across the graveyard.

"Here mark his devilry—*they were all fellows he had brought from Acquitaine—who had never seen the Queen*—and who beheld now nothing more than a couple of youths caught in the infamous and deadly practices of black magic.

"After them came a whole pack of the baser sort, carrying torches and lanterns and accompanied by several of those fierce dogs of the kind men take with them when they hunt highwaymen and night ruffians, and these, with the enthusiasm of the chase, and the delight of seeing the quarry cornered, and the hope that now the Devil-worshippers were caught the misfortune of France would cease, were beside themselves, leaping, shouting and pushing forward across the gravestones, and only held in check by the pikes of the Duke's men from Acquitaine.

"It may be imagined that though some of them may have glimpsed her golden chariot in the distance, none knew the Queen.

"And she stood with her back against the wall, facing them in the moonshine, so pale now compared with the angry red dancing light of the coarse resin torches of the crowd.

"As for the other youth, the student I mean, he stood numb and bewildered and frightened to death, yet (with the instinct to stand by the woman) staying where he was though none held him. Isabeau looked up at François.

"'You must save me,' she said haughtily, and she signed furiously to her lover to leave her—but he, poor fool! did not understand and

24

instead drew nearer to her, clapping his hand to his outmatched sword.

"'Why should I save you, little witch?' cried the Duke in a loud voice, and he beckoned his followers nearer. 'See justice done to these two,' he said, 'who were so manifestly raising the Devil! What shall their punishment be?'

"And they shouted violently, 'Death'—and Isabeau cowered a little, and then looked at François again and saw what revenge he had prepared for her—she must declare herself before these churls or be done to death by them; there was no pity in Duke François—she knew it in an instant.

"I think that in that instant, too, she had taken her resolve. Pride is a deadly sin, but always a brave one.

"She folded her arms on her bosom and looked sideways at the mob, who ever pressed nearer with shouts of hatred.

"'Tell them who you are,' said the Duke. 'Give them, sweet, your name and quality.'

"She shot a glance up at him and hell-fire flashed in her eyes; she said nothing. He swung her round to face her persecutors. At that the student sprang forward, hardly knowing what he did—or what had happened. 'Whom do you touch—do you know who this is?' he cried, himself not knowing who Duke François was. But the Queen turned on him with all she knew of royalty in her looks and gesture.

"'Silence!' she commanded, 'or I curse you!'

"He fell back at that and was seized by the Duke's guard. He hung his head, he had no great desire to speak, nor for anything on the earth, for he saw that her love had vanished in a flash—that she thought no longer of him... that she was the Queen now, and no longer his lover...

"'Speak!' cried François. 'Will you not speak?'

"Surely he had never believed she would carry it so far... but her sole answer was to laugh.

"She stood full in the moonlight, a small figure, but dauntless; she slipped the royal signet from her finger and dropped it into the rank grass—she had only to show it to gain instant safety, remember.

"But she set her foot on it instead, and laughed at François.

"He had come to shame her and he saw she was minded to baulk him, and in his rage and his fury at the sight of pride carrying her so far he stepped aside and with a gesture offered her to the rage of the crowd.

"His men lowered their pikes and the people surged forward— little knowing on whom they were wreaking vengeance at last.

"And she did not speak... she put her cloak before her face and set her back against the tomb.

"And so died the Queen of France; when the crowd had finished with her she need not have feared recognition.

"Her tattered corse was flung into a ditch—and the Duke rode over it when he left the graveyard; maybe some of her blood was on his horse's hoofs.

"At least he respected her pride; it was given out that she was dead of sudden fever, and there was a gorgeous funeral—with a gorgeous doll in her place, while her bones were nosed by swine.

"The student escaped," added the monk, "or how should I be telling you this?

"And the next deadly sin is Greed, as shown in the tale of the Merchant and the Citron Pies..."

A WEDDING CHEST

Vernon Lee

Violet Paget (1856–1935), who later adopted the name Vernon Lee, was born in France and moved restlessly about the Continent with her family before settling in Italy, where she spent most of her life. Obsessed with history from a very young age (little Violet and her playfellow, the future painter John Singer Sargent, used to wander around Rome, digging up "antique marbles" with their umbrellas), she published her first work of cultural history, *Studies of the Eighteenth Century in Italy*, in 1880. Lee went on to write many learned books: of history, travel, and literary and art criticism, among other subjects; devotees of the weird, however, remember her gratefully for such exquisitely crafted tales of horror as "A Phantom Lover," "Amour Dure," and "A Wicked Voice." Often Lee's fantastic tales feature hapless protagonists, like the young historian Spiridion Trepka in "Amour Dure," who are irresistibly drawn to their doom by their obsessive entanglements with the past. In other stories, Lee's fascination with, and scholarly mastery of, the past manifest themselves in brilliantly realized historical settings. One particularly chilling example is the present *conte cruel*, set in the Umbrian capital of Perugia during the Quattrocento, as we learn from the provenance of the painted *cassone* that gives the story its title.

"A Wedding Chest" first appeared in the jointly published bilingual monthly *Les Lettres et les Arts / Arts and Letters: An Illustrated Review*; it was subsequently included in Lee's 1904 collection *Pope Jacynth and Other Fantastic Tales*.

TO
MARIE SPARTALI STILLMAN
1879–1904

o. 428. A panel (five feet by two feet three inches) formerly the front of a *cassone* or coffer, intended to contain the garments and jewels of a bride. *Subject*: "The Triumph of Love." "Umbrian School of the Fifteenth Century." In the right-hand corner is a half-effaced inscription: *Desider... de Civitate Lac... me... ecit*. This valuable painting is unfortunately much damaged by damp and mineral corrosives, owing probably to its having contained at one time buried treasure. Bequeathed in 1878 by the widow of the Rev. Lawson Stone, late Fellow of Trinity College, Cambridge.[*]

By Ascension Day, Desiderio of Castiglione del Lago had finished the front panel of the wedding chest which Messer Troilo Baglioni had ordered of Ser Piero Bontempi, whose shop was situated at the bottom of the steps of St. Maxentius, in that portion of the ancient city of Perugia (called by the Romans Augusta in recognition of its great glory) which takes its name from the Ivory Gate built by Theodoric, King of the Goths. The said Desiderio had represented upon this panel the Triumph of Love, as described in his poem by Messer Francesco Petrarca of Arezzo, certainly, with the exception of that Dante, who saw the Vision of Hell, Purgatory, and Paradise, the only poet of recent times who can be compared to those doctissimi viri P. Virgilius, Ovidius of Sulmona, and Statius. And the said Desiderio had betaken himself in this manner. He had divided the panel into four portions or regions, intended to represent the four

---

[*]   Catalogue of the Smith Museum, Leeds.

phases of the amorous passion: the first was a pleasant country, abundantly watered with twisting streams, of great plenty and joyousness, in which were planted many hedges of fragrant roses, both red and blue, together with elms, poplars, and other pleasant and profitable trees. The second region was somewhat mountainous, but showing large store of lordly castles and thickets of pine and oak, fit for hunting, which region, as being that of glorious love, was girt all round with groves of laurels. The third region—*aspera ac dura regio*—was barren of all vegetation save huge thorns and ungrateful thistles; and in it, on rocks, was shown the pelican, who tears his own entrails to feed his young, symbolical of the cruelty of love to true lovers. Finally, the fourth region was a melancholy cypress wood, among which roosted owls and ravens and other birds of evil omen, in order to display the fact that all earthly love leads but to death. Each of these regions was surrounded by a wreath of myrtles, marvellously drawn, and with great subtlety of invention divided so as to meet the carved and gilded cornice, likewise composed of myrtles, which Ser Piero executed with singular skill with his own hand. In the middle of the panel Desiderio had represented Love, even as the poet has described: a naked youth, with wings of wondrous changing colours, enthroned upon a chariot, the axle and wheels of which were red gold, and covered with a cloth of gold of such subtle device that that whole chariot seemed really to be on fire; on his back hung a bow and a quiver full of dreadful arrows, and in his hands he held the reins of four snow-white coursers, trapped with gold, and breathing fire from their nostrils. Round his eyes was bound a kerchief fringed with gold, to show that Love strikes blindly; and from his shoulders floated a scroll inscribed with the words—"Sævus Amor hominum deorumque deliciæ." Round his car, some before, some behind, some on horseback, some on foot, crowded those who have been famous for their love. Here you might see, on a bay horse, with an eagle on his helmet, Julius Cæsar, who loved Cleopatra, the Queen of Egypt; Sophonisba and Massinissa, in rich and strange Arabian garments; Orpheus, seeking for Eurydice, with his lute; Phædra, who died for love of Hippolytus, her stepson; Mark Antony; Rinaldo of Montalbano, who loved the beautiful Angelica; Socrates, Tibullus, Virgilius and other poets, with Messer Francesco Petrarca and Messer Giovanni Boccaccio; Tristram, who drank the love-potion, riding on a sorrel horse; and near him, Isotta, wearing a turban of cloth of gold, and these lovers of Rimini, and many more besides, the naming of whom would be too long, even as the poet has described. And in the region of happy love, among the laurels, he had painted his own likeness, red-haired, with a green hood falling on his shoulders, and this because he was to wed, next St. John's Eve, Maddalena, the only daughter of his employer, Ser Piero. And among the unhappy lovers, he painted, at his request, Messer Troilo himself, for whom he was making this coffer. And Messer Troilo was depicted in the character of Troilus, the son of Priam, Emperor of Troy; he was habited in armour, covered with a surcoat of white cloth of silver embroidered with roses; by his side was his lance, and on his head a scarlet cap; behind him were those who carried his falcon and led his hack, and men-at-arms with his banner, dressed in green and yellow parti-coloured, with a scorpion embroidered on their doublet; and from his lance floated a pennon inscribed: "Troilus sum servus Amoris."

But Desiderio refused to paint among the procession Monna Maddalena, Piero's daughter, who was to be his wife; because he declared it was not fit that modest damsels should lend their face to other folk; and this he said because Ser Piero had begged him not to incense Messer Troilo; for in reality he had often pourtrayed Monna

Maddalena (the which was marvellously lovely), though only, it is true, in the figure of Our Lady, the Mother of God.

And the panel was ready by Ascension Day, and Ser Piero had prepared the box, and the carvings and gildings, griffins and chimæras, and acanthus leaves and myrtles, with the arms of Messer Troilo Baglioni, a most beautiful work. And Mastro Cavanna of the gate of St. Peter had made a lock and a key, of marvellous workmanship, for the same coffer. And Messer Troilo would come frequently, riding over from his castle of Fratta, and see the work while it was progressing, and entertain himself lengthily at the shop, speaking with benignity and wisdom wonderful in one so young, for he was only nineteen, which pleased the heart of Ser Piero; but Desiderio did not relish, for which reason he was often gruff to Messer Troilo, and had many disputes with his future father-in-law.

For Messer Troilo Baglioni, called Barbacane, to distinguish him from another Troilo, his uncle, who was bishop of Spello, although a bastard, had cast his eyes on Maddalena di Ser Piero Bontempi. He had seen the damsel for the first time on the occasion of the wedding festivities of his cousin Grifone Baglioni, son of Ridolfo the elder, with Deianira degli Orsini; on which occasion marvellous things were done in the city of Perugia, both by the magnificent House of Baglioni and the citizens, such as banquets, jousts, horse-races, balls in the square near the cathedral, bull-fights, allegories, both Latin and vulgar, presented with great learning and sweetness (among which was the fable of Perseus, how he freed Andromeda, written by Master Giannozzo, Belli Rector venerabilis istæ universitatis), and triumphal arches and other similar devices, in which Ser Piero Bontempi made many beautiful inventions, in company with Benedetto Bonfigli, Messer Fiorenzo di Lorenzo and Piero de Castro Plebis, whom the Holiness of our Lord Pope Sixtus IV. afterwards summoned to work in his chapel in Rome. On this occasion, I repeat, Messer Troilo Baglioni of Fratta, who was *unanimiter* declared to be a most beautiful and courteous youth, of singular learning and prowess, and well worthy of this magnificent Baglioni family, cast his eyes on Maddalena di Ser Piero, and sent her, through his squire, the knot of ribbons off the head of a ferocious bull, whom he had killed *singulari vi ac virtute*. Nor did Messer Troilo neglect other opportunities of seeing the damsel, such as at church and at her father's shop, riding over from his castle at Fratta on purpose, but always *honestis valde modibus*, as the damsel showed herself very coy, and refused all presents which he sent her. Neither did Ser Piero prevent his honestly conversing with the damsel, fearing the anger of the magnificent family of Baglioni. But Desiderio di Città del Lago, the which was affianced to Monna Maddalena, often had words with Ser Piero on the subject, and one day well-nigh broke the ribs of Messer Troilo's squire, whom he charged with carrying dishonest messages.

Now it so happened that Messer Troilo, as he was the most beautiful, benign, and magnanimous of his magnificent family, was also the most cruel thereof, and incapable of brooking delay or obstacles. And being, as a most beautiful youth—he was only turned nineteen, and the first down had not come to his cheeks, and his skin was astonishingly white and fair like a woman's—of a very amorous nature (of which many tales went, concerning the violence he had done to damsels and citizens' wives of Gubbio and Spello, and evil deeds in the castle of Fratta in the Apennines, some of which it is more beautiful to pass in silence than to relate), being, as I say, of an amorous nature, and greatly magnanimous and ferocious of spirit, Messer Troilo was determined to possess himself of this Maddalena di Ser Piero. So, a week after, having fetched away the wedding chest from Ser Piero's workshop (paying for it duly in Florentine lilies), he seized the opportunity of the festivities of St. John's Nativity, when it is the habit of the citizens to go to their gardens and vineyards to see how the country is prospering, and eat and drink in honest converse with their friends, in order to satisfy his cruel wishes. For it so happened that the said Ser Piero, who was rich and prosperous, possessing an orchard in the valley of the Tiber near San Giovanni, was entertaining his friends there, it being the eve of his daughter's wedding, peaceful and unarmed. And a serving-wench, a Moor and a slave, who had been bribed by Messer Troilo, proposed to Monna Maddalena and the damsels of her company, to refresh themselves, after picking flowers, playing with hoops, asking riddles and similar girlish games, by bathing in the Tiber, which flowed at the bottom of the orchard. To this the innocent virgin, full of joyousness, consented. Hardly had the damsels descended into the river-bed, the river being low and easy to ford on account of the summer, when behold, there swept from the opposite bank a troop of horsemen, armed and masked, who seized the astonished Maddalena, and hurried off with her, vainly screaming, like another Proserpina, to her companions, who, surprised, and ashamed at being seen with no garments, screamed in return, but in vain. The horsemen galloped off through Bastia, and disappeared long before Ser Piero and his friends could come to the rescue. Thus was Monna Maddalena cruelly taken from her father and bridegroom, through the amorous passion of Messer Troilo.

Ser Piero fell upon the ground fainting for grief, and remained for several days like one dead; and when he came to he wept, and cursed wickedly, and refused to take food and sleep, and to shave his beard. But being old and prudent, and the father of other children, he conquered his grief, well knowing that it was useless to oppose providence or fight, being but a handicraftsman, with the magnificent family of Baglioni, lords of Perugia since many years, and as rich and powerful as they were magnanimous and implacable. So that when people began to say that, after all, Monna Maddalena might have fled willingly with a lover, and that there was no proof that the masked horsemen came from Messer Troilo (although those of Bastia affirmed that they had seen the green and yellow colours of Fratta, and the said Troilo came not near the town for many months after), he never contradicted such words out of prudence and fear. But Desiderio of Castiglione del Lago, hearing these words, struck the old man on the mouth till he bled.

And it came to pass, about a year after the disappearance of Monna Maddalena, and when (particularly as there had been a plague in the city, and many miracles had been performed by a holy nun of the convent of Sant' Anna, the which fasted seventy days, and Messer Ascanio Baglioni had raised a company of horse for the Florentine Signiory in their war against those of Siena) people had ceased to talk of the matter, that certain armed men, masked, but wearing the colours of Messer Troilo, and the scorpion on their doublets, rode over from Fratta, bringing with them a coffer, wrapped in black baize, which they deposited overnight on Ser Piero Bontempi's doorstep. And Ser Piero, going at daybreak to his workshop, found that coffer; and recognizing it as the same which had been made, with a panel representing the Triumph of Love and many ingenious devices of sculpture and gilding, for Messer Troilo, called Barbacane, he trembled in all his limbs, and went and called Desiderio, and with him privily carried the chest into a secret chamber in his house, saying not a word to any creature. The key, a subtle piece of work of the smith Cavanna, was hanging to the lock by a green silk string, on to which was tied a piece of parchment containing these words: "To Master Desiderio; a wedding gift from

Troilo Baglioni of Fratta"—an allusion, doubtless, *ferox atque cruenta facetia*, to the Triumph of Love, according to Messer Francesco Petrarca, painted upon the front of the coffer. The lid being raised, they came to a piece of red cloth, such as is used for mules; *etiam*, a fold of common linen; and below it, a coverlet of green silk, which, being raised, their eyes were met (*heu! infandum patri sceleratumque donus*) by the body of Monna Maddalena, naked as God had made it, dead with two stabs in the neck, the long golden hair tied with pearls but dabbed in blood; the which Maddalena was cruelly squeezed into that coffer, having on her breast the body of an infant recently born, dead like herself.

When he beheld this sight Ser Piero threw himself on the floor and wept, and uttered dreadful blasphemies. But Desiderio of Castiglione del Lago said nothing, but called a brother of Ser Piero, a priest and prior of Saint Severus, and with his assistance carried the coffer into the garden. This garden, within the walls of the city on the side of Porta Eburnea, was pleasantly situated, and abounding in flowers and trees, useful both for their fruit and their shade, and rich likewise in all such herbs as thyme, marjoram, fennel, and many others, that prudent housewives desire for their kitchen; all watered by stone canals, ingeniously constructed by Ser Piero, which were fed from a fountain where you might see a mermaid squeezing the water from her breasts, a subtle device of the same Piero, and executed in a way such as would have done honour to Phidias or Praxiteles, on hard stone from Monte Catria. In this place Desiderio of Castiglione del Lago dug a deep grave under an almond-tree, the which grave he carefully lined with stones and slabs of marble which he tore up from the pavement, in order to diminish the damp, and then requested the priest, Ser Piero's brother, who had helped him in the work, to fetch his sacred vestments, and books, and all necessary for consecrating that ground. This the priest immediately did, being a holy man and sore grieved for the case of his niece. Meanwhile, with the help of Ser Piero, Desiderio tenderly lifted the body of Monna Maddalena out of the wedding chest, washed it in odorous waters, and dressed it in fine linen and bridal garments, not without much weeping over the poor damsel's sad plight, and curses upon the cruelty of her ravisher; and having embraced her tenderly, they laid her once more in the box painted with the Triumph of Love, upon folds of fine damask and brocade, her hands folded, and her head decently placed upon a pillow of silver cloth, a wreath of roses, which Desiderio himself plaited, on her hair, so that she looked like a holy saint or the damsel Julia, daughter of the Emperor Augustus Cæsar, who was discovered buried on the Appian Way, and incontinently fell into dust—a marvellous thing. They filled the chest with as many flowers as they could find, also sweet-scented herbs, bay-leaves, orris powder, frankincense, ambergris, and a certain gum called in Syrian fizelis, and by the Jews barach, in which they say that the body of King David was kept intact from earthly corruption, and which the priest, the brother of Ser Piero, who was learned in all alchemy and astrology, had bought of certain Moors. Then, with many alases! and tears, they covered the damsel's face with an embroidered veil and a fold of brocade, and closing the chest, buried it in the hole, among great store of hay and straw and sand; and closed it up, and smoothed the earth; and to mark the place Desiderio planted a tuft of fennel under the almond-tree. But not before having embraced the damsel many times, and taken a handful of earth from her grave; and eaten it, with many imprecations upon Messer Troilo, which it were terrible to relate. Then the priest, the brother of Ser Piero, said the service for the dead, Desiderio serving him as acolyte; and they all went their way, grieving sorely. But the body of the child, the which had been found in the wedding chest, they threw down a place near Saint Herculanus, where the refuse and offal and dead animals are thrown, called the *Sardegna*; because it was the bastard of Ser Troilo, *et infamia scelerisque partum*.

Then, as this matter got abroad, and also Desiderio's imprecations against Ser Troilo, Ser Piero, who was an old man and prudent, caused him to depart privily from Perugia, for fear of the wrath of the magnificent Orazio Baglioni, uncle of Messer Troilo and lord of the town.

Desiderio of Castiglione del Lago went to Rome, where he did wonderful things and beautiful, among others certain frescoes in Saints Cosmas and Damian, for the Cardinal of Ostia; and to Naples, where he entered the service of the Duke of Calabria, and followed his armies long, building fortresses and making machines and models for cannon, and other ingenious and useful things. And thus for seven years, until he heard that Ser Piero was dead at Perugia of a surfeit of eels; and that Messer Troilo was in the city, raising a company of horse with his cousin Astorre Baglioni for the Duke of Urbino; and this was before the plague, and the terrible coming to Umbria of the Spaniards and renegade Moors, under Cæsar Borgia, *Vicarius Sanctæ Ecclesiæ, seu Flagellum Dei et novus Attila*. So Desiderio came back privily to Perugia, and put up his mule at a small inn, having dyed his hair black and grown his beard, after the manner of Easterns, saying he was a Greek coming from Ancona. And he went to the priest, prior of Saint Severus, and brother of Ser Piero, and discovered himself to him, who, although old, had great joy in seeing him and hearing of his intent. And Desiderio confessed all his sins to the priest and obtained absolution, and received the Body of Christ with great fervour and compunction; and the priest placed his sword on the altar, beside the gospel, as he said mass, and blessed it. And Desiderio knelt and made a vow never to touch food save the Body of Christ till he could taste of the blood of Messer Troilo.

And for three days and three nights he watched him and dogged him, but Messer Troilo rarely went unaccompanied by his men, because he had offended so many honourable citizens by his amorous fury, and he knew that his kinsmen dreaded him and would gladly be rid of him, on account of his ferocity and ambition, and their desire to unite the Fief of Fratta to the other lands of the main line of the magnificent House of Baglioni, famous in arms.

But one day, towards dusk, Desiderio saw Messer Troilo coming down a steep lane near Saint Herculanus, alone, for he was going to a woman of light fame, called Flavia Bella, the which was very lovely. So Desiderio threw some ladders, from a neighbouring house which was being built, and sacks across the road, and hid under an arch that spanned the lane, which was greatly steep and narrow. And Messer Troilo came down, on foot, whistling and paring his nails with a small pair of scissors. And he was dressed in grey silk hose, and a doublet of red cloth and gold brocade, pleated about the skirts, and embroidered with seed pearl and laced with gold laces; and on his head he had a hat of scarlet cloth with many feathers; and his cloak and sword he carried under his left arm. And Messer Troilo was twenty-six years old, but seemed much younger, having no beard, and a face like Hyacinthus or Ganymede, whom Jove stole to be his cupbearer, on account of his beauty. And he was tall and very ferocious and magnanimous of spirit. And as he went, going to Flavia the courtesan, he whistled.

And when he came near the heaped-up ladders and the sacks, Desiderio sprang upon him, and tried to run his sword through him. But although wounded, Messer Troilo grappled with him long, but he could not get at his sword, which was entangled in his cloak; and before he could free his hand and get at his dagger, Desiderio had him down, and ran his sword three times through his chest, exclaiming, "This is from Maddalena, in return for her wedding chest!"

And Messer Troilo, seeing the blood flowing out his chest, knew he must die, and merely said—

"Which Maddalena? Ah, I remember, old Piero's daughter. She was always a cursed difficult slut," and died.

And Desiderio stooped over his chest, and lapped up the blood as it flowed; and it was the first food he tasted since taking the Body of Christ, even as he had sworn.

Then Desiderio went stealthily to the fountain under the arch of Saint Proxedis, where the women wash linen in the daytime, and cleansed himself a little from that blood. Then he fetched his mule and hid it in some trees near Messer Piero's garden. And at night he opened the door, the priest having given him the key, and went in, and with a spade and mattock he had brought dug up the wedding chest with the body of Monna Maddalena in it; the which, owing to those herbs and virtuous gums, had dried up and become much lighter. And he found the spot by looking for the fennel tuft under the almond-tree, which was then in flower, it being spring. He loaded the chest, which was mouldy and decayed, on the mule, and drove the mule before him till he got to Castiglione del Lago, where he hid. And meeting certain horsemen, who asked him what he carried in that box (for they took him for a thief), he answered his sweetheart; so they laughed and let him pass. Thus he got safely on to the territory of Arezzo, an ancient city of Tuscany, where he stopped.

Now when they found the body of Messer Troilo, there was much astonishment and wonder. And his kinsmen were greatly wroth; but Messer Orazio and Messer Ridolfo, his uncles, said: "'Tis as well; for indeed his courage and ferocity were too great, and he would have done some evil to us all had he lived." But they ordered him a magnificent burial. And when he lay on the street dead, many folk, particularly painters, came to look at him for his great beauty; and the women pitied him on account of his youth, and certain scholars compared him to Mars, God of War, so great was his strength and ferocity even in death. And he was carried to the grave by eight men-at-arms, and twelve damsels and youths dressed in white walked behind, strewing flowers, and there was much splendour and lamentation, on account of the great power of the magnificent House of Baglioni.

As regards Desiderio of Castiglione del Lago, he remained at Arezzo till his death, preserving with him always the body of Monna Maddalena in the wedding chest painted with the Triumph of Love, because he considered she had died *odore magnæ sanctitatis*.

DARK LOT OF ONE SAUL

M. P. Shiel

Matthew Phipps Shiell (1865–1947) was born in the British West Indies, in Montserrat, of a lay preacher father who may have been of mixed race. When he was a boy, his father brought him to the uninhabited Caribbean island of Redonda and declared him to be its king. (Affected belief in the mythical principality's autonomy has persisted, within certain literary circles, ever since, even extending to the granting of spurious titles.) Shiell moved to England in 1885, lopped one of the Ls off his surname, and tried his hand at several different vocations before turning to writing works of detection, horror, fantasy, and science fiction. For some years, during the "yellow nineties," he eked out a precarious existence in London, much like his friend and neighbour there, the great Welsh fantasist Arthur Machen, who said of Shiel, "He tells of a wilder wonderland than Poe dreamed of." The comparison with Poe is particularly apt in Shiel's case, as he clearly modelled many of his stories deliberately after specific tales by the haunted Baltimore author: Brian Stableford has called the present selection, for instance, a "transfiguration" of Poe's 1841 story, "A Descent into the Maelström." Greater success came to Shiel with the coming of the new century, as novels such as *The Yellow Danger* (1898), *The Purple Cloud*, and *The Lord of the Sea* (both 1901) were popular successes. (He is best remembered today for *The Purple Cloud*, a post-apocalyptic work of science fiction second only, among his contemporaries, to the novels of H. G. Wells.)

The remarkable tale "Dark Lot of One Saul," which appeared in periodical form in 1912 before being republished in the 1928 collection *Here Comes the Lady*, begins with its roots sunk in the soil of real history before veering off into psychedelic fantasy: Shiel's narrator, born around 1540, comes of age in the time of the famed Elizabethan "Sea Dogs," royally sanctioned explorer-privateers who, when not plundering Spanish vessels, engaged in (indeed pioneered) the practice of enslaving and selling African people to the Spanish colonies in the West Indies. The voyage with Sir John Hawkins (1532–1595) and Sir Francis Drake (1540–1596) and the three English ships named here, as well as the 1568 Battle of San Juan de Ulúa and its aftermath, are all historical, as is the arrival of the Inquisition in New Spain (Mexico) in 1571.

hat I relate, ladies, is from a document found in a Cowling Library chest of records, written in a very odd hand on fifteen strips of a material resembling papyrus, yet hardly papyrus, and on two squares of parchment, which Prof. Stannistreet recognizes as "trunk-fish" skin; the seventeen pages being gummed together at top by a material like tar or pitch. A Note at the end in a different hand and ink, signed "E. G.," says that the document was got out of a portugal (a large variety of cask) by the Spanish galleass *Capitana* between the Bermudas and the Island of St. Thomas; and out of knowledge that at this point a valley in the sea-bottom goes down to a depth of four thousand fathoms affords, as will be noticed, a rather startling confirmation of the statements made in the document. The narrator, one Saul, was born sixteen to twenty years before the accession of Queen Elizabeth, and wrote about 1601, at the age of sixty, or so; and the correspondence of his statements with our modern knowledge is the more arresting, since, of course, a sailor of that period could only know anything of submarine facts by actual experience. I modify a few of his archaic expressions, guessing at some words where his ink ran.

*

This pressing paucity of air hath brought me to the writing of that which befel, to the end that I may send forth the writing from the cave in the portugal for the eye of who may find it, my pen being a splinter broken from the elephant's bones, mine ink pitch from

45

the lake, and my paper the bulrush-pith. Beginning therefore with my birth, I say that my name in the world was James Dowdy Saul, I being the third child of Percy Dowdy Saul and of Martha his wife, born at Upland Mead, a farm in the freehold of my father, near the borough of Bideford, in Devon: in what year born I know not, knowing only this, that I was a well-grown stripling upon the coming of Her Grace to the throne.

I was early sent to be schooled by Dominie John Fisher in the borough, and had made good progress in the Latin Grammar (for my father would have me to be a clerk), when, at the age of fifteen, as I conjecture, I ran away, upon a fight with Martin Lutter, that was my eldest brother, to the end that I might adopt the sea as my calling. Thereupon for two years I was with the shipmaster, Edwin Occhines, in the balinger, *Dane*, trading with Channel ports; and at his demise took ship at Penzance with the notorious Master Thomas Stukely, who, like many another Devon gentleman, went apirating 'twixt Scilly and the Irish creeks. He set up a powerful intimacy with the Ulster gallant, Master Shan O'Neil, who many a time has patted me upon my back; but, after getting at loggerheads with Her Grace, he turned Papist, and set out with Don Sebastian of Portugal upon an African expedition, from which I felt constrained to withdraw myself.

Thereupon for a year, perhaps two, I was plying lawful traffic in the hoy, *Harry Mondroit*, 'twixt the Thames' mouth and Antwerp; till, on a day, I fell in at "The Bell" in Greenwich with Master Francis Drake, a youth of twenty-five years, who was then gathering together mariners to go on his brigantine, the *Judith*, his purpose being to take part in Master John Hawkins' third expedition to the settlements in Espaniola.

Master Hawkins sailed from Plymouth in the *Jesus*, with four consorts, in October of the year 1567. After being mauled by an equinox storm in Biscay Bay, we refitted at the Canaries, and, having taken four hundred slaves on the Guinea coast, sailed for the West Indies, where we gained no little gold by our business. We then proceeded to Carthagena and Rio de la Hacha; but it should now be very well known how the *Jesus* lost her rudder; how, the ships' bottoms being fouled, we had perforce to run for San Juan de Ulloa in the Gulf of Mexico; and how, thirteen Spanish galleons and frigates having surprised us there, the Admiral de Bacan made with us a treaty the which he treacherously broke at high noon-day, putting upon us the loss of three ships and our treasure, the *Minion* and the *Judith* alone escaping: this I need not particularly relate.

The *Judith*, being of fifty tons portage only, and the *Minion* of less than one hundred, both were now crowded, with but little water aboard, and the store-chests empty. After lying three days outside the sandridge, we set sail on Saturday, the 25th September, having heard tell of a certain place on the east reaches of the Gulf where provisions might be got. This we reached on the 8th October, only to meet there little or nothing to our purpose; whereupon a council was called before Master Hawkins in the *Minion*, where one hundred of us proffered ourselves to land, to the intent that so the rest might make their way again to England on short rations.

The haps of us who landed I will not particularize, though they were various, God wot, remaining in my head as a grievous dream, but a vague one, blotted out, alas, by that great thing which Almighty God hath ordained for a poor man like me. We wandered within the forests, anon shot at by Indians, our food being roots and berries, and within three weeks reached a Spanish station, whence we were sent captives into Mexico. There we were Christianly behaved to, fed, clothed, and then distributed among the plantations—a thing amazing to us, who were not ignorant of the pains put upon English sailors in Spain; but in those days no Holy Office was in Mexico, and on this count were we spared, some of us being bound over to be overseers, some to be handicraftsmen in the towns, etc. As for me, after an absence from it of seven months, I once more found myself in the township of San Juan de Ulloa, where, having ever a handy knack in carpentry, I had soon set myself up for a wright.

No one asked me aught as to my faith; I came and went as I thought good; nor was it long but I had got some knowledge of the Spanish tongue, stablished myself in the place, and taken to wife Lina, a wench of good liking, daughter of Señora Gomez of the *confiteria*, or sweetmeat-store; and out of her were born unto me Morales and Salvadora, two of the goodliest babes that ever I have beheld.

I abode in San Juan de Ulloa two years and eleven months: and these be the two years of quietness and happiness that I have had in this my life.

On the 13th afternoon of the month of February in the year 1571 I was wending homeward over the *prado* that separated my carpentry from the *confiteria* of my mother-in-law, when I saw four men approaching me, as to whom I straightway understood that men of San Juan they were not: one was a Black Friar, so hooded and cowled, that of his countenance nothing was discovered, save the light of his eyes; another was bearded—of the Order of Jesus; another wore the broad chapeau of a notary, and the fourth had the aspect of an alguazil, grasping a baton in his hand. And, on seeing them, I seemed to give up heart and hope together: for a frigate hulk had cast anchor that morning beyond the sandridge, and I conjectured that these men were of her, were ministers of the Holy Office, and had heard of me while I was awork.

I have mentioned that no Inquisition was in Mexico afore 1571: but within the last months it had been bruited in San Juan that King

Phillip, being timorous of English meddling in the gold-trade, and of the spread of English heresy, was pondering the setting up of the Holy Office over Espaniola. And so said, so done, in *my* case, at any rate, who, being the sole heretic in that place, was waylaid on the *prado* in the afternoon's glooming, and heard from the alguazil that word of the familiars: "follow on"; to be then led down the little *callejon* that runneth down from the *prado* to the coast, where a cockboat lay in waiting.

To the moment when they pushed me into the boat, I had not so much as implored one more embrace of my poor mate and babes, so dumb was I at the sudden woe: but in the boat I tumbled prone, although too tongue-tied to utter prayer, whereupon an oarsman put paw upon me, with what I took to be a consoling movement: a gesture which set me belching forth into lamenting. But with no long dallying they put out, having me by my arms; and beyond the sandridge I was took upon the poop's ladder into the frigate, led away to the far end of the forecastle's vault, and there left with a rosca loaf, four onions, and a stoup of water in the sprit room, a very strait place cumbered by the bulk of the bow-sprit's end, and by the ends of a couple of culverins.

I know not yet whither it was the will of my captors to carry me, whether to Europe, or to some port of the Spanish Main; but this I know that the next noon when I was led apoop, no land was visible, and the sea had that hard aspect of the med-sea.

Our ship, the which was called the *San Matteo*, was a hulk of some four hundred tons portage, high afore, and high stuck up apoop, her fore castle having two tiers, and her poop's castle three, with culverins in their ports. Her topsides were so tumbled home, that her breadth at the water may have been double her breadth at her wales, and she had not the new-fangled fore-and-abafts of Master

Fletcher, such as the *Judith* wore to sail on a wind. But she was costly built, her squaresails being every one of the seven of heavy florence, broidered in the belly, and her fifty guns of good brass fabric. She was at this time driving free afore the wind under full spread, but with a rolling so restless as to be jeopardous, I judged. In fact, I took her for a crank pot, with such a tophamper and mass of upper-works, that she could scarce fail to dip her tier of falcons, if the sea should lash.

I was brought up to the master's room, the which was being used as an audience-chamber, and there at a table beheld five men in file. He in the centre, who proved to be both my accuser and judge, presently gave me to know that the evidence against me had been laid before the Qualifiers of the Office—which Qualifiers I understood to be none other than themselves there present—and been approved by the said Qualifiers; and when I had given replies to a catalogue of interrogatories as to my way of life in San Juan, I was then straightway put to the question. My breast, God wot, was rent with terrors, but my bearing, I trust, was distinguished by Christian courage. The interview was but brief: I demurred to kiss the cross; whereupon the President addressed me—he being the Dominic that I saw on the *prado*, a man whose mass of wrinkles, although he was yet young, and his wry smile within a nest of wrinkles, I carry still in my mind. My rudeness, he said, would prove to be but puny: for that during the day I should be put to a second audience in order to move me to a confession, and after to the screws.

For that second audience I waited, but it came not: for, huddled up in a corner 'twixt the sprit's end and a culverin's end, I became more and more aware that the *San Matteo* was labouring in the sea, and by evening mine ears were crowded with the sounds of winds, so that I could no more hear the little sounds of the cook's house, the which was not in the hold, as with English vessels, but in a part of the fore castle abaft my cell. No food was brought me all that day, and I understood that all had enough to trouble them other than my unblest self.

I fell into a deep sleep, nor, I believe, awaked until near the next noon, though between noon and midnight was but little difference in my prison. I now anew knew, as before, of a tumult of winds, and understood by the ship's motion that she was now fleeing afore the gale, with a swinging downhill gait. Toward night, being anhungered, I got to thumping in desperate wise upon my prison, but no signal was given me that any heard me, and doubtless I was unheard in that turmoil of sounds.

And again I fell into forgetfulness, and again about midday, as I conjecture, bounded awake, being now through the door, the which a stripling had just opened. He tumbled toward me with a bowl of tum-tum and pork, and, having shot it upon my lap, put mouth to mine ear with the shout: "Eat, Englishman! Thou art doomed for the ship!"

He then fell out, leaving me in a maze. But I think that I had not ended the meal when the meaning of his words was but little uncertain to me, who was versed in the manners of the sea, and of Spanish seamen in especial; and I said within myself "the *San Matteo* is now doubtless near her end; the sun hath gone out of the sky; the course peradventure lost: and I, the heretic, am condemned to be thrown away, as Jonah, to assuage the tempest."

The rest of that day, therefore, I lay upon my face, recommending my spirit, my wife, and my children to my Creator, until, toward night, three sailors came in, laid hands on me, and hauled me forth; and I was hardly hauled to the castle's portal, when my old samite coif leapt off my head, and was swept away.

Surely never mortal wretch had bleaker last look at the scheme of being than I that night. There remained some sort of disastrous glimmering in the air, but it was a glimmer that was itself but a mood of gloom. A rust on the nigh horizon that was the sun was shining on high above the working of the billows, then hurling itself below, with an alternate circular working, as it were a dissolute or sea-sick thing. The skies were, as it were, tinted with inks, and appeared to be no higher beyond the sea than the mizzen-top, where sea and sky were mixed. I saw that the poop's mast was gone, and the *San Matteo* under two sails only, the mizzen-top sail and the sprit sail: yet with these she was careering in desperate wise like a capon in a scare from the face of the tempest, taking in water with an alternate process over her port and starboard wales, and whirled to her top-castles in sprays: so that she was as much within the sea as on it. Our trip from my prison to the poop's castle must have occupied, with his halts, no less than twenty minutes of time, so swung were our feet between deep and high: and in that time a multitude of sounds the most drear and forlorn seemed borne from out the bowels of the darkness to mine ears, as screams of craziness, a ding-dong of sea-bells, or cadences of sirens crying, or one sole toll of a funeral-knell. I was as one adream with awe: for I understood that into all that war of waters I was about to go down, alone.

Lashed to the starboard turret of the poop's castle by a cord within the ring at its paunch was a portugal, such as be employed to store pork on big voyages; and, sprawling on the deck, with his paws clutching within a window-sill of the turret, was the Jesuit, his robes all blown into disarray, with him being the ship's master, having a hammer's handle sticking out of his pouch, and four others, the particulars of whose persons mine eyes, as though I had scores of eyes that night, observed of their own act.

As I staggered near the lax keeping of my guardians, the portugal was cast aslant to his lashing, and I could then descry within it one of those 30-inch masses of iron ballast, such as be named dradoes; by the which I understood that I should not be tossed forth coffinless, as Jonah, but in the portugal: inasmuch as the corpse of many a Jonah hath been known to "chase i' the wake," as mariners relate, to the disaster of them in the ship; and the coffining of such in ballasted casks has long been a plan of the Spanish in especial.

On my coming to the turret, he whom I took to be the master put hand upon me, uttering somewhat which the hurricane drowned in his mouth, though I guessed that he egged me to go into the portugal: and indeed I was speedily heeled up and hustled in. Resistance would have been but little difficult to me, had I willed, but could have resulted only in the rolling overboard of others with me: nor had I a spirit of resistance, nay, probably lost my consciousness upon entering, for nothing can I remember more, till the top was covered in, save only one segment of it, through which I on my face glimpsed three struggling shapes, and understood that the Jesuit, now upheld 'twixt two of the shipmen, was shouting over me some litany or committal. In the next moment I lay choked in blackness, and had in my consciousness a hammer's banging.

Whether awake or adream, I seemed to recognize the moment when the portugal's mass splashed the ocean; I was aware of the drado's bulk tumbling about the sides, and of a double bump of the iron, the one upon my breast, the other upon my right thigh.

Now, this was hardly owing to the water's roughness, for my last glance abroad before going into the portugal had shewn me a singular condition of the sea: the ship appeared to have driven into a piece of water comparatively calm, and pallid, a basin perhaps half-a-mile in breadth, on a level rather below the rest of the ocean that darkly rolled round its edge; and the whole seemed to me to move with a slow wheeling: for I had noted it well, with that ten-eyed unwittingness wherewith I noted everything that night, as the mariners' apparel, or the four-square cap of the Jesuit crushed over his nose, or the porky stench of the portugal...

Down, swiftly down, and still profounder down, I ripped toward the foundry of things, to where the mountains and downs of the mid-sea drowse. I had soon lost all sense of motion: still, I divined—I knew—with what a swiftness I slid, profoundly drowned, mile on mile, and still down, from the home of life, and hope, and light, and time. I was standing on the drado, no less steadily than if on land, for the drado's weight held the portugal straight on end, the portugal's top being perhaps one inch above my head—for my hands touched it, paddling for some moments as though I was actually adrown, like the paddling pattes of a hound in his drowning. But I stood with no gasping for a good span, the portugal was so roomy; and it proved as good-made as roomy, though soon enough some ominous creakings gave me to know that the sea's weight was crushing upon his every square inch with a pressure of tons; moreover, both my palms being pressed forth against the portugal's side, all at once the right palm was pierced to the quick by some nail, driven inward by the squeezing of the sea's weight; and quickly thereupon I felt a drop of water fall upon my top, and presently a drop, and a drop, bringing upon me a deliberate drip, drip: and I understood that the sea, having forced a crack, was oozing through atop.

No shock, no stir was there: yet all my heart was conscious of the hurry of my dropping from the world. I understood—I knew—when I had fared quite out of hue and shape, measure and relation, down among the dregs of creation, where no ray may roam, nor a hope grow up; and within my head were going on giddy divinations of my descent from depth to depth of deader nothingness, and dark after dark.

Groan could I not, nor sigh, nor cry to my God, but stood petrified by the greatness of my perishing, for I felt myself banished from His hand and the scope of His compassion, and ranging every moment to a more strange remoteness from the territories of His reign.

Yet, as my sense was toward whirling unto death, certain words were on a sudden with me, that for many a month, I think had never visited my head: for it was as if I was now aware of a chorus of sound quiring in some outermost remoteness of the heaven of heavens, whence the shout of ten thousand times ten thousand mouths reached to me as a dream of mine ear: and this was their shout and the passion of their chanting: "If I ascend up into Heaven, He is there; if I make my bed in Hell, behold, He is there; if I take the wings of the morning, and dwell in the uttermost parts of the sea, even there shall His hand lead me, His right hand shall hold me."

But the lack of air, that in some minutes had become the main fact of my predicament, by this time was such, that I had come to be nothing but a skull and throat crowded with blood that would bound from me, but could not; yet I think that in the very crux of my death-struggle a curiosity as to the grave, and the nature of death—a curiosity as frivolous as the frolics of a trickster—delayed my failing; for I seemed to desire to see myself die.

Still upon my top, with a quickening drip, drip, dropped the leak, and this in my extremest smart I ceased not to mark.

But there came a moment when all my sentience was swallowed in an amazing consciousness of motion. First I was urgently jerked against the portugal, the which was tugged sidewards by some might: some moments more, and the portugal bumped upon something.

By a happy instinct, I had stiffened myself, my feet on the drado, my head pressed against the top piece; and immediately I was aware of precipitous rage, haste the most rash, for a quick succession of shocks, upon rocks, as I imagine, quick as you may say one, two, three, knocked me breathless who was already breathless, racking the cask's frame, and battering me back, so to say, out of my death into sense. And or ever I could lend half a thought to this mystery of motion-on-the-horizontal down by the ocean's bottom, I was hounded on to a mystery still more astounding—a sound in the realm of muteness—a roar—that very soon grew to a most great tumult. During which growth of tumult I got the consciousness of being rushed through some tunnel, for the concussions of the cask on every side came fast and more frightfully faster; and I now made out, how I cannot tell, that the direction of my race was half horizontal, and half downward, toward the source of that sounding. How long the trip lasted my spirit, spinning in that thundering dark, could hardly sum up: it might have been a minute or live, a mile or twenty: but there came a moment when I felt the portugal lifted up, and tossed; it was spinning through space; and it dropped upon rock with a crash which ravished me from my consciousness.

So intemperate was this mauling, that upon returning to myself after what may have been many hours, I had no doubt but that I was dead; and within myself I breathed the words: "The soul is an ear; and Eternity is a roar."

For I appeared at present to be a creature created with but one single sense, since, on placing my fingers an inch afore my face, in vain I strained my vision to trace them; my body, in so far as I was any longer cognizant thereof, was, as it were, lost to me, and blotted out; so that I seemed to be naught but an ear, formed to hear unceasingly that tumult that seemed the universe: and anew and anew

I mused indolently within me: "well, the soul is an ear; and Eternity is a roar."

Thus many minutes I lay, histing with interest to the tone of the roar, the which hath with it a shell's echoing that calleth, making a chaunting vastly far in the void, like an angel's voice far noising. What proved to me that I was disembodied was the apparent fact that I was no longer in the portugal, since I at present breathed free; nevertheless, upon becoming conscious in the course of time of a stench of sea-brine, and presently of the mingling therewith of the portugal's stink of pork, I straightway felt myself to be living flesh; and, on reaching out my fingers, felt the sufficient reason of my breathing, to wit, that the portugal's bottom had been breached in, and a hoop there started by his fall, for the staves' ends at that part at present spread all asprawl. I was prostrate upon my back, and the drado and broken portugal's bottom lay over my legs, so that the portugal must have toppled over on his side after striking on his end.

The next circumstance that I now observed was a trembling of the ground on which I lay, the which trembled greatly, as with a very grave ague.

I set myself then to talk with myself, recalling, not without an effort of my memory, the certain facts of my predicament: to wit, firstly, that I had been cast in a cask from a bark called the *San Matteo*, not less than a century agone, I thought; I had then beyond doubt gone down toward the bottom of the sea; here some sea-river had undoubtedly seized and reeled me through some tunnel beneath the sea's base: and the under-tow of this sea-river's suction it was which must have occasioned that basin-like appearance of the sea's surface with a circular working, observed by me some moments before my going in the portugal. This salt torrent, having caught my cask, must have hurtled me through the tunnel to a hollow hall or vault in the bowels of the earth at the tunnel's mouth, and had then hurled the portugal from the tunnel's mouth down upon some rock in the grotto, and so broken the portugal's bottom. The cave must contain the air which it had shut in in the age of the convulsion of nature which had made it a cave, peradventure ere the sea was there, thus permitting me to breathe. And the roar that was roaring should be the thundering of the ocean tumbling down the walls of the hall from out the tunnel's mouth, the preponderousness of which thundering's dropping down occasioned that ague of the ground which was shaking me.

So much I could well sum up; also, from that echo's humming, whose vast psalmodying haunts the waterfall's thunder, I judged that the hollowness of the hall must be large beyond thought. More than this I understood not; but, this being understood, I covered my face, and gave myself to lamenting: for, ever and again, together with the thunder and his echo, worked certain burstings and crashes of the cataract, brief belchings breaching on a sudden, troubling the echo with yet huger rumours, madding sad to hearken to; and my hand could I not descry, stared I never so crazily nigh; and the ague of the ground was, as it were, a shivering at the shout of God-omnipotent's mouth: so that sobs gobbled forth of my bosom, when I understood the pathos of this place.

On throwing my hands over my eyes to cry, I felt on them a slime crass with granules, perhaps splashed upon me through the open end of the portugal on his tumble, the which when I had brushed away, with much anguish I got my head round to where my feet had been. No doubt had I but I should of necessity perish of thirst and the dearth of food; but that I might come to my doom at liberty, I crept forth of my prison, as a chick from the rupture of his shell.

A tinder-box was in my pouch, but, in the swound of my comprehension, I did not then remember it, but moved in darkness over a slime with my arms outstretched, drenched ever with a drizzle, the source of which I did not know. Slow I moved, for I discovered my right thigh to be crushed, and all my body much mauled; and, or ever I had moved ten steps, my shoe stepped into emptiness, and down with a shout I sped, spinning, to the depth.

My falling was stopped by a splash into a water that was warm, into which I sank far; and I rose through it bearing up with me some putrid brute that drew the rheum of his mucus over my face. I then struck out to swim back to the island from whose cliff I had tumbled: for I saw that the cavern's bottom was occupied by a sea, or salt pond, and that upon some island in this sea the cask must have been cast. But my effort to get again to the island availed not, for a current which seized me carried me still quicker, increasing at the last to such a careering that I could no more keep me up over the waves; whereupon an abandonment of myself came upon me, and I began now to drown, yet ever grasping out, as the drowning do; and afore I swooned I was thrown against a shore, where, having clutched something like a gracile trunk, I dragged my frame up on a shore covered over with that same grainy slush, and tumbled to a slumber which dured, I dare say, two days.

I started awake with those waters in mine ear whose immortal harmony, I question it not, I will for ever hear in my heart; and I sat still, listing, afeared to budge, lest I should afresh blunder into trouble, while mine eyeballs, bereft of light, braved the raylessness with their staring. My feet lay at a sea's edge, for I could feel the upwashing of the waves, the which wash obliquely upon the shore, being driven by a current: but near as they were, I could hear ne'er a splash, nor anything could hear, except the cataract's crashing, joined with the voice of his own echoing, whose music tuneth with the thundering a euphony like that of lute-strings with drum ahumming, and anon the racket of those added crashings, when masses more ponderous of the cataract drop; and I did ever find myself listing with mine ear reached sideward, drawn to the darksome chaunting, forgetting my hunger, and the coming of death: listing I wot not how long, perhaps hours, perhaps night-longs: for here in this hall is no Time, but all is blotted out but the siren's sorrow that haunts it: and a hundred years is as one hour, and one hour as a hundred years.

I remarked, however, immediately, that the waves which washed my feet were not warm like that part of the water where I had fallen into the lake; so that I understood that the lake is a cauldron of different temperatures at different parts, the waters which roll in from the ocean being cold, but the lake warmed by flames beneath the cave: indeed, each region of the cave, so far as my feet ever reached in it, is always warm to the hand, and the atmosphere warm, though thick, and sick with stinks of the sea.

After a long while I found the tinder-box within my pouch, wherein also I found a chisel which I was bringing to my house to sharpen on the night of my capture, and also a small gar or gimlet. So I struck a flash that cut mine eyes like a gash, and I kindled a rag, the which glowed a rich gore-colour upon an agitated water rushing past the shore; and although only a small region of the dark was lit up, I could see sufficient of the shore's sweep to understand that I was standing on a mainland made of granite, but not altogether without marl on the ground, nigh behind me being a grove of well-formed growths resembling elms, all gnarled and venerable, yet no taller than my belly, although some do come to my neck. Their leaves be milk-white, and even of a quite round shape, and they do for ever shake themselves with the ground that shakes, and produce a globose fruit, the which is blanched, too, and their boles pallid. I saw long afterwards another dwarf of just the same shape, only his fruit oozeth a juice like soap's water, that maketh a lather. On the lake also I have lately seen by the torch's light near the island a weed with leaves over two yards long, the which be caused to float on the water by small bladders attached to it; and also the marshy spot by the promontory is the forest of bulrushes, that show a tuft, or plume, at their summit, and they do shake themselves, their stem being about three feet high, and they shoot out a single root that groweth visible over the ground seven feet or more in his length, besides which, I observed none other shrubs, save a pale purple fungus, well-nigh white, growing on these rocks where I write, and in the corridor which is on this side of the pond of pitch.

But in that minute's glimmering, while my rag's light was dancing on the waves, I knew what super-abundance of food lay for me in this place, to be had by only putting forth of my hand: for in that paltry area of the water I saw pale creatures like snakes seven or eight feet long, tangled together in a knot, and some more alone, and four globose white beings, so that I could see that the lake is alive with life; and they lay there quite unaware of the light that pried on their whiteness, so that I decided that they be wights deprived of eyes. A very long time later on, probably many years, I came upon the stream to the lake's left, by the promontory, the which is thronged with oysters, with many sorts of pearl, and conch shells: but at the first I saw it not.

To have the creatures of the lake, I take stand to my knees in the water's margin (for farther I may not enter for the strength of the current), lean forward with the torch, and abide the coming of the creature of my liking, the which resembles the creatures called a trunk-fish in the tropics, being of triangular form, with freckles. The species of the creatures of the lake be few, though their number great; and, as all the plants be very pigmy, so all the animals be of great bigness, save one thing resembling a lizard, a finger in his length, that I have seen on the reefs, and his tail is formed in the shape of a leaf, and engorgeth itself grossly, and it gazeth through great globose eyeballs that glare lidless, but they be blind eyeballs; and one only wight of the lake has eyes, but they do hang by a twine out of his eye-sockets, and dangle about his countenance, and be blind. As to their catching, this I managed at starting without so much as a torch, but by the touch alone; nor do their sluggish natures struggle against my grabbing, but by their motions I understand the wonder that they have what creature he might be who removeth them from their secret home. The flesh of one and all is soft and watery, yet cruel tough, and crude to the tongue. My repasts at starting were ate raw; but afterwards I made fires with the tree-trunks, the which being dry-timbered, I could chop down with the chisel and a rock for my hammer. Later on when I did find out the rock-hall, I laid my fire there: but almost all the rags of my garments, except my jerkin, had been burned up for tinder, before I unearthed the marsh of bulrushes, whose pith served me from thenceforth both for tinder and food, and at present also for parchment: for, boiled in the hot rivulet in the rock-hall, the pith and fish together giveth an excellent good food, when, being voided of moisture, and pounded, they become a powder or flour; so that when I had once come at the bulrushes, where, too, are the oysters, being put upon the plan of boiling, I no more roasted my food as before.

For what appeared a long period, as it were long weeks, I mollified my thirst by soaking my body on the shore's verge, where the waves break; but thirst became a rage in my throat, like that lust of light in mine eyes, so that sometimes, pronouncing a shout, I did desperately drench my bowels, drinking my fill of the bitterness, the which, I am convinced, is more bitterer than the bitterness of the outer sea. By this time I had roamed exploring far around that part of the shore on which I was cast up, and had found about me a boundless house of caves, chambers, corridors, with dwarf forests, and stretches of sponges of stone, boulders, and tracts of basalt columns, a fantastic mass to me of rock and darkness, all racked, and like the aspen dancing, to the farthest point of my wandering, all inhabited by the noise of the waters' voice, and stinking of the sea with so raw a breath, that in several spots the nostrils scarce can bear it. There be shells of many shapes and dimensions upon the land, many enamelled with gems and pearl, sea-urchins also, star-fish, sea-cucumbers, and other sea-beasts with spines, mussels nigh to the promontory on the lake's left, corals, and many kinds of sponges, many monstrous huge and having a putrid stench, some, as it were, sponges of stones, others soft, and others of lucid glass, painted gallant with hues of the rainbow, and very gracious shaped, as hand-baskets, or ropes of glass, but crude of odour. Till I had set up my hearth in the rock-hall, I rambled about without any torch, for the cause that I knew not yet well the inflammable mood of the wood, nor had yet tumbled upon the sulphur, nor the pitch, with which to lard the torches; and, walking dark, with just a flash anon, I did often count my footsteps, it might be to a thousand, or two, till tired out. But spite of my ramblings, my body had knobs like leprosy, and was lacerated with my scratching, and racked with the rushing through me of the salt draughts which I drank, afore ever I chanced upon fresh water. That day I descended by three great steps that are made as by men's hands, and that lie peradventure half a mile from the lake, into a basalt hall, vastly capacious, so that forty chariots could race abreast therein; and the walls be as straight as the walls of masons, the roof low, only some twenty foot aloft, flat and smooth and black, and at the remote end of it a forest of basalt columns stands.

There I marked that the air was even warmer than the warm air near the lake, and it was not long ere I had advanced into a hot steaming, with a sulphur stench, the which I had no sooner perceived than I fell upon my hands over a heap which proved, when I had struck a flash, to be slushy sulphur. I also saw a canal cut through the floor across the rock-hall's breadth, as regular as if graved there, this being two feet deep, as I discovered, and two feet across, through which canal babbled a black brook, bubbling hot, the floor on each bank of the canal being heaped with sulphur. I had soon scooped up some of the fluid with the tinder-box, and upon his cooling somewhat, I discovered it to be fresh, though sulphurous, and also tarry, in his taste; and thenceforth I had it always cooling in rows of conch shells by the rock-hall's left wall.

And during all the years of my tarrying in this tomb, the rock-hall hath become, in some manner, my home. There, in a corner nigh the three steps, I made up a fire; I put round it stones, and over the stones a slab, and plaiting my beard into my hair behind me, I there broiled my meat, until the time when I took to boiling the mixed trunk-fish and bulrush in the canal's boiling brook; and for a long while I kept the fire ever fed with wood from the tiny forests: for that I loved his light.

But, as to light, I have nineteen times beheld it in this dark from other causes than mine own fires, seventeen times the light being lightning: for lightning I must call it, the land lightning like the sky: and this I understand not at all. But I was standing by the water's margin, bent upon catching my white blindings, when the cavern became far and wide as it were an eye that wildly opened, winked five million to the minute, and as suddenly closed; and after a minute of thick darkness as afore, it opened once more, quick quivered, and closed. And there all ghast I stayed, in my heart's heart the ghast thought: "Thou, God, Seest Me." But though mine eyes staggered at the glare, I fancy that in fact it was but faint, and the ghost only of a glare, for of the cave's secrets little was thereby revealed unto me: and sixteen times in like wise his wings have quivered, and the wildness of his eye hath stared at me like the visitations of an archangel: and twice, besides, I have beheld the cave lighted by the volcano.

But it was long before ever the volcano came that I fell in with the mescal: for it was no long time after that surprise of lightning that, in pacing once to the shore to take up some trunk-fish which I had thrown in the slush there—I think eight or twelve years may then have gone over me—I happened to bruise in my fingers one of the pigmy globose fruit, and there oozed out of it a milk that I put to my lips. It was bitter, but I did swallow some drops unawares, the result whereof was wondrous: for even ere I reached the beach, an apathy enwrapped my being; I let myself drop down by the breakers' brim; my brow and body collapsed in a lassitude; and my lips let out the whisper: "pour on: but as for me, I will know rest." I was thereupon lapped in trances the most halcyon and happy; the roaring rolled for me into such oratorios as my mouth may not pronounce, though I appeared, so to speak, to *see*, more than to hear, that music; and in the mean time mine eyes, fast closed, had afore them a universe of hues in slow movement and communion, hues glowing, and hues ghostly and gnomelike, some of them new hues to me, so that I knew not at all how to call them, with cataracts of pomegranate grains pattering, waves of parrot green, wheels of raspberry reeling, dapplings of apple and pansy, pallid eyeballs of bile and daffodil, pellucid tulips, brooks of rubies, auroras, roses, all awork in a world earnester than Earth, that it were empty to attempt to tell of.

I had heard tell at San Juan of the shrub which they do name "the mescal button," chewed by the Mexicans to produce upon them such revelations of hues; and I have concluded that this shrub of the cave must be of nature akin. But though the gift of it transfigured that stink-pit beneath the sea into a region of the genii for me, I was aware that to munch thereof was presumptuous, for the troubles that his rancour bringeth upon the body of men were quickly obvious upon me. But I made never an attempt to abandon his happiness, for it wheeleth through the brain to so sweet a strain, and talketh such gossip to the organs of the consciousness, as I do not suppose to be true of the very lotus, nor of that pleasant root that is known as nepenthe.

I have spent years on years, nay, as it seems to me, eras on eras, in one dreaming by the sea's rim, while my soul, so to speak, passed into the cataract's inmost roar, and became as one therewith. I lay there naked, for at first I had preserved my jerkin and shirt to serve for tinder, until I tumbled upon the discovery of the bulrush-pith, whereupon I employed the jerkin and shirt to contain the pith and fish for their boiling; so after the last of my trouser's rags had shredded from around my legs, and my shoes, too, from my feet, through great periods of time I have lain there naked, though enveloped to my belly in my hair and beard, idly dreaming, finding it too dreary a trial to seethe my food, and often eating raw, having long agone let the fire in the rock-hall go out. In the end I have shirked even the burden of bending in the sea's surf, or of journeying to the mussel stream, to get at my grub, and will spend considerable periods with never a hit other drink or meat than that bittersweet milk of the mescal.

From this life of sloth twice only have I been disturbed by fright, the first time when the volcano came, the second time when I observed the increasing dearth of air to breathe; and on each occasion I was spurred to take torch and search further afield than e'er before what the vault holds—in both searches meeting with what

turned out serviceable to my needs: for in the first search I butted on
the bulrush bush, which I believe I butted on years ere I observed
this increasing dearth of air; and it was the increasing dearth of air
which sent me peering further a second time, and then I saw the
pond of pitch. This latter is beyond the forest of basalt columns at
the far end of the rock-hall; and it was in passing to it through those
columns that I saw the beast's bones, that be bigger, I believe, than
several elephants together, although the beast resembles an elephant,
having straight tusks, exceeding long; and his jaw hath six huge teeth,
very strange, every several tooth being made of littler ones, the which
cling about it like nipples; and there among those pillars his ribs may
have rested for many a century, some of them being now brittle and
embrowned; and beyond the pillars is a passage, perfectly curved,
having a purplish fungus growing upon his rock; and beyond the
passage is a cavern than whose threshold I could no farther advance,
for the bed thereof is a bitumen sea, which is half-warm and thick
at the brink, but, I think, liquid hot in the middle; and all over his
face broods a universe of rainbows, dingy and fat, which be from
the fat vapours of the pitch bringing forth rainbows, not rainbows of
heaven, but, so to say, fallen angels, grown gross and sluggish. But
years ere this, I think, I had seen the bulrushes: for, soon after the
volcano came, in roaming over the left shore of the cataract's sea—the
which left shore is flat and widespread, and hath no high walls like
the right side—I walked upon a freshet of fresh warm water, and
after following it upward, saw all round a marsh's swamp, and the
bush of bulrushes. This is where the oysters be so crass, and they be
pearl oysters, for all that soil be crass with nacreous matter of every
sort, with barrok pearls, mother-of-pearl, and in most of the oysters
which I opened pearls, with a lot of conch shells that have within
them pink pearls, and there be also the black pearl, such as they have

in Mexico and the West Indies, with the yellow and likewise the white, which last be shaped like the pear, and large, and his pallor hath a blank brightness, very price less, and, so to say, bridal. As to the bulrush his trunk is triangular (like the trunk-fish), some five inches wide at the bottom, and giveth a white pith good for food. I came, moreover, upon the discovery after a long time that, since this pith lieth in layers, these, being steeped in water, and afterwards dried, do shrink to a parchment, quite white and soft, but tending to be yellow and brittle in time.

But for these two adventures, first to the bulrushes, and then to the pond or sea of pitch, I cannot remember that that long trance I had by the shore was broken by any excursion. But I had a rough enough rousing in that hour when, upon opening mine eyes, I beheld, not the old darkness, but all the hall disclosed in scarlet, and felt the cavern in movement, not with that proper trembling that I knew, due to the pre ponderousness of the cataract's mass over the earth's fabric, but racked with an earthquake's racking: and when mine eyes, now shyer than the night-bird's, recovered their courage, I observed the sea's whole surface heaved up like sand-heaps, dandled up with the earthquake's dancing. Now also for the first time I saw aloft to my right the tunnel's monstrous mouth, out of which the cataract's mass tumbleth down, the mouth's top rim being rounded, like the top lip of a man's mouth crying aloud. I saw also the cataract rolling hoary across his whole breast's breadth, woolly with flocks and beards of froth, as it were Moses' beard, except at the centre, where it gallops glassy smooth and more massy, for there the sea cometh out from the tunnel's inwards to stretch itself out in that mouth that shouteth aloud. I saw also the roof like a rufous sky of rock, and right before mine eyes lay an island, long and narrow, upon the which I had been cast at the first, for there yet lay the portugal on

68

the right end of the island, that right end lying quite nigh the cataract, and the island's left end some twenty yards from the lake's left end. And I saw the lake in his entirety by spying over the island's centre, where the land lies low, the lake having an egg's form, perhaps two miles in his length, I being at the egg's small end. I saw also that the cave's right side, where the wall rises sheer, is washed directly by the lake's wheeling career; and since the cataract there crashes down, along that right side I cannot advance; nor along the cave's left side can I advance so much as a mile, for there a headland juts out into the lake, dividing that side of the cave into two great rooms. I saw also nigh the far shore of the lake four more small islands of rock, and I was shewn, from the lake's ocean-like aspect, that his waters be vastly profound, his bottom being doubtless housed far down in the planet's bowels. All was lit up, and some distance beyond the lake's far boundaries I saw the mouth of some cave, through which came up a haze of radiance sparkling, and vaulting stones, and therewith some tongues of flame, which now showed, and now withdrew their rouge.

I gathered that some volcanic action was going on under the cavern, and as I there stayed, agape at it, I saw arise out of the lake in the remote distance, and come toward me, a thing, with the which I so long had lived, and known it not. His body lay soft in curves on the billows nigh a furlong behind his uplifted head, and I could not fly, nor turn mine eyes from the pitifulness of his appearing in the light. His head and face be of the dimension of a cottage, having a shameful likeness to a death's-head, being bony, skinny, and very tight-skinned, and of a mucky white colour, with freckles. It hath a forehead and nose-ridge, but, where eyes should be, stands blank skin only; and it drew nigh me with the toothless house of his mouth wide open in a scream of fear, distrusting Him that made it: for the air was waxing still hotter, and it may have had an instinct of calamity, peradventure from some experience of the volcano's fierceness a century since. It travelled nigh under the island's right end through the cataract's foam, and then close under me, nor could see me look at his discovered nudity, nor could my rooted foot flee from it; and on it journeyed, circling the lake's surface with the dirge of his lamentation. Immediately after I lost my reason through the fierceness of the heat, and reeled; and when I came back to myself the cave was as black as ever. And once again, long afterwards, I saw flames flutter in the cave beyond the lake, a grey dust rained over the lake's face, the great creature arose, and a grove of the trees at this end were seared with heat; but since then the event has never been seen.

But it was soon subsequent to this second convulsion that I made an observation: to wit, that unless I was well under the rule of the mescal fruit—when I do scarce seem to breathe—I became aware of an oppression of the chest. And this grew with me; so that I began to commune within me, saying: "Though the cavern be vast, the air that it containeth must be of limited volume, and I have inhaled it long: for whereas when I hither came I was a young thing, I am now old. My lungs have day by day consumed the wholesome air; and the day approacheth when I must surely perish."

At the commencement it was only when I lay me to rest that the trouble oppressed me, but, sat I up, it passed; then after, if I sat, it oppressed me; but, stood I up, it passed: so that I understood it to be so that a lake of noxious vapour lay at the bottom of the air of this place, a lake due to my breathing, that each year grew in depth and noxiousness, the longer I breathed: this vapour having a sleepy effect, not happy like the mescal's, but highly unhappy, making me nightmares and aches of my body. In the beginning I got relief by going to live in other regions than in the rock-hall and on the beach: but in every direction my way hath now been blocked, for I have now inhabited in turn every cranny of the cavern whereto I am able to penetrate, and the vapour is in all, troubling also the shrubs of all sorts, the which let fall their heads, and shed their health. There remain some coigns among the rockeries, wherein, when I toil aloft to them, I may yet breathe with some freedom; but that my days are numbered I know. My God! my God! why hast Thou created me?

But soon after understanding the manner of my undoing, I began to argue in myself as regards the cavern and his architecture as never formerly, arguing that whereas so great volumes of water came in, and the vault was not filled, there must needs be some outlet for an equal volume to flow out. I was led to conjecture that the tunnel which admits the sea into the cavern is at some sea-mountain's summit; that the cavern must be in the mountain's bowels; and that the outflow out of the cavern must be down another much longer tunnel, leading down to the mountain's bottom into the sea. I therefore conceived the notion that, if I could reach the portugal, get it repaired, and, in it, introduce myself into the tunnel of outflow (the which I knew to be beyond the headland on the lake's left, where the lake's two wheeling currents meet), then I should be carried down and out into the bottom of the sea, should thereupon rise to the sea's surface—for the unweighted portugal would certainly float with me—and there I might bore a hole or two in the portugal's upper belly for air, and be picked up by a ship before my stores were done, and before my death from hunger or suffocation, I being well drugged with the mescal, and so but little breathing or eating. As to introducing myself into the tunnel of outflow, nothing more was necessary than to get the portugal to the headland's end, get myself into it, and roll myself in the portugal from the headland's end into the lake: where the currents would not fail to bear me toward the place of outflow, and I should be sucked down into the tunnel.

I meditated that the stupendousness of the attempt in no fashion lessened my chance: for that laws will act exactly on the immense scale as on the small. The portugal I could get to by going into the lake at the egg's-point of the lake, whence the current would carry me away along the left shore toward the inland, the left end whereof I might catch by continually swimming strong to the right; and lest I should be dashed to fragments in my grand journey through the tunnel, I determined to pad the portugal's inside with the bulrush pith; and moreover I devised a sliding-door in the portugal's side, the which when I should reach the sea's surface would be furnishing me with breathing: in the making whereof I did not doubt but that my former craft in carpentry would help me out. That I might be struck blind by the moon's brightness, and surely by the sun's, upon opening mine eyes up there above I reflected: but I price eyes as of but paltry value to a man, and should estimate it no hardship to dispense with mine, such as they are. On the whole, I had no fear; and the reason of my fearlessness, as I at present perceive, lay in this: that in my heart I never at all intended to attempt the venture. It was a fond thought: for, granting that I got out, how could I live without the cataract? I should surely die. And what good were life to me there in the glare of day, without the mescal's joys, and without the secret presence of the voice, and the thing which it secretly shouteth? In such separation from the power of my life I should pass frailly away as a spectre at daybreak: for by the power of the voice is my frail life sustained, and thereon I hang, and therein I have my being. And this in my soul I must have known: but in the futile mood that possessed me, I made three several attempts to gain the portugal, terrified the while at mine own temerity; and twice I failed to make the left end of the island, for the current carried me beyond—toward the tunnel of outflow, I doubted not; yet were my terrors not of that horror mainly, but of the monster in the lake's depth, the which stayeth there pale and pensive, meditating his meditations: for I knew that if my foot or hand just touched his skin, I must assuredly reel and sink, shrieking mad, since I swam dark, but having an unlighted torch in my hand, the tinder-box being tied within my beard; and the first twice I was hurled to land upon the headland, but the third time upon the island's left end, and the rock of which I clambered up with my hands lacerated by shells. And after lighting the torch, I wrought my steps toward the island's right end; and there lay the portugal even as I had left it twenty, forty, years ago, the slime on his side yet wet from the waterfall's aura that haunts the island. And in that spot I saw, not the portugal alone, but moreover a sword's hilt, a human skull, and a clock's racket, thither tossed by the cataract. The portugal was still good, for the pitch which is on it: and having cast out the drado by an effort of all my strength, I struck out four of the nails from the three bottom pieces that had been sprung, nailed the three pieces, and the broken hoop of wood, too, to the side of the portugal, and so consigned the portugal to the waters, the which, I was assured, would bear it to the small end of the lake's egg-shape, as they had borne me upon mine ancient fall from the island.

But I had myself no sooner been spued again upon the mainland, more dead than alive, and there found the portugal stranded, then I knew myself for a futile dreamer, wearying myself without sincere motive: for that I should really abandon the cavern was a thing not within the capability of nature. And there by the shore's edge I left the portugal lying a good while, abiding for the most part upon the crags of these rocks that be like gradients on the right side of the hall, until that day when it was suggested to my spirit how strangely had been given me both ink and paper in this place, the knowledge moreover how to get the portugal forth of the grot with a history of that thing which my God in song hath murmured unto me, having furtively hid me with His hand, though a seraph's pen could never express it; nor could I long resist the pressure of that suggestion to write, and send forth the writing in the portugal.

For the portugal's mending I had the gimlet, the chisel, mescal-timber, and some of the nails from the sprung bottom, which could be spared; nor was the job hard, since the one started hoop could be nicely spliced. I rolled and got the portugal up to this level ground in the rocks, surrounding myself, as I wrought, with tarred torches, which I stuck in the rocks' cracks: for down below it is reluctantly if a fire will now burn; and at this height also the torches do burn with shy fires.

Or ever the portugal was repaired, I had got ready the pages for writing, having divided fifteen of the bulrush piths into strips, then wetted, and dried them; but there be spongy spots in them where the lampblack that I have manufactured out of the pitch runneth rather abroad under the spling of fish-bone that serves for my pen, hurting the fairness of my writing. That I could write at all I rather doubted, on the count that I have not for so long handled pen nor spoken, and on the count moreover of the trembling: for not only the pen trembleth by reason of mine age, but the parchment trembleth by reason of the vault's trembling; and between these two tremble-ments, in a sick sheen which flickers ever, these sheets have, letter by letter, been writ. The fifteen sheets of pith, moreover, have proved too little, and I am writing now on the second of two sheets that are sections of a fish's skin.

But now it is finished: and I send it out, if so be a fellow in the regions above may read it, and know. My name, if I have not yet writ it down, was James Dowdy Saul; and I was born not far from the borough of Bideford in the county of Devon.

My God! My God! why hast Thou created me?

I ask it: for the question ariseth of itself to my mind because of the crass facts of my predicament; yet my heart knoweth it, Lord God, to be the grumble of an ingrate: for a hidden thing is, that is winninger than wife, or child, or the shining of any light, and is like unto treasure hid in a field, the which when a man findeth, he selleth all, and buyeth that field; and I thank, I do thank Thee, for Thy voice, and for my lot, and that it was Thy will to ravish me: for the charm of Thy secret is more than the rose, exceeding utterance.

VERSCHOYLE'S HOUSE

Vincent O'Sullivan

Despite the esteem in which he has long been held by connoisseurs of the weird—Montague Summers included no fewer than three of his stories in his landmark *Supernatural Omnibus*, and Jessica Amanda Salmonson calls him "one of the world's great authors of horror fiction"—Vincent O'Sullivan (1868–1940) has remained a relatively obscure figure even among devoted readers of horror today. Born in New York City, O'Sullivan studied at Oxford before gravitating to London, where he found himself at the centre of the Decadent movement which flourished in the Yellow Nineties. He numbered among his friends the poet Ernest Dowson, the artist Aubrey Beardsley (who provided a cover and frontispiece, respectively, for two of O'Sullivan's books), and the immortal writer Oscar Wilde, who once quipped that Vincent was "really very pleasant, for one who treats life from the standpoint of the tomb." In 1896 O'Sullivan's first collection of stories, *A Book of Bargains*, appeared; a Decadent production through and through, it contains most of his better-known stories, including "The Business of Madame Jahn," "When I Was Dead," and "The Bargain of Rupert Orange." Perhaps O'Sullivan's greatest weird work, however, is the present novella, which first appeared in the 1907 collection *Human Affairs*. The historical backdrop for this disturbing tale of supernatural possession is the English Civil War and its aftermath, a turbulent period which also provides the setting for Adrian Ross's nearly contemporaneous novel *The Hole of the Pit*.

A host of historical figures are referenced here, among them Charles I, Oliver Cromwell, and the courtier, natural philosopher, and astrologer Sir Kenelm Digby (perhaps O'Sullivan's original inspiration for the villainous Verschoyle). The tale is particularly impressive in its mastery of the language of a bygone age, especially in Verschoyle's letters (I wonder if H. P. Lovecraft might possibly have read this novella before writing *The Case of Charles Dexter Ward*, with its similarly archaic correspondence?).

ir John Holdershaw, living retired in Paris in the year 1689, went one day to the Comédie, where was acted a piece by Boursault with which he was much discontented. When he had returned to his lodgings, he wrote in his notebook, after violently censuring the play, what follows: "In the first act, before I went asleep, there was a part (but 't is true writ here by Mons. Borsalte in a vein of fooling) which minded me (though far enough off), and my countryman Mr. Amcotts too, of a story told in our country of old Mr. Verschoyle, in King Charles and Oliver Protector's time: And I did promise a gentleman last night I would write it down for him; but what with watchings and silly healths my fingers and head tremble woundily of a morning."—Some time later he composed his differences with King William's government, and returned to live quietly on his estates. His life in the country seemed to weigh heavily upon him, and it was, as he said, "To tear myself from my chagrins, and the slow hours, and the thoughts of poisonous devouring rascals who have drawn me in, and now undermine me in the country, that I have undertook to reach down some bright pictures hanging in my mind, which soon must fade otherwise." Accordingly he wrote out various pieces concerning the adventures of his life, and also three or four tales he had picked up here and there; among them the one he had been reminded of at Paris. It is chiefly from Sir John's narrative that the ensuing pages have been taken.

I

In the early part of 1645, on a cold dull morning, King Charles, walking slowly, against his wont, in the Christ Church meadow at Oxford, read carefully some papers he had taken out with him. Two gentlemen in attendance, Mr. William Legge of the Bedchamber and a certain lord, loitered a few paces behind. After a while, the king paused, and half turning looked at the lord, who hastened forward.

"Here is a report that concerns your country, my lord", said the King, and he put his finger on a closely written paper.

The nobleman, who was short-sighted, bent over to see better, and then he smiled in spite of himself. "It is old Mr. Verschoyle," he said.

But the King was in no laughing humour. "He is little better than a traitor!" he exclaimed warmly. "Nay, I think him worse. He claims to be loyal and well-affected, and yet, though it appears he has a great estate, he has lent neither money nor any comfort in those troubles, nor shewn any affection to me or my cause save by vain words. He deserves to be disjusticed, and his house beset. I tell you truly, my lord, the carriage of this Mr. Verschoyle and men like him, who will not declare themselves freely, but float up and down with the tide of the war, has given me as much grief as almost any misfortune since this damnable rebellion. Yes, men who act as this man, I tell you, would be glad of my ruin. They go all ways in the world to destroy their king. For what is that they do, but making a common cause, giving countenance, and taking hands with the rotten-hearted villains who go about seducing the honest tenantry of the country from their devotion?—Has this man any excuse? Is he hampered? Has he compounded? The report says not."

"Sir, he is old", answered the nobleman, who was of the Privy Council, and had himself suffered many thousand pounds' loss for the King. "He is all but seventy; some say more. He was at court in the Queen's time, and continued there some years after your royal father came into England. I have heard he was much noticed by the Lord Chancellor Bacon, at whose house he pried curiously in crucibles, and alembics, and the arts of nigromancers; searching spells, the philosopher's stone, and the principle of life. He married but a few years ago in his old age the young daughter of Sir Thomas Foulkes, who went to Italy long before our troubles began, and who, returning to England to marry his daughter, died suddenly on the wedding night, having been, as they say, slain by Verschoyle with his wizardries. His daughter, a great heiress, had been betrothed from her young age to her cousin Sir Edward Morvan, now or lately with Sir Richard Byron at Newark, and a very true servant of your Majesty; but her father was so besotted by old Verschoyle's charmings (for it could be nothing else) that she was forced to the old man's bed. Where her fortune now is", continued the lord, seeing that the King listened, "or what enjoyment she has of it, none can say. As for Mr. Verschoyle himself, when I taxed him with his passiveness in regards your Majesty's service, going to his house myself to that end, he burst forth in a thousand excuses and reasons to shew why he could not further the cause: as that his tenants were sullen and unruly, that he had a great charge of servants for his lady's needs, and was put to it to maintain the tenants in their holdings. And in truth, Sir, for these four or five years he has lived in a mean poor way, his family ill-clad, and keeping but two old horses in his stable. Some maintain he has great sums bestowed in the Low Countries, and with merchants at Genoa. In truth", concluded the nobleman, who had his own reasons for wishing that part of the country to remain free of soldiery, "I humbly think that to despatch a troop for the harrying and wasting of his house and lands would do your Majesty small service—no, not now, nor any time later."

As he listened, the King kept rapping impatiently on the papers he held. "Has he discovered himself?" he now inquired. "Has he ever told out boldly in any company what side he is on in these struggles?"

"Sir", returned the nobleman, with some change in his demeanour, "I have been shewn a little tract which, though he did not put his name, 'tis certain he wrote, and the title was, if I remember right: 'Problems necessary to be Determined by All that have or have not taken Part on Either Side in this Unnatural War'".—At this the King stared for an instant with amazed and angry eyes, and then almost against his will, as it were, smiled out at his attendant. "Yes", pursued that one, smiling now himself, "and the inside was as dark and double-dealing as the title, the writing being so close and folded no man could tell what foot the writer stood upon. Nevertheless, that he has some agreements with the Roundheads I know well, from a sure hand; but" (added the speaker with a serious want of tact) "he claims to be uxorious and governed by his wife, whose cousins are deeply engaged on that side.—If he were harried and his house fired", said the lord, again reverting to his anxiety, "the cause would be little better off; for if he were killed his tenants would rebel and surely would not pay, and if he escaped, seeing his monies lie abroad, he could doubtless without difficulty, by the strict relations he has maintained in London, obtain a pass from the Parliament to go beyond seas."

"And a good ending too", said the King vehemently; "a most desirable ending, to rid this distracted kingdom of him and all like him.

He is worse in my sight than a declared rebel. A strange time", quoth the King somewhat bitterly, "a strange bad time with no blessing on it, when men can fence and argue and try all means to find out how little they can do for their lawful sovereign. When I see", he continued graciously, "what you, my lord, and other loyal subjects suffer in my cause even here in this town; packed together, living coarse and meanly, with only the sad spectacle of war and sickness; while it consoles and cheers me in these trials, yet it does incense me the more against base wretches even as this man who use cunning and tricks to lie snug at home."—He had, however, notwithstanding his indignation, evidently taken notice of his attendant's hint as to the inexpediency of dragooning Mr. Verschoyle in his house; and he had besides more important affairs to engage him than that gentleman's contumacy. And therefore it was that after a pause he merely said, with that mixture of melancholy and dignity which was his greatest charm and enabled him to pass grandly through the most galling situations, frequent enough since the war began, wherein circumstances compelled him to forego his most cherished desires—well, perceiving something like that to be the situation now, he deliberately quenched his anger and only said, looking meanwhile afar off vaguely at the bare trees and spectral river, where the morning mist still hung, as if he watched a scene enacting there,—"Whensoever it shall please God", said the King slowly, "to enable me to look upon my friends like a King, they shall thank God for the pains they have spent in my cause." And having said that, he drew forth another paper and fell to talking of a different matter.

But if the King, at the time he was comminating Mr. Verschoyle, had been suddenly transported from Oxford to Mr. Verschoyle's house, his wrath, instead of dropping, must have sensibly increased.

It chanced to be the day that Mr. Verschoyle gathered in his rents; and there were the tenants coming up to the door quietly, and laying on the table in the panelled hall where Mr. Verschoyle himself sat by a rousing fire,—not, as you might fancy, just half or a quarter of what they owed, which in those troubled times, when most of the great estates were disorganized, and the tenants froward and demoralized, many landlords would have been glad to get,—but, wonderfully enough! the full amount as ever, and that without sulks, or murmuring, or making the disturbed state of the country an excuse for their unwillingness to pay. It is true that these peasants, when they came out from the dark house blinking into the daylight, bore a look of astonishment and relief as though they had just passed safely through a danger, and some of them replaced curious rustic charms and amulets which they had kept in their hands while they were indoors carefully back in their clothes; but their uneasiness was not provoked by parting with a sum of money. On the contrary, they rejoiced that they had got that business over: now they might sleep another year without affliction, or terror of marauding, burning troops, the rumour of whose wild doings elsewhere had reached them vaguely; or worse still! of those witches and devils who come by night in the country places, laying waste the land, tearing the careful thatch from roofs, and leaving in their train strange languors and wasting diseases among the strong men and the cattle, and slowness, palenesses and faintings among the unmarried girls. The truth is, Mr. Verschoyle's reputation as a wizard pervaded the countryside; to encounter him at night would kill a child in the mother's womb; if he entered your house it was an omen of the most deadly; to affront him was more than the boldest dared to do. Better to eat grass and bitter herbs, and lie cold at night, than to see old Verschoyle at your door asking for his rent. Had not the daughter of Will Lees, off there in the fen, whose father had withstood the esquire to his face that his thin undrained land yielded not the rent put upon it, from a fine buxom girl fallen suddenly into such a decay and consumption that her flesh took on the colour of blue and her bones rattled;—being vexed with no natural sickness, but undeniably by magical art, as was proved the night she died. For her mother sitting by her, the girl fell to groaning that one was pulling her out of bed by the feet, and upon the mother asking who was pulling her, says the poor creature: "'Tis Squire Verschoyle who has sat this hour at the foot of the bed." Yes, and when the corpse was borne to the churchyard, and the grave was found to be too short, all were convinced that the wizard had distorted the thin body so that it might not lie easily in its place of burial.

Still, though there were reasonable terrors for every hour under Mr. Verschoyle, there were immense advantages also. It was owing to his magic power, people thought, that there was so little sickness on the land, and that since the war broke out they had lived unharassed by soldiery. Indeed, so important seemed these advantages to Mr. Verschoyle's tenants, that although they did not love him at all, and trembled in his presence, they would not have exchanged him for any other landlord in England. Little they cared for King or Parliament! In the struggle which was now devastating the country they were not partizans; or rather, owing to their master's skilful training, they were solely partizans of Mr. Verschoyle. He had already induced in them that temper which later blazed out generally in the South and West, when the peasantry, or "Clubmen" as they were called, banded themselves together to drive both armies impartially from their neighbourhood. This temper which, as we know, was roused in the "Clubmen" by plundering and ruthless exactions, Mr. Verschoyle called up, so to speak, in advance by descriptions of these miseries, and threats, kept purposely vague, of their imminence, and the consequent withdrawal of his protection; so that his tenants were at last determined to chase from their fields the troops of either side. It was not, however, that they seriously feared invasion: the King no doubt was great, and the Parliament great too, but what were they against the powers of the unseen world? Under the government of those incalculable powers whose weapons their squire, old Mr. Verschoyle, possessed and occasionally brandished, they did, no doubt, live in a perpetual tremor; but that was alleviated after all by the genuine advantages already mentioned.

And these advantages, these striking immunities, were certainly solid enough, considering the time, to make people who enjoyed them put up with a great deal, though the causes of them of course were to be looked for elsewhere than the common people imagined. That the estate had escaped invasion from the contending armies, and demands for free quarters, was largely sheer luck. It lay remote from the theatre of war, one boundary of it being desolate coast; it was not a good country wherein to manœuvre squadrons; and, perhaps chief of all, there were no fortified or garrisoned houses anywhere near to attract attention. The northern boundary of Mr. Verschoyle's estate touched a tract of land which had belonged to his father-in-law, lately dead, and was now merged in his own; while his only neighbour was Sir Edward Morvan, whose house stood about fifteen miles away to the west. He was therefore free from local influences and a neighbouring gentry who might from one reason or another have driven him to take action in the war, as happened in other parts of the country where the conflict, during the first years of it at any rate, was greatly embittered by little local provincial jealousies and quarrels, men taking that fair opportunity to pay off old rancours which had been gathering for years before the war, and which had nothing to do with the high matters they were ostensibly fighting for.

Furthermore, he was careful even now, but especially a little later on—say, just after Naseby, when affairs took an unmistakable turn against the King—he was careful to pay with scrupulous regularity the monies exacted by assessment from the land.

These seem to be the chief causes why Mr. Verschoyle and his tenants had dwelt hitherto unmolested, and it will be seen he had himself done hardly anything to bring this happy condition about, though of course like many others he had taken the trouble to get Protections both from the King and the Parliament, upon which however he was too shrewd to depend. But on the other hand, that his people had been so little afflicted by that terrible fever and ague which was always lurking in the cottages up and down England, may fairly be put down to his credit. For a man of that age he took an extraordinary interest in drainage and sanitation, the importance of which he probably understood from the valetudinary Bacon, in whose house he had spent so much time; and when after the death of King James he came into the country for good, he set himself to overhaul the dwelling-houses on his estate,—not, it must be confessed, from any genial feeling for the welfare of his tenants, but simply from a scientific concern to have things as they should be.

No; magic had doubtless nothing to do with the unusual prosperity of Mr. Verschoyle and his tenants; and yet as they saw him this day and every day that he took his rents, it is no wonder that the stoutest quailed. The hall where he sat, panelled to the ceiling with black oak, was gloomy enough, and the gloom was thickened by the stained glass which filled the high windows. Watching Mr. Verschoyle as he sat there taking money, none could doubt that he knew his reputation and condescended to the lowest tricks to maintain it. He had never changed from the dress of King James's reign; but his daily costume, all but the deep ruff, was at this moment concealed by a black cloak stained with crimson, cast about his shoulders, while on his head he had placed a kind of mitre scrolled with cabalistic signs. At the table, covered with large books heavily bound and clasped, was seated near him a one-eyed rascally-looking man, devoted soul and body to Verschoyle, who served as his steward, and might well be taken for his familiar in unholy rites. And as the brief afternoon waned, and the night seemed gradually to advance in veritable wafts of blackness across the chamber, where the fire now glowed redly through the twilight, those who had been late in leaving home and had unwisely tarried till this hour, found something terrific and portentous in those two figures. Neither spared any shameful mummery to strike terror into the simple peasants who stood before them awe-stricken. Old Verschoyle would clutch the money they tendered with his huge hands and mumble over it certain charms and spells, and then pass it along to the steward who, while pretending to go through the like indecency, would diligently count the pieces. Nor did the old man shrink from the poorest antics of the mountebank. It happened, to give one instance, in the course of the afternoon that a man who had brought his wife with him actually ventured to complain, whereupon Mr. Verschoyle, noting that the hall was pretty full and a performance would not be wasted, picked up some grains of a powder he had carefully laid by him, cast them into a glass of water, and spreading his great hands over it as the liquid turned red, cried out in a terrible voice, "Blood, Blood!"—upon which the one-eyed droll with horrible contortions began to drink it. The woman, who was with child, was taken with a trembling fit, and she and her husband passed haggardly away, all present shrinking from those blighted ones.

It would seem as if Nature, foreseeing the part he was to play in his old age, had carefully prepared for him an adequate appearance;

every wrinkle on that extraordinary visage seeming to be laid there to produce a duly calculated effect. Towards the end of 1636, upon one of his visits to London, becoming as time went on rarer and rarer, he was seen at some gathering by the painter Van Dyck who, after considering him for a little, holding meanwhile his under lip between his thumb and finger as his manner was when he was taking in a subject, drew near at last, and accosting Mr. Verschoyle with much civility offered to make his portrait. This portrait still exists in the possession of my worthy friend, Nicolas Ursal, Esquire, of Fraynes, and any one who examines it carefully can see that Van Dyck welcomed here a genuine subject, coming to him perhaps as a relief amid the endless round of fashionable portraits—apt to become insipid in the long run even for a man so enamoured of elegance and the dainty fragile things of life as he was—and painted this one happily, "with his heart", as people say. With what force and inspiration, with what indescribable *brio*, the great bald skull, the beaked predatory nose, the long beard, beneath which you divine the firm pitiless mouth, even to the old-fashioned vesture of the last reign—yes, with what conviction all these are rendered; leaping out as it were from a picture of which the dominant tone, nevertheless, is sombre. But what perhaps shews most of all that Van Dyck was interested in this work, is the certainty we have, that instead of falling back, as was his languid, somewhat insolent wont, upon the hired models with well-shaped hands he kept by him to supply delicate hands to his troop of sitters, here he has rendered Mr. Verschoyle's hands just as he found them: thick, broken-nailed, knotty, cruel—"Grand hands of a strangler", said the artist to himself, smiling admiringly, as he painted them in with gusto. Nor are the very height and clumsy massiveness of the model's frame evaded or attenuated to gentler proportions in the picture.

Mr. Verschoyle's conversation, too, Van Dyck must have found a distraction from that of the people he usually dealt with. Verschoyle's coarse abusive wit, his command of vituperation and the large phrase, entertaining as it sometimes was, he shared however with some others; notably with his friend Sir Kenelm Digby. But what was piquant in his character was the conjunction of baseness—an ignoble occupation with the meanest and most sordid things,—and a strange idealism, dreamy, yet coldly speculative rather than enthusiastic. In his youth he had been a hard-drinking, hard-fighting, unscrupulous scoundrel. One of his maxims had been that if you start by refusing to say "By your leave" to the world, the world will end by saying it to you. He had played a thousand pranks; he is said to have accompanied Sir Walter Raleigh on his wild voyage to the Oroonoko. Later, when he was almost middle-aged, he had been entertained, as we have already learned, for some time at Gorhambury; accepted, we may be sure, by the subtle, refining owner of the place, to whom all other gifts save mental ones seemed almost negligible, for some gift, keenly descried, which separated him plainly from the crowd. But in his studies, pursued untiringly at that beautiful seat, he had felt himself bound to follow the system of learning advocated by his entertainer, which implied a contemptuous intolerance of the fantastical and unnecessary, and a grave impatience of such speculations as by their nature were not susceptible of logical demonstration, excepting only (possibly from other than religious promptings, and perhaps on the whole, less sincerely than he would have it appear) the mysteries of the Christian faith,—well, Mr. Verschoyle followed in all that but a certain distance, and had then boldly struck off into a path of his own; devoting himself with passionate intensity to uncertain, godless, ill-reputed studies: the arts of the nigromancer, spells, witchcraft, the notation of omens, alchymical divinings, the transmutation of base metals, the present resurrection of the dead; with curious wayward meditations upon the influence the spirits of those we have known in life have after their death for good or ill upon the fortunes of the living. Even by jealous professional operators he was acknowledged to be at this time the most excellent proficient in England, and perhaps in Europe, for resolving horary questions; and beyond that, he was reported so well versed in the Black Art as to practise the circular way of invoking spirits with a success to which none other could pretend. Neither did his master expressly discourage him in these pursuits, watched him rather with a kind of bantering scepticism: such studies were mazy and confused, he thought, and ended, it was to be anticipated, nowhere, nor could anyone declare certainly how much of them was verity and how much vanity. Besides, either from deep policy, or—with that baffling tortuous mind who can tell?—perhaps from genuine piety, he let it be known that he considered "similar enquiries must be bounded by religion or else they would be subject to deceit and delusion"; and how far amid these magical labyrinths could one travel without encountering Sathanas himself, and tendering a hand for his powerful yet fatal aid as he prowled there in his congeries? So at least men should be encouraged to think; and all means and figures, even fables and old wives' tales, should be employed to prevent the world from wandering vaguely after high and vaporous imaginations to the manifest injury of a laborious and sober inquiry of truth. For such imaginations begat hopes and beliefs of strange and impossible shapes, and therefore (Verschoyle often heard him say it with his fine meaning smile, using almost the very words he had written, as they sat pleasantly at table, where the sweet breath of the flowers came and went through the windows "like the warbling of music")—therefore it was to be noted in those sciences which held so much of imagination and belief as magic, alchemy, astrology, and the like, that in their propositions the description of the means was ever more monstrous than the pretence or end. And these frivolous experiments, he was wont to add a little scornfully, were as far differing in truth of nature from such a knowledge as we require, as the story of King Arthur of Britain or Hugh of Bordeaux differed from Caesar's Commentaries in truth of story. But furthermore, it was for Mr. Verschoyle and experimenters like him to observe, that however entrancing these occult studies, these dizzying voyages through the uncharted seas of knowledge, harrowed by tempests and lit by ruddy flames—even Hell-fire itself!—beating above, around, what do I say? on the very hands and face of the desperate navigator, whereof one might concede, if you wished, that the gains would be so well worth the hazards once the headlands passed, the haven won—ah yes, however exciting and bewildering these quests which enhanced the discreet enthusiasm of the scholar with something of the passionate intention of the gamester, there were other studies, in effect, so much more real, so much more worth while: kingcraft, statecraft, the law even, which had the reputation of being so dry, but which, as people knew, he himself had shewn at various times, and notably in his Charge upon the poisoning of Sir Thomas Overbury, could be rendered on due occasion vivid, flexible, entertaining as a romance. And had you not the arts (though this appeal Mr. Verschoyle, who was unfamiliar with the fine arts, might not be expected to take in, any more than, coarse and full-feeding himself, he could understand that delicacy of the senses which induced in the Lord Keeper a sickness and faintness if a servant came into his presence shod in neat's leather)—but had you not the arts which came pleasantly to the spirits: poetry, the falls of low music in bowers on a moonlit night, sculpture, the cadences of rhetoric? Nor were these mere toys, as

men of weak judgment might conceive, but all related among themselves and to the great order of the world. Consider for example the
trope of music to avoid or slide from the close or cadence—well,
was not that common with the trope of rhetoric? Again; is not the
delight (as he wrote so charmingly and truly) of the quavering upon
a stop of music, the same with the playing of light upon the water?

By some such reasonings did the illustrious sage endeavour to
draw his guest to honourable learning, albeit lightly and intermit-
tently, as one who cared little whether his arguments took effect
or no. After all, the broad placid river of learning was fed by innumerable rills, and it might be unwise to divert or dam up even the
most apparently turbid. So too perhaps he had reasoned when he
seemed willing to examine seriously the "Sympathetick Powder" of
the youthful Kenelm Digby, that wonderful salve which was vouched
to heal though a man were bleeding to death at a distance of thirty
miles, and consequently made such a heavy demand upon human
credulity;—going so far, they say, in his complaisance as a willingness
to register the drug among the observations he proposed adding,
had he lived, by way of appendix to his Natural History. And yet
the compound itself, both in its constituent parts—moss of a dead
man's head, man's grease, and the rest,—and in the odd method of
utilizing it,—never touching (as one might anticipate according to
the practice of the craftiest chirurgeons) the wound itself with the
salve, but dressing and anointing instead each morning the weapon
wherewith the wound was given; only laying at the same time upon
the wound a linen cloth wet in the patient's urine:—ah, what else
could all that be but one of those gross attempts to block and darken
true science of which he wrote so sternly: "The impostor is prized,
and the man of virtue taxed. Nay, we see the weakness and credulity of men is such, as they will often prefer a mountebank or witch

before a learned physician." But when the "Powder of Sympathy" was put before the world he was old, and perhaps more tired than he seemed; he had fallen from extraordinary glory and had drunk his full of gall and humiliation; all the powers and honours he had so feverishly struggled and schemed for all his life may now, tardily, have taken on a dun and uncertain look; and noting that, he may have disposed himself to regard all things else with an ironical tolerance. And of that tolerance Mr. Verschoyle, for one, reaped the benefit. This last, for his part, the large, sanguine, sophistical projector, had been taken with a veritable enthusiasm for the "Powder of Sympathy"; and when not long after he made the acquaintance of the man who had promulgated its virtues, he found him congenial and they became friends.

That romantic figure, buccaneer, swashbuckler, duellist, braggart, alchymist, poet, architect, courtier, theologian—what else? who passes to and fro so vividly and gallantly across the stage of the seventeenth century, generally feared, always admired, though never quite respected or trusted,—"a teller of things strange", as Evelyn calls him good-humouredly; who constantly vapoured and hectored, but with such an air that men dared not laugh at the one or resent the other;—how could he fail to attract one of Mr. Verschoyle's nature and intellect? For this was the man who would be found in years to come declaring himself a Cavalier and Catholic, and yet managing the amazingly dexterous exploit of keeping a foot at once in the court of Cromwell and in that of the widow of the late King: a man, who was completely untroubled, it would seem, by moral principles, or scruples, or restraints, and who seriously believed and acted upon what he wrote, "That no man is to be lamented for finding any means, whatsoever it be, to please and gratify himself", which however did not prevent him from discussing doctrinal points of a religion he held apparently with no ardour, and so little of the spirit that one is led to believe he joined the Church of Rome for little else than the pleasure of flaunting in the face of the world the paradox of a man taking immense risks for what he did not care a straw about. Sir Kenelm's notion of friends was that "those are to be esteemed good that are the least ill"; and he found Mr. Verschoyle, although many years older than himself, a man so young, so eager, so curious, so loud too and turbulent on occasion, so indifferent to other men's censures, that he lived much with him, and took great delight in his qualities and conversation. The very bulk and size of the two men, and their tendency to domineer, made them appropriate companions. After Sir Kenelm's return from his piratical cruise in the Mediterranean, but especially after the death of his wife, when he retired to Gresham College to pursue the study of chemistry, and to divert his melancholy by learned discoursings, he was often to be seen in Mr. Verschoyle's company, clad in the sad-coloured clothes he now affected which, like the straggling beard he had grown since his bereavement, matched congruously enough with the other's presence.

As for Verschoyle, that part of his nature which had been least valued at Gorhambury, the gross and coarse part, which was on the whole the strongest part, he was not at the trouble of modifying to please Digby, who had indeed himself the same proclivities, though, if you will, more interrupted and softened. But though all that was very saliently there, still intellectual curiosities, a passion, never at rest in either, for rending the veil which hid the secrets of Nature, had almost as much to do with their friendship. Many discourses did they have together of rare chymical secrets, of antimonial cups, of unheard-of medicines. They watched the stars, and cast horoscopes. With the help of one Evans who lived in Gunpowder-alley, a most horrid wizard, reputed to be the familiar of the dark angel Salmon, they called up a spirit; and they being all within the body of the circle, after powerful invocation it came first in the shape of a toad, speaking high and shrilly, which proved it to be not Gabriel or Michael or any blessed Heavenly angel, who when they do speak, says one of the wisest masters and operators, "it is like the Irish, much in the throat". But when Verschoyle undaunted, and to the great fear of the adept, who though he had taken some cups to hearten him was in a sad trembling state, commanded the fiend in a terrible voice to leave off his tricks and come forth there was heard a very dismal groan, and a thing dreadful, unformed, rolling at Verschoyle's feet worshipped him as its Master, and Lord of the Powers of Hell.

So we are told; but be that as it may, there can be no doubt that Sir Kenelm Digby had at one time, whatever he may have thought later, a great respect for Mr. Verschoyle's parts and curious learning. There is still extant a letter of his addressed to Verschoyle wherein, after equalling his friend for deep knowledge and high speculations to "a Brachman of India" he had met with in Spain, and protesting in his large way that Verschoyle "had ravished the secrets of Nature, and made the lodestone a thing of no wonder", he goes on:—"Persuaded of those conferrings, that I say will come drily to yourself which it freshens me to witness. Sir, I have seen you do that by magical arts which would blast the eyes of ignorant vulgars and analphabetes to behold." And in a letter to another correspondent, written from Paris, he speaks ungrudgingly in a like strain, and quotes with seeming approval a saying of Verschoyle's to the effect, that a system of philosophy or religion should be like to a coat whereof the cloth is strong and good, so that the shape can be changed many times to accommodate the needs of the body.

Later, some years before the war, they fell apart, and gradually ceased even to correspond. Whether they quarrelled, or whether

Sir Kenelm's public acceptance of the doctrines of the Church of Rome, however wide and untrammelled that acceptance might be, and though Sir Kenelm seems to have held to the old distinction between the Church of Rome and the Court of Rome, considering himself bound only to the first—whether that made intercourse undesirable, or what else it was that put an end to their friendship, cannot now be determined. Certainly Mr. Verschoyle, for his part, who as he grew older became more than ever unwilling to compromise himself for trifles, as he deemed opinions and disputes about religion, would have steered clear of Sir Kenelm Digby after his appeal to the English Catholics for funds on the Queen's behalf had been discovered by the Parliament. If Verschoyle had ever had it, he had lost long ago that generosity of mind which was so constant a trait in Sir Kenelm's character. The wise man, he considered, was he who professed the religion of the dominant party in the State, and did as little as he could, without offending that party, to harass the minority. For himself, privately, he inclined to the doctrine of those old curious subtilizers of ethics whose aim has been to distinguish acts from being, what we do from what we are, pronouncing the last alone pleasing and interesting to the gods: a doctrine which he was to find roughly adopted, and urged somewhat crudely as the effect of knowledge and the Spirit of God, by the sects called Ranters and Seekers of his own time; though, unlike him, the sectaries sheltered their equivocal teaching under the name of Christ,—calling to men to hearken to Christ within them, and maintaining that all impulses of nature, even towards things commonly forbidden, were the workings of Christ in humanity; thus in their turn curiously arriving—but by what different roads!—at almost the same landing-place as the Illuminati of Spain, or the believers in the revelation of Anthony Buckuet in France.

But it must not be understood that he was foolish enough to advertise his indifference in matters of religion: on the contrary he assumed at one time what may fairly be called, considering the personage and the way he took himself, an appalling piety, carrying his insincere mummery so far as to deceive the eminent and judicious Bishop Juxon; the prelate regarding this penitent, whose scandals and ill-practices had been the talk of two courts, with great contentment. It remained for the good Mr. Nicholas Ferrar, to whose convent-like house, the Hall at Gidden, or Gidding, in Northamptonshire, Verschoyle in his fervour, pretending the need to search his conscience, had asked leave to make a visit, and was thereupon graciously welcomed—it needed Mr. Ferrar with his saintly eyes to discern the genuine nature, the rank nature, the bias to sin underlying the mockery of this conversion which had duped the Bishop and other men of the world. On the second evening since his arrival, after evening prayers, which as it was an extreme cold winter night had been recited in the parlour where there was a fire burning instead of in the church, as was the ordinary use of that family, Mr. Ferrar takes Verschoyle and gently draws him before a table of brass placed on the wall of the room by the venerable Mrs. Mary Ferrar, which bore an inscription upon it composed perhaps by Herbert of Bemerton, and smiling always lays his finger on these words which made part of it:—"He who any ways goes about to disturb us in that which is and ought to be amongst Christians (though it be not usual in the world), is a burthen whilst he stays, and shall bear his judgment, whosoever he be." He did this, however, not pointedly, but rather laid his hand on the tablet as if by chance, talking meanwhile of his mother who had set it up there, and her quiet life; for he was very sensitive and gentle, and would not hurt the feelings of his guest. But it would have been all one had he been harsh and blunt: Mr. Verschoyle was not sick of that disease called tenderness of conscience, and never took an affront save when it suited his convenience; and now, not at all disconcerted, and apparently indifferent to this rebuke—if that be not too rough a word for what was done so dreamily—he lingered on a day or two more, howling at night over his sins, claiming to see his sweet Jesus, and raving out other blasphemous and hypocritical indecencies too odious to repeat. When at length he took himself away, the family offered up special purifying orisons: had they been as Popishly disposed as many fancied, they would certainly have exorcized their dwelling-place with consecrated water. As it was, for days following there was an uneasiness, an indescribable *malaise* in the house, an unwonted sluggishness and untowardness troubling its calm and sedateness, as though the Father of all Evil had in reality passed there.

Yes, the base part of Mr. Verschoyle's nature was by far the strongest, and it was that which as he grew old, coagulating into avarice, had most to do with his retirement into the country. And yet, just as in his youth it was a mixture of dreaming and rapacity which had sent him voyaging to the other side of the earth with Sir Walter Raleigh in search of gold, so now in his old age, mingled curiously with the habits of the miser which led him to reside constantly on his estate for the purpose of grinding money out of his tenants, there was also something of the temper of the fastidious builder of visions—visions of Heaven or Hell, of sweet faces or places, of fantastical nether worlds, what matters it?—who prefers to live solitary, to sacrifice many sympathies, and adopts an unfriendly and repellant attitude towards mankind, simply from the fear that others may do or say that which would disturb the rhythmic life he has so carefully organized; even as a shriek tearing through a happy dream awakens the sleeper to the trifling of fools or the desolation of tears. But to gain high and worthy ends, he never thought of making the sacrifices or going to the trouble and inconveniences he did to gain bad; and the bad of course predominated. All his life he had been able at any moment to relinquish his favourite studies and intellectual pursuits, but he had never been able—anyhow he had never cared to abjure rapine, lust, riot, all of which, now that he was old, had rolled themselves into avarice, not so much from the love of money itself, as because that was the only field open at last for the exercise of the undying instincts of the bird of prey, the robber and marauder, the overbearing tyrant. This eagerness to gain treasure, to wrench from others their property, which in the Middle Age would have sent him pillaging and ravaging the land with a horde at his back, and which he had never been quite free of even in those early years when the harsher vices sit unnaturally on a man; those hard propensities which led him, for example, as it was currently told, so far as to perjure himself early in the present reign in his desperate efforts to escape the fine imposed on him for declining the obligatory honour of knighthood, increased as he became aged and rose up about him like a ruining tide, drowning as it were all else except what was indeed akin, his passion for domination, which, in its turn he gratified, not arrogantly, but rather by stealthy covered ways and serpentine windings gaining his ends, bringing people to his mind. The scandal of his marriage, a business in which he enthralled and intimidated the already dying Sir Thomas Foulkes, and tore the young heiress almost from the very arms of her lover to share his unholy bed, was the crowning instance of his predatory capacities. After that, saving his pride in his house which he cherished and dealt with as a jewel, all his mental powers seemed willingly abandoned to the poorest sort of men's dealings with each other, tricks of bailiffs, usurers, lawyers, which had not even boldness to lend them glamour.

But his house was indeed worthy of the sedulous care he bestowed on it. Built in the time of Henry the Seventh, and enlarged by Mr. Verschoyle's father during the early years of Elizabeth, it was now become a captivating example of the middle-sized Tudor dwelling. Time, with his hand of grey, touching the stones had happily moulded them, and the storms of over a century, extremely violent in that coastward region, confusing various early crudities of the building, had but enhanced its mellowness of tone. At the end of a long summer day, when the gardens drowsily breathed a thousand sweets, and the voices of labourers ending their work in the fields might be heard faintly on the long terraces—in those flying lights the house took on a wonderful dignity and charm; so much indeed that its young mistress, in her first lonely and unhappy summers there, was fain to linger out of doors till night fell suddenly, scarfing up the outlines, and leaving only a dark mass, grim and somehow terrifying, premonitory of the wafts of blackness to be encountered inside. But not only summer, the breath of all the seasons lingered there wooingly, increasing the singular charm of the house; and it was probably to be seen at its best towards sunset on a windless day of autumn, when a chill was in the air urging to swift movement out of doors, and that vague odour of burning wood and leaves which pervades the country in fine autumn weather suggested agreeably the bright fire on the hearth to greet one returning. Then in the changing afternoon the house stood out clearly, with the smoke rising straight from its chimneys, and behind it the sun waning amid the wild colours of a sky orange, crimson, golden; while even as one gazed came swimming into all that glory, lucid, serene, spiritual, bringing an unutterable conviction of termination and requiem, the evening star. Yes, the sky thickened, it was almost night; now truly "the labourer's task was over"; the mill ceased, birds nested, the sheep were folded; but for the call of a crow winging homeward, the far cry of a teamster to his horses, a watchdog's bark at some distant farm, the land already reposed. Ah,—as one mournfully watching the house through her tears in a kind of ecstasy would think,—could death but come in the evening as easily and sweetly, quieting the turmoil of hearts and consciences, as the fields were stilled at the rising of yon star!—But, in effect, in all conditions, whether under snow or beaten by rain, the house offered itself seductively to the imagination. From the windows could be heard the muffled beat of the surf, and the great clamour of the sea as the tide came in. Strange birds driven ashore by the hard weather would whirl with anxious cries about the chimneys, or perch on the jutting stone-work under the roof. And on all sides rolled away and away to the horizon the plain, its level interrupted only by church-tower, or windmill, or cottage, widely dispersed, so that you could follow for miles with the eye the course of a road lying like an idly thrown piece of white tape among the fields. At the opening of the drive, opposite the entrance gate, stood the parish church, with the dead lying around it just off the high-road, who might be thought, not too fancifully! to have part and interest still in the small noise of the countryside and the few passengers who went by the way. The living was now vacant, the last incumbent having been so harassed by Mr. Verschoyle that the sexton coming to the church one morning at dawn found the body of the vicar swinging by the neck from a pillar in the gloomy aisle.

Not the least comely feature of the place were the gardens, planted at the side of the house and running far back in the rear. Mr. Verschoyle had always cherished these gardens; he had desired the celebrated John Tradescant to control the ordering of them and to embellish them with his fancies: and indeed they were very stately, and of great curiosity and beauty. Contrived with so much skill that even in that bleak clime they offered somewhat of refreshment at all seasons, it was here the young mistress of the place loved best to spend her long pale days, tending by preference the sadder flowers which she watered, as one might surmise, with her tears. Apparently free to wander whither she chose, yet her movements in reality strictly confined to the gardens and terraces, she reminded herself in her great longing for the free air of the outer lands, and in her narrow imprisonment there, of a cart she had once seen in an Italian city conveying prisoners condemned to the galleys through the streets. The cart, although covered over, had an air-hole on the top, and through this hole appeared—so significantly, so poignantly!—a pair of coarse grimy hands waving aimlessly, as if the hopeless wretch within was thus blindly trying to identify himself, to take a last contact with the lovely freedom of the streets. Like those hands, from the same mad longing, her eyes, as she leant on the balustrade of the terrace on a calm evening, not seldom reverted to a certain far away point on the coast; there, it was said, the smugglers, coming from the Low Countries on fine dark nights, were wont to run in their contraband goods. Well, might not those men, desperate as they were, be persuaded by the gift of the few jewels she had left to land her on the shores of the Continent; and then, somehow—never mind how—would come Italy, help, freedom! So dreaming, she would remain for an hour at a time with her elbow on the stone, resting her chin in her hand; till the mere sight of Mr. Verschoyle passing in the distance sufficed to remind her despairingly how futile it was to struggle against his will, how she was helpless as a young fluttering bird in his big hand. Nay, those very smugglers,—with whom, moreover, in all likelihood he had dealings,—would even they have the hardihood to oppose him?

Whenever she thought of freedom, she thought with passionate longing of Italy. As a young girl she had lived much at Genoa in the family of the Duchess Paola Adorno Brignole-Sale whose name she bore, and whom she was thought to resemble. However that might be, in the English Paola, at any rate, what you saw was a young woman's face which indicated that however unusual and terrible the griefs she might have to suffer in her life, she would never meet them with large tragic utterance and demeanour, but rather in the spirit of a rebuked child, pouting and surprised, and quite ready to laugh through her tears at the first intimation that the storm was over. There was in her face a sort of distressed notification that she was not being caressed—the action she could understand best; and a sort of wonder that it was omitted. She was not a tall woman, and her face would have been conventionally pretty had it not been for a look—one would call it high-bred, save that undeniably high-bred people constantly do such abject things—but at all events a nobleness of mien which assured you that on any trying occasion she would not be found trivial and common. Yes, that; and furthermore a look of mingled terror and sadness in the large brown eyes, such as might cloud the eyes of a child who has witnessed, and partly understood atrocious violences, degrading scenes. But, as it happened, in Paola's eyes the terror prevailed over the sadness; for though she loved her lover, Sir Edward Morvan, and grieved miserably because she was deprived of his sweet company, still, as she was not one of those deep-natured, high-souled women who entangle their fate with one man, and losing him lose all, she might have consoled herself in happier circumstances even for that loss; whereas from her terror of the old man her husband there was no escape, and no consolation to modify it. Besides its very real action, increased daily by a thousand artifices, it remained with her always imaginatively, a prolongation of the sort of fear—but how much intensified! which had haunted her for a few hours in her happy childhood when she had seen a painting of the flames striking the feet of the lost let down into Hell.

To her, now, as she stood in the waning light, a black calash drawn over her head beneath which her brown eyes looked forth so mournfully, a vellum-bound volume of Petrarch she had carried out in the early afternoon clasped in her fragile long-fingered hand, was borne faintly the voices of the tenants as they plodded homeward after the rent-paying; a laugh breaking forth now and then, or a child's playful cry, as she listened enviously—the bewitched young lady whom the country folk hardly ever saw, and spoke of under their breaths—trying to decide herself to go indoors and face the desolation, the appalling shadows, the night. And with a sickening of heart she pictured what awaited her: the evening meal in the long half-lit room which she was forced to eat, not only in the presence of her husband, but of the odious one-eyed droll his steward, who was now grown so great with Verschoyle that he must sit at table with his master. All the time that the supper lasted, Verschoyle would pour out a stream of truculent wit directed against all the neighbourhood; the one-eyed wretch, who was himself pretty often the butt, chuckling and sweating and choking with obsequious laughter. Then, the supper over, Mr. Verschoyle and this mean fellow would sit down by the fire in the dark hall to a game of gleek; but if upon these dispositions Paola offered to retire, she was loudly bidden to remain.

"My lady's windows look towards Sir Edward Morvan's house which is known to be unwholesome, is it not?" he would ask with a meaning laugh of the one-eyed steward, who would of course set up another sniggering laugh of acquiescence.

That man had not always been one-eyed: Paola would sob in the wildest fear when she recalled the monstrous deed which had deprived him of sight. One night, when she had been married but a few months, they were eating their meal, after the manner just described, in the gloomy panelled room. All seemed to be going no worse than usual, when Mr. Verschoyle suddenly fell silent, and after a minute brusquely ordered the servants out of the room. Then he pitched back his chair with a clatter, and towering in his immense size, menacing and formidable, he seized the weazened little steward by the ear and dragged him from his place.

"Here, you!" he said. "You eat your victuals with me without a due sense of what you are about. You lack virtue, sirrah; you have need of a congruent gymnastic to keep your mind in humility. Begin your pious exercises. Kneel down and pray to me. I am God."

The poor mean fellow, taken utterly aback by this command, fumbled pitifully. It was more than he dared to do.

"Come sir," cries Verschoyle in a loud authoritative voice, "leave off your fooling and pray as you are desired. Pray, sing a hymn in my honour, you prick-eared rascal: 'tis all that will serve your turn in this world or the next. My lady had a Puritan to her father and is an Italian papist herself, and Sir Edward Morvan, they say, is a good State-Protestant. Shew her a new form to take up with in our pleasant home. Give her a chance to hear your cackle. Out with our Turnbull Street litany and the canticles of the Pict-Hatch fornicators, where you was bred, you caitiff. Come, begin down on your knees!"

But the man was recalcitrant: it was too much. His spirit was not as yet quite broken by Verschoyle, and certain rests of religion, or at all events of superstition, made him recoil from the blasphemy. And in effect, though he stood there trembling all over, he had the courage to stammer out a refusal. But he had scarcely time to get the words out of his mouth, before his master snatched up a candlestick and laid open his face, cutting into the nerve of the eye so that he was blinded. Paola, standing meanwhile with her back against the wainscot, her hands spread out, her eyes dilated, heard his lamentable squeal as he sunk to the ground; and then the lights flashed and wheeled, the chamber rocked, and she saw no more. But before many days the steward, his head craftily swathed, was again at his work, closeted mysteriously with the tyrant, and more devoted to his interests than ever.

Such were her painful reveries as she stood at dusk, uncertain, in the gardens. It was cold and dreary; the moisture dropped from the trees; she shivered, drew her cloak about her, and decided. But as she went strolling reluctantly towards the house, she saw her husband suddenly a few paces in front of her as if he had surged out of the ground,—coming on her, in fact, as he always did, noiselessly, before she was aware. He had laid aside his indecent foolish hat and charlatan's robe, and stood there, with his bare skull unscreened from the wintry airs and his ragged beard blowing over his shoulder, huge and black and sinister, threatening somehow, though he was smiling, ominous, presaging disaster. He had a letter in his hand, and as he came up to her—"My sweet chuck," he cried with a horrid shew of affection which made her wince, "here comes Ned Morvan home."

The blood fluttered into her face and fell away again, like the light of a candle that is carried past a window. She remained silent.

"This is his letter," said Mr. Verschoyle waving it. "He comes home from the King's armies under a pass of the Prince, and doubtless one from the Parliament too, so he may lie snug. A brave lad, Ned Morvan, and a whiteboy wherever he goes. He will be truly welcome here. Perhaps he means to diet with us now he is home", he added, and peered through the dusk to see how this stroke took.

He did not think it necessary to explain that he was afraid to shew Morvan the cold shoulder and forbid him the house, lest the other might turn it into an affront to his cause and bring down a cavalier troop. Besides, he had heard a rumour that Morvan had the King's warrant to search out all those in that part of the country whose loyalty was equivocal or flaccid, and to put the estates of those who refused to contribute to the royal cause at the mercy of the soldiers. After a pause, finding that his wife did not speak, he thought it worth while to drop carelessly the news that Morvan had been wounded in a skirmish.

"Wounded?" she breathed, looking at him with startled eyes.

"Who knows but he may have lost an arm or a leg?" said old Verschoyle considering her with his cruel eyes, and enjoying her dismay. "Nay, Ned used to be a pretty sprig enough, but if a musket shot has removed his nose—"

His quick ear had caught the sound of a footbeat advancing from the house. "As you see, he is even now coming towards us, so his wound must be of the slightest", said Mr. Verschoyle. And lowering his voice—'Tis a wound in the left side, I misdoubt me," he added with malevolent intention.

Then peering through the dark towards the house, where Paola could see nothing, "Ned, Ned, you come in pudding-time!" he shouted heartily.

Even as he spoke a pale young man who limped slightly, apparently between twenty-five and thirty years old, wearing his hair long, as most gentlemen did of both parties, and dressed elegantly in a habit trimmed with gold, with silver points and buttons, stepped out of the pleached alley hard by where they were standing, and greeted them debonairly with gay laughter.

II

The spring was early that year, and Sir Edward Morvan, riding light-heartedly, often with a song on his lips, to and fro between Verschoyle's house and his own, a journey he was making four or five times a week, might see the new-dropt lambs in the meadows, and innumerable violets on the roadside bank penetrating with their cool fragrance the mild air. Ah, how good it was to be in this secluded land, when all over the country men were battling and marching, lying hard at nights, risking their lives! That had been his own life till a few weeks since; later on, in a few days, a few weeks, some vague time always drawing near and always pushed farther off, that would have to be his life again. But not just yet; if the gods were kind, not yet. And as he rode thinking of all that, he would feel his wound, perfectly healed by this time save for a little superficial soreness, to excuse his slackness. Because, for once, Mr. Verschoyle had got hold of a wrong story: Morvan had no warrant from the King to raise money in the country, nor any business whatever there beyond the healing of his wound. And he had certainly exaggerated its severity in his letters to the Newark garrison—nay, he was quite equal to opening the wound afresh if the Governor, impatient as he well might be of this prolonged furlough, had threatened to send a surgeon to report on his condition. But the Governor did nothing of the kind; on the contrary, Morvan seemed to be utterly neglected and forgotten at headquarters; and to the letters he so laboriously composed (Paola sometimes aiding him with the intelligence and fineness of a woman in love) he received no reply at all. This was unusual, even when large free allowance was made for the hindering of messengers, and to one of another character might have seemed disquieting and suspicious; but Morvan was never a man to split straws or ponder might-be's, and lazily took it for granted that the Governor was satisfied with those elaborate reasons he had put forward for not joining.

And thus day after day went by him flowingly, hazily, as a man lounging half-asleep on a hot day might watch the ripples and eddies of running water. There was a dreaming ecstasy in every hour of this wonderful spring, the most wonderful, Morvan thought, certainly the most delightful he had ever lived. To see Paola, the woman whom he loved with a great consuming love which left no room for anything but itself, and who had been stolen from him by machinations the most nefarious—to see her not once or twice, which was the limit of his hope when he first came home, but every day without restraint for long sweet spells—that was an astonishing happiness against which, if the old legends were true, some great retributive punishment must be rolling up. Well, he would face that with equanimity, come when it would, take it without murmuring, even welcome it and think himself all the same the gainer, if it were the penalty exacted from him in exchange for the present smile of her face in his, and the touch of her hand. In the meanwhile, it was enough for his life that every night his pillow was gladdened by the thought that he was going to see her in the morning.

And the strange part was that they were left, as I have said, as untroubled, as much to themselves, as lovers could desire, Mr. Verschoyle appearing but seldom, and then only to ask with marked concern after Morvan's wound, and to bestow his benediction—it actually seemed like that—upon the pair; afterwards vanishing—well, by magic! hiding himself for days and days so inscrutably that none in the house knew where to look for him, and yet revealing himself in disquieting apparitions, now to a lonely passenger over a windy heath, and then, almost at the same hour, as those colloguing at the ale-house painfully took note, to a woman miles and miles away, as if he indeed possessed the receipt of fern-seed, and walked invisible by the aid of those black arts he was supposed to have at command. Beyond question, Sir Edward Morvan regarded Mr. Verschoyle with infinite rancour and hatred: he had come home prepared for the worst reprisals if the other should give him the shadow of an excuse to take offence: but seeing now the old man's complaisances and loose ways his stronger feelings were almost extinguished by contempt. A miserable old dotard (so he thought), who by the long-continued practice of debaucheries dozed in his understanding, and he lamented more than ever the sacrifice of his beautiful Paola.

III

But if Morvan had known what Verschoyle was about while he was dallying, he would have changed his tune more than a little. Sir Richard Willis, who had lately succeeded Byron as Governor of Newark, amazed and furious at Morvan's long desertion of the shaken and sore-pressed garrison, without any excuse offered for his dilatoriness, had finally complained bitterly to the newly-appointed Commander-in-chief of the King's forces. In accordance with that, two letters desiring Morvan to return to his duty, one written chidingly, but the other couched in very peremptory terms, were despatched from Prince Rupert's headquarters; but they were carefully intercepted by Verschoyle, who was plotting nothing less than to ruin the cavalier with his own party, and had up to this managed to stop all expresses riding between Sir Edward and the army. Some weeks before the time we are now arrived at, Morvan being rather anxious, notwithstanding his insouciance, at the failure of letters from Newark, had himself applied directly to Prince Rupert for an extension of his furlough, using in the business a safe man, one his father, who in his time had been involved in some delicate affairs, had often employed. This man came up with Prince Rupert at Beeston Castle, and having delivered his master's letters, which were treated as mere rigmaroles and feignings, he was entrusted with a very angry letter written by the Prince himself, in which Sir Edward was commanded upon his loyalty to join without delay, under pain of being esteemed a renegade and punished as such. The man carried also a very strong message from Morvan's closest friend, acquainting him with the bad odour he had fallen into, wondering at his supineness, and urging him to loose all that held him and return suddenly to his place.

The messenger made good speed, and coming skilfully into his own country congratulated himself on having passed through the area occupied by soldiery. As he journeyed along the familiar road, not more than five miles now from home, riding at a smart trot, sitting loosely in the saddle, and not paying much attention, suddenly he made out in front of him on the bleak unsheltered road three horsemen halted, whose steel he could see gleaming in the late afternoon sun. He thought a moment, chagrined and weary, studying his mount, and then decided to run for it; but as he wheeled his horse he found that he must have ridden past two more who were lying concealed in the dyke-side, and who, once he was passed, had scrambled on to the road to bar his way. Here was an end to the hope of flight; for the wide dyke bordering the road on either side without any "take-off" made a rush across country impossible. But alert and resourceful, he covered his wheel about by acting as if his horse had shied, and pulling up to a foot-pace he approached the main band with an open look, smiling, thinking he might by free manners and effrontery win through without question. The men were every one well armed, but only the leader, a one-eyed man in whom Sir Edward's servant after some hesitation and with infinite astonishment recognized Mr. Verschoyle's steward, was equipped like a soldier. This droll had furnished himself out with an old buff coat, and an iron back and breast, and had clapped a "pot" or headpiece on his skull which being too big for him hung awkwardly askew. He had further girded on an extravagantly long sword which, even on the mild old nag he bestrode, was more than he could handle. Altogether, he presented an appearance something between a bully of Alsatia and a guy ready for Bartholomew Fair.

He it was who summoning up a terrible voice, imitated from his master, ordered the oncomer to stand, and then demanded whither he was bound. The messenger answered, to Sir Edward Morvan's, adding carelessly that he had been to attend the market of a distant town. But the other frowning prodigiously began to vapour and talk big, saying that Sir Edward was a foul malignant, full of factious designs and immodesty, whom well-affected men were about to purge from that honest part of England, since he was naught but a riotous and drunken cavalier and dammy, lewd and a swearer, a man vastly insufficient and scandalous, who lacked healing and savoury counsel. When he had harangued in this style for some minutes, he suddenly threw up his arm, whereupon the two men behind came down the road at a canter, and the messenger found himself hemmed in.

"Give up what you are carrying", snarled the leader seizing the servant's bridle. "Expand, produce, cough it up. In the market you come from there's a king sitting on rotten eggs. The man Morvan is one of them, and you are even now carrying to him messages for the disordering of this peaceable country, which I command you in the Parliament's name to surrender."

The intrepid messenger protested that he carried nothing; and seeing that he must fight, he suddenly pressed his knees on his horse and rode smash against a big hulking fellow, whose small pole-axe, which hung in a ribbon tied about the wrist, he snatched before the other could recover from the shock, and then turning about he reached the one-eyed leader such a swinging blow on the pate that if it had not been for the steel cap he wore his head must have been cleft. As it was, the knock fetched him off his horse into the mud. Seeing one of them down, the messenger laid about him with such fury that had the road been wider, as he was so much a better horseman than any of his assailants, he might have got clean off. But the narrowness of the road and the wide stream on each side gave them the advantage, and after a sharp tussle, in which one got a desperate wound in the side, they closed up and secured the messenger, whom they succeeded in mastering at last only by their numbers and the bad ground. Seeing that the fight was over, the one-eyed captain, who had meanwhile been sitting ruefully by the waterside bathing his head and trying to collect his wits, hoisted himself into the saddle and gave the order to march. And as they marched, what must the worthy captain do to hearten them after the conflict but break out into various prayers and ejaculations, of the kind used by the precisians, for the mercy vouchsafed; and then struck up a psalm which he sang violently through the nose; all by way of convincing the prisoner, if by any chance he should escape, that he had been captured by one who belonged to the party of the Saints in the Parliament army; though in truth the other was far too shrewd to be taken in by this impudent travesty of those stern and godly men.

After a sufficiently long march, variegated by this kind of thing, and by halts while the pious captain drank freely of strong waters to keep, as he explained, his head from swimming with obscene vapours, they drew up to a cottage, standing very lonely in a wood, which the prisoner, who knew every yard of the country, recognized as being on that old estate of Sir Thomas Foulkes which now of course belonged to Mr. Verschoyle through his wife. The house was uninhabited and almost bare; but the captain, kicking the door open, swaggered in with a great bustle, sat himself on the only stool, and clapping his sword on the table glared round him ferociously, while two men brought in the prisoner and the others laid the fellow who had been hurt in a corner. Then, after telling the captive, whom he kept standing before him sorely bound, that he had a mind to hang him up forthwith, he once more ordered him to declare where he came from, and to give up the letters he carried. The man however persisted in denying that he carried papers, and immediately they began to search him; but nothing at all could be found. Matters being thus at a stand, Mr. Verschoyle's captain shouted that he was too old a bird to be cozened, and directed that the prisoner's fingers should be burnt with match. But the messenger, although he suffered atrocious pain, held dauntlessly to what he had said. The captain seeing him thus firm, and being terrified to return home empty-handed, fell into a miserable blasphemous passion strangely at variance with his late psalm-singing, and roared out to twist a rope tight round the prisoner's head, swearing that he was resolved to make him know his master, and what he might trust to if he did not speedily confess. Then at last, after holding out till he was utterly crushed by pain and almost delirious, the messenger shewed where the letters were cunningly hid in a double-lining of his sleeve; but no sooner had the agony ceased than he seemed ashamed of what he had done, and though they renewed the match-burning twice, and also tortured him abominably with water, not all the threats in the world could force him to give any further information. So, after spending some time at this business, the captain finally was fain to be satisfied with what he had got, and rode off in the darkness, leaving the messenger in charge of two louts who sat all night sotting together, but always wide awake enough to prevent any move to escape, even if the prisoner, who lay half dead, had been in any condition to attempt it. And before the next day was over, the man had been carried miles and miles to the north, and the letters were safe in Verschoyle's hands, who used them to elaborate his snares.

IV

This very morning, the most perfect of that perfect season, Morvan riding along heedlessly, now singing, now smiling out good-humouredly at the fair-lighted day, passed over, all unsuspecting, that part of the road where his messenger had been waylaid some weeks before. He was annoyed, as much as he could be in his beatific state—lying, as it were, dulled by love's drowsy medicine—about the messenger's miscarriage, and grumbled now and then without conviction at the stupidity which he supposed had led the man to be taken by the Roundheads. But he had fallen of late, as we have seen, into such a contempt of Mr. Verschoyle that it never came into his mind to look for that hand in the business. He did not perceive, he was really perhaps with all his handsome audacity and physical gifts too stupid to perceive, that Verschoyle was not at all a man like himself, or governed by the motives of his generation; but rather a survival from the reign of Elizabeth and the early years of James, with all the peculiar subtilties, refinings, and roundabout methods of those times. A man too having in him the spirit of that large body of men in Elizabeth's time whose horror of the violent sins—murder, ravage, piracy,—was perfunctory and as it were spectacular; while in their breasts was a very real ferocity, in its essence barbaric and of the Middle Age, though softened and polished in a thousand ways and subdued to the ends in view: and with that, an almost complete freedom from harassing trammels of conscience, and a distinct preference for considering the fortunes of the soul as vague and matter for scholastic disputation, while the fortunes of the body were to be zealously pursued with unrelenting activity. Had Sir Edward estimated Verschoyle aright, he would have kept his eye upon all sorts of covers expecting him to emerge: he would have been most on his guard when he found the other vacant, senile, mildly foolish. But Verschoyle had always been taken by Morvan for a frantic beast who tore from people whatever of theirs he wanted; yet one whose roar you might hear, and whom you might descry so to speak afar off bounding on his prey, however little you could do to arrest the onset. At present, none too soon! the teeth of the beast seemed to have fallen, his fire dying, almost extinct; the frantic beast was become, in fact, now happily at last so insignificant, so little to be reckoned with, that Morvan as he turned in at the gate today, perceiving the gaunt black figure prowling in the churchyard, waved a recognition with an air of scornful tolerance.

It is so hard for the young to rate at their due value the powers of the old! Morvan, seeing the old man so weary, so unwary, so trembling and incurious, had almost allayed even the fears of Paola, who, however, as she owed them to numberless stronger experiences, could not be induced entirely to forget. Still, for all that, she was happy now and content with an immense wide happiness she had not known since her marriage; and when Sir Edward, his horse comfortably stalled, strolled out of the house on to the long lawn, his heart followed his eyes and lingered upon the exquisite picture she made in the distance as she stood under a blossoming almond tree, wearing a painted calico gown and white hood—graciously lovely, buoyant, full of laughter, fragrant, delicate, and young as the primroses, hyacinths, daffodils, blue violets she cherished there. These long white days, veritable holidays, which she watched drop into darkness one by one as threaded crystals into wellwater, she had arrived never to regret;—looking forward rather with a childlike expectation of indefinite felicity, and welcoming the gleam of the new jewel ere the ripple of the one just sunk had quite died away. Were not these hours today more suave, the sunshine over there on the old wall against which the flowers were opening more genial, than at the same time yesterday? And tomorrow surely would be fairer still. Anyhow, the blessed sweetness of wandering there together—yes, literally hand in hand, lingering over trifles, looking for nests in the hedges, playing a thousand childish pranks in mere youthful folly and high spirits—what was better in life than that? The shadow of age seemed exorcized from the garden, leaving nothing old save the grey old house which looked blandly on this spectacle of young love, as though it gathered a warmth from youthful merriment, blitheness, and frolic, of which it had seen so little. And the tyrant, the ogre, the demon, where was he? Banished too by some good fairy; perhaps still prowling coldly in the place of graves.

But the long happy day of love was over. The sun fell; the wind, rising, blew chill from the wolds; the birds, tired of their loves and quarrels, sought the nest; it was time to go in. They passed through the broad shadows, cast by the last rays of the sun upon the fine-shorn lawn, round to the front of the house, and passing through the empty hall where a great fire blazed, made their way to a small wainscotted parlour which overlooked the terrace. Here too a fire was set, but the logs fallen together gave but a red glow on the hearth; and while they stood warming themselves the day gradually died from the windows, leaving the old room in that tender light when afternoon merges into evening. Then, after they had talked a little at random, saying tumultuously they knew not what, they fell into an intense silence, holding hands, gazing pensively into the fire. What was the use of speech? But Sir Edward, noticing a theorbo-lute leaning against a chair, took it up, and after preluding a little, sang these verses, which he had made in the time of their separation, to a sweet and plaintive air, composed probably by Henry Lawes, though it is not be found in his *Ayres and Dialogues:*—

I wonder if the lovers of old time
   Like me upon the smoke of love were fed;
When in their lady's praise they made a rhyme
   Were they so drear and little comforted?
Absence and sighings are my palmer's share:
Love that sees not the lover is despair.

I pay with scorns the heat of the clear sun
   Since that it falls in groves where she is not,
Young quires make music, but I will have none,
   Since by them all her name hath been forgot.
Days wind to months, and months creep into years
But all my portion is disgusts and fears.

If the one hour that brings the patient moon
   To hang in Heaven its little silver crook
I could but see her, then the nights were soon,
   The days were early after that one look.
'Tis now the lover's anguish and complaint,
Which if endured for God would make a saint.

And then in a dying fall he sang low over again the melancholy cadence:—

> Absence and sighings are my palmer's share:
> Love that sees not the lover is despair.

His voice was indistinct, trembling with love. As the last note fainted and failed, he put down the lute and bending over Paola took her head between his hands and kissed her on the mouth. She rose with an indraw of breath like a sob, naive, pale; and in a burst of tenderness, of despairing passion, threw herself against him, pliant, powerless, mad with happiness, with adoration. He seized that delicate head which drooped upon him like a too-heavy flower; he breathed the odour of her hair, stammering meanwhile some words, feverish and incoherent. But as they clung together in a disordered insatiable embrace, losing themselves utterly, suddenly they heard a cough in the room.

They started apart and stared into the darkness. Who was it? The door was fast closed with a stock-lock, and they must have noticed any one coming from outside. However, before they could speak, they heard a great clapping of hands together, with the voice of Mr. Verschoyle calling loudly for lights; and as the servant entered, there was revealed the old husband seated at a table, a velvet skull-cap on his head, and holding to his face a pomander-ball over which his eyes glittered on the two before him, who, amazed, were asking themselves uneasily how he had got in, and how long he had been there.

"That was a good song, Edward", he called out cheerily, "a sweet ditty and well sung. Living here retired in a poor country-house, 'tis seldom our ears are refreshed with carols. There was parson", he went on, broadening his accent like a rustic, "he used to give us a stave o'nights. But a's gone, dead and gone; a was took off at Christian-tide come two years. A is a main loss is parson, a main sad loss; but a was not a man of God. There was no fervent prayer and savoury conference about parson. Should's ha' heard him read the Book of Sports in church o'Sundays afore the war came. He owed much to me which he forgot: till I put him here he was an old curate living on ten pound a year and unlawful marriages. A weak man, Edward, weak and deboshed, vastly lewd, given over to wenching and the devil. A had more bastards to his charge than any man in parish. He used to say he made a scruple about the ring-marriage, like a nonconformist divine. But like yourself, a was a rare hand at a song and talking bawdy, Edward,—that he was; thof his songs had none of your fantastical French turns about them, and suited better with a tavern or play-house than a godly abode. Was't not so, madam?" he asked, looking straight at his wife.

She stood resting her elbow on the shelf above the fireplace, leaning her head on her hand, her other slim hand lying against her skirt, with that admirable dignity and unruffled demeanour she had always in reserve for trying situations.

"Sooth, sir," she answered, "my little knowledge of these matters I owe to you."

She said it in such a fine grave way that any one else but Verschoyle must have been disconcerted, and even he judged it convenient to give over his odious clowning and laments for a man whom all the country knew he had plagued out of existence. He called Morvan's attention to the pace of a horse led up and down on the terrace.

"Why dost leave us so early, Ned?" he cried hospitably. "The nights be warm and thou knowest the road. Here 'tis uncommon trist at night after you go. I wax old and am only good for the chimney-side, and my wife sighs and mutters charms and passes Popish stones through her fingers to put the black spot on us; and I go all of a dither, what with fear of Sathanas, and the ultimate fire, and the end of a life of sin, which must ever afflict the old age of the saints; thof your secure and sensual sinners may carouse to their coffin, and make a health of perdition. So we continue till the night is near spent. We have conduct, but we lack revelry and songs. Why not tarry yet a little?"

Old as the man was, Morvan felt like knocking him down. In the few minutes this scene had been transacting, he had made up his mind that he must contrive, at whatever cost, the escape of Paola from the house of this monster, and fly with her over seas. But now, angry and bewildered, he could find for Verschoyle's question only a dull reply.

"Because, sir", he said fiercely, "I am resolved never to tarry in any man's house who considers me an intruder."

"Faith, then", replied Mr. Verschoyle with a loud laugh, "I'm thinking you'll deprive many of your company!" And with that, as he saw Sir Edward was bowing formally to Paola, he reached down a candlebranch from the sconce and preceded his guest to the court-yard, whither the horse had been led in. Morvan followed him in a passion of anger and hatred: wounded vanity never forgives, and the speech last uttered was the key, as it were, which locked finally from the outside the door of the chamber wherein all the injuries he had entertained from the same source were heaped up. His host stood on the threshold watching him while he mounted.

"It looks like a storm in the sky tonight", he said. "God grant thee a good home-coming, Edward". And as Sir Edward rode off without any reply, or even Good-night, he turned back into the house singing in a strong trolling voice, most weird in so ancient a man:

Absence and sighings are my palmer's share:
Love that sees not the lover is despair.

V

The wind was rising as Morvan rode forth, clouds were rolling together, and some drops of rain began to fall. Once on the road, he started homeward at a brisk trot, pressing his animal a little so as to put as many miles as he could behind him ere the wind, which always in storms swept with great fury across that open land, had risen to its full force. But he had barely covered two miles when he noticed his horse grow sluggish under him, and with some dismay found that it was running lame. He dismounted, and felt tenderly all round the lame leg to discover where the mischief lay and if it might be remedied; but the horse, as he found, had picked up nothing in the hoof, and for anything less simple it was as good as useless to waste time in the darkness. What he did ascertain after a minute was that the horse, between its hurt and the wind and darkness, was grown too nervous to go forward unless it were led; so, as he cared not to return to Verschoyle's house for hospitality after his malevolent parting of just now with the squire, he resigned himself as cheerfully as he could to trudge the twelve miles and more which lay between him and home. He made, however, but poor headway; and what with leaning against the wind, and trying to soothe the horse which started and shied at the least noise, he ran some risk, well as he knew the road, of breaking his neck in the obscurity, or at least of tumbling into one or other of the ditches full of water which bordered a good part of the route. Thus hindered, it was close on midnight when he drew near to the park gates.

For some miles he had observed a glare in the sky without giving himself much concern about it: some barn, doubtless, carelessly ordered, where a spark falling had been blown into flame by the great wind. But now that he was almost on the skirts of his park he made out that the fire must be pretty near his own house: a heavy smoke mingled with the scudding clouds, which were reddened by a great light whereof the palpitating centre seemed to be the mansion itself: the eastern lodge, perhaps, where a keeper dwelt, was in flames, or worse still! the stables. He would learn all about it, of course, when he reached a cottage hard by which served as a kind of gatehouse, where he was used upon his return from journeys to hand over his horse. But when he did actually come up to the cottage, hoping to shelter there for a little, he found to his great astonishment that it was deserted, though the gates near at hand stood wide open. Somebody would pay for that, by Heaven!—that was the last straw of an awkward day. And it was in a rousing temper that Sir Edward, wet, footsore, thirsty, his arm nearly wrenched off by holding a jibbing horse, tramped up the avenue, the boughs over his head soughing and moaning in the storm.

The avenue was over a mile long. Morvan had advanced about two hundred yards when something white rushed at him from the bushes.

"Oh, Sir Edward! Sir Edward! Lo, now, Sir Edward!"—and the words dwindled to an incoherent wail.

He thought he recognized a maid-servant from the house, and inquired petulantly what was the matter with her.

"Oh, Sir Edward, sir, 'tis the soldiers, please you sir. Mr. Bates stood me here, and cautioned me not to let your honour go up to the house, for the soldiers were there all burning and firing."

"Nay, clear thy noddle, thou silly little fool!" cried Morvan impatiently. "What soldiers? Are they the Roundheads?"

But this was more than the maid could say, and when she fell once more to "Oh, Sir Edward, please you, Sir Edward!" he brushed by her and went striding up towards the house whence there came now to his ears, notwithstanding the gale, a great noise of voices. He was pushing on rapidly, when at a bend of the avenue he ran sharp against Will Bates, his faithful body-servant, a sturdy man who had attended him to the war. Bates was now moving cautiously towards the gate, followed by a stable-lad leading two horses on the grass border of the path.

"How is this, Bates?" exclaimed Morvan peremptorily. "Wherefore is all this noise?"

But Bates himself seemed alarmed. "For God's sake, Sir Edward", he said in a whisper, "get you to horse and let us be gone. 'Tis a party of dragoons from the King's army. They summoned the house towards eight o'clock, and finding you was away, entered with great shouts and went about pillaging and firing, their officers never quelling them that I did see, but triumphing and rejoicing, and calling you a damnable traitor. So that all's ruined. But they said 't was your honour they was after, and when they catched you they would slaughter you, for that you was worse than the rebels, and served with the King to steal his secrets and then deserted, and that you was a what y'call and traitor. And I said that you was none, and they took me prisoner saying they would hang me up with my master, and so they put me in the little room over the stable, not knowing the trap in the floor. But I got out, and found Jock here, and took the two bays in the grass field and lay here to stop you, sir, for 'tis plain they mean your life."

Morvan grew paler and paler as he listened. "I am no traitor", he said sternly, "and I am going up to face them. Come you with me. Who is their commander?"

"Sir, I do not know. But two of their officers talking a little apart together under the window of the stable, I heard them say they had all their informations from old Mr. Verschoyle, and they took it ill he had given them the wrong hour for your home-coming.—Don't go up to the house, Sir Edward", said Bates imploringly; "prithee, let us be gone. 'Twill serve nothing to go up."

"Rot thee!" shouted Morvan furiously. "Get thee gone, with a murrain! Save thyself, trembler! Thou art as pitiful a coward as yon poor wench. Am I to see my house burn and stand here idle?"

But Bates never moved. "For my life, I value it no more than another man", he said simply. "If Sir Edward goes up, I will go too. But 'tis useless; all's one ruin. Tomorrow they mean to fell the trees, and fetch the horses and cattle away. When I came down they were drinking and tobacconing in the stables; but they think you are on the road, and now as they have waited so long they will be spreading out to seize you. Mount now, Sir Edward, in God's name! or 'twill be too late. Nothing can be saved by your going up," said honest Bates, and took the freedom to push his master towards the horses. "There will be no persuasion, they'll not listen, they are mad to slaughter you. One of them swore they would cut yourself down afore they cut down your trees. Nay, sir, they may have missed me by this time, which will set them running; for they mean to hang me tonight, and only waited till they catched you to finish us together."

While he was talking he had passed the bridle of the lame horse to the boy, and twisting a lock of his own horse's mane round his finger, stood looking anxiously at his master, ready to jump into the saddle when Sir Edward had led the way. But Sir Edward was reluctant, and stood without moving. He trusted Bates; he knew that if Bates turned his back on a burning house and assaulting soldiers affairs must be indeed at a desperate pass. But to stand by while his wide fair house was plundered and burned without striking a blow, to be branded shamefully as a traitor to the King in whose cause he had been wounded, to run away from the doom of a traitor without defending himself, without ramming the charge back in their teeth— ah, no, his nature revolted against that. But even while he stood there deliberating, the trample of horses, the clang of accoutrements, and the sharp words of command were heard further up the avenue.

"Blood, Sir Edward, 'tis too late!" whispered Bates lamentably. "Here they come!"

By instinct Morvan swung himself into the saddle. From the very first he had felt in his heart that the game was up. He breathed a deep malediction against the destroyers of his father's house, and the greybeard fiend whose machinations had rendered him homeless.

"Lead on, Will", he said. "Ride where you can".

The two horses moved with little noise over the turf, and then swerving out of the avenue struck into the plantations, guided by their riders without the least embarrassment or uncertainty through the tangle. Bates led and did all the marking and listening, for Sir Edward was so stunned and furious that he could bestow no care on the passages of his escape; and it was only the long-trained hand of the fine horseman, the rider of the great horse, apt at all the graces of *manège*, acting now as it were by habit, distinct from the rider's will, which cleverly steered the fretting mare over the rough ground. The soldiers, however, were already beating the plantations; one or two of them who had got drunk were calling out ribaldries against Sir Edward; and just as Bates skilfully brought up against a little opening in the hedge, the fugitives were detected by some troopers posted hard by. These immediately ordered them to halt and give the word, and getting no answer, fired almost at random into the darkness, calling loudly meanwhile for their mates to bring up a lantern, and railing out against Judas Iscariot, and the Puritanical traitor. But while they were groping, baffled by the thick night, Sir Edward and his man had pushed through the hedge, and taking the open, tore along blindly at a free gallop. The soldiers had no chance over that difficult country in the black night against two riders who had known every field from childhood. They followed gallantly; several plunged horse and man into the dykes; three at least, encumbered with their heavy fighting gear, were drowned. A few more shouts were heard, a few more scattered shots, and then the pursuit was abandoned; and the two flying rode on unhindered till the dawn broke upon their haggard faces. A little after sunrise they arrived at a hut standing lonely on the moors in a hollow between hills. This was the end of the journey.

While Bates dismounted and set about making a fire, Sir Edward still sat his horse, overwhelmed, as it seemed, by his misfortunes. He knew he was guilty of no treason; yet here he was a runaway, proclaimed up and down England as a traitor, his goods seized, his house burned, and miles and miles from Paola, with all hope gone of rescuing her. As he thought of these things, he turned in his saddle and childishly shook his fist in the direction of Verschoyle's house.

"From today there is no quarter between you and me", he muttered. "Ten years if need be I'll pursue you, but I shall have you at last, God aid me!"

For the moment, however, there was nothing more exciting to be done than to lie concealed, and send Bates out to forage, who might pick up by the way some trustworthy information concerning the destruction which had fallen. And in effect before long Bates had cunningly established communications here and there, and from the news he brought in Sir Edward was able to piece together a story.

There could be no doubt he had been ruined by Mr. Verschoyle. The Prince, finding his orders neglected and his letters unnoticed, was become angry and suspicious; and Mr. Verschoyle had succeeded, not only in conveying damaging reports to His Highness's ears, but had also fastened on Morvan many imprecise and black discredits, contrived to blast his integrity with Lord Digby, Legge, Ashburnham, Warwick, and others who were in the private counsels of the King. But there was one letter, above all else, which definitely lost Sir Edward with the Royalists. In this letter, written in cypher by Sir Richard Willis a few weeks after Morvan first came into the country, the writer, while strictly enjoining his correspondent to delay not his return to Newark, at the same time, very unfortunately as it turned out for the other, gave some tactical details of a sally which he was planning. Now this letter, having been warily trapped by Verschoyle's servants, and the express riding with it persuaded he had delivered the paper to none other than Sir Edward Morvan himself, was presently carried to a division of the Parliament army under Massey, together with the key of the cypher, which Morvan in the mazedness and insouciance of those blissful days had left lying about, and a servant in Verschoyle's pay had purloined. When Rupert defeated Massey's force at Ledbury, these papers among others found their way to the Commander-in-chief's own hands. The Prince disliked Sir Edward already, and was prepared to find in him all sorts of treacheries since he knew him to be a friend of the Lords Goring and Wilmot, and of Daniel O'Neil; and when he reached Oxford early in May he did not measure his words in passionately denouncing Morvan before the King. The upshot was that a troop was detached to carry fire and sword against the traitor. It is said[*]

---

[*]   Memoirs relating to the Family of Morvan, vol. II (Privately printed, 1828).

that the commander of the party had orders to put Morvan to death on the place, and having taken his informations timed his attack for the hour when that one was usually returned home.

So if his horse had not gone lame he would now be dead of a shameful death, and unavenged. His ruin, as he gathered from the report of Bates, was well-nigh complete: the soldiers had carried away everything; his tenants had been intimidated and ordered not to pay their landlord any more rent; altogether, he was undone and his two sisters—fortunately with their aunt in Yorkshire when the soldiers came—were likely to beg their bread. Morvan, as he brooded over this disaster, was filled with rage against the Prince and the King's other advisers in this business, for their readiness to condemn him unheard. True, Morvan had been of the party amongst the King's followers against Prince Rupert, whom he regarded as a young foreigner battling mainly for his own hand; a soldier of fortune whose methods of warfare were questionable, and who had on his side all the broken rakes, the men of prey, and the low-fortuned nobility and gentry of the country,—in fact all those disorderly and refractory persons who brought dishonour on the King's arms and made the name of cavalier a byword for lewdness, and rapine, and swearing. He even went so far as to suspect the Prince of hiding a design to shoulder out the old King and set himself up instead. These opinions upon His Highness he had expressed pretty freely up and down, and Rupert was no doubt acquainted with them; hence it was reasonable enough that when the opportunity offered the King's nephew should shew no reluctance to rid himself of an avowed enemy. That was as far as Prince Rupert went; but leaving him aside, Morvan had been loyal to King Charles and his cause to the full measure. He had not only served at his own charge, but at the first setting up of the Royal standard he had brought a strong company into the field which as the war went on had been gradually dispersed. In common with many another man of his level serving in the Royal army, Sir Edward had taken the King's side more from sentiment than from any strong convictions as to the righteousness of the cause; and like many another man at all stages of the world, he found the justice of the cause strangely diminished by the harsh treatment he had suffered in his own person from its upholders. Still, for that cause he had fought even to shedding his blood: he might have got leave to travel, as many did at the beginning of the troubles; but he had remained and taken the brunt, and now this was his reward! As a matter of fact, he had almost as many friends out for the Parliament as riding for the King; and in his present desperate fortunes, with his eagerness to get even, to assuage his soreness, to counteract his ruin, and above all, to lay a heavy retributive hand on that old vile rat and sorcerer Verschoyle, he was vastly disposed to revise his convictions, and to throw in his lot with those whom he no longer hesitated to consider as the honest party in the State.

Ultimately, that is what he made up his mind to do. Having first sounded some of his friends on the Parliament side to ascertain what welcome he might expect within their lines, he set forth one night attended by Bates, and notwithstanding some dangers and hindrances made a rapid journey to Oxford, which the New Model under Fairfax was at that time investing. When he presented himself at headquarters, being very sensitive to slights after his late trials and because of his present equivocal position, he found himself irritated and baffled by the general's reserved, frigid demeanour, wherein he seemed to detect a note of irony. But one or two of his friends who stood by during the interview assured him that his impression was wrong, that those dry sombre manners were ordinary with 'Black Tom', and that on the whole he had been received very honourably.

Any how, whether that was the truth or not, Fairfax must at least have thought well of his qualities as a soldier, for he had not been many days with the army before he was appointed to a rather important post. A few weeks later he drew his sword against the King in person at Naseby.

VI

In the Manuscript of Sir John Holdershaw which we follow, at that part corresponding to the place we have now reached are inserted various excerpts from the Royalist News-letters, Mercuries, and pamphlets, which leave no doubt that Sir Edward Morvan's defection was deeply resented by that party. Ever since Marston there had been a pretty constant trickling of officers and soldiers from the King to the Parliament, and the lapse of a man of Morvan's standing could hardly fail to draw many waverers in its wake. Beyond that, his action must have the worst effect upon those little squires and men of middling estate up and down the country, ostensibly for the King, but who watched the wind, and whose *lâchetés* have been covered over for us of a later day by the noble unswerving loyalty of the greatest part of the Cavaliers; just as on the opposite side the unquestionable religious fervour and conviction of a section of the Parliament army stands forth so conspicuously, that some of us are led to attribute to that army as a whole a higher credit for godliness than perhaps it deserved.

But the writers against Morvan, to say the truth, somewhat over-reached themselves; for though their evident game was to prove that they were well rid of him, their violence revealed their mortification. They did not regulate their attacks by any sense of decency, but rather fell on with a brutal freedom, fleshing their pens, and howling. The result, as might be expected, is a body of writing incredibly scurrilous, noisy, and confused, floundering in all that bad taste and licentiousness of vituperation which really seem often the only things that count in political writings and speeches. Here, however, it is purposed to pluck but few weeds from all this garbage; basing ourselves upon the opinion of a gentleman who himself served the King without flinching to the end:—That to write invectives is more criminal than to err in eulogies. Our one great difficulty is the almost impossibility we are in to select among these indecencies so as to avoid shocking a fastidious age; and we take leave to premise that the specimens offered have been chosen rather because they are the least offensive than because they are the most witty—wit, alas! not being always inseparable from propriety, but on the contrary too often flourishing amid filth, as fair plants use to spring from the dung laid about their roots. Nay, so far are we here from the spirit of true wit, that perhaps the most regrettable feature of those examples we are permitted by the aforesaid considerations to lay before the reader, is a dull, barbarous mood of contumely, fatal to those lighter graces which alone can render a malign way of writing tolerable.

For instance, one author, after railing scandalously at "That notable hee-whore, who by his lewd embracements and chamberings with the rebels, hath dared, as we may say, to make the royal cause a cuckold",—thus bursts forth:

> "Temples of Venus fall apart!
>   Ye bordelloes fall down!
> The bawds have given up their trade
>   Since Morvan's on the town."

Another delivers a laboured assault in a long dull pamphlet entitled, "God's Deliverance from the Lousy; Exemplifyed in the Filthy, Accursed, and Poysonous Seditions and Treachery of Sir Ed. Morvan, Kt." From this wearisome compilation, which is full of lies, and among other fictions relates that Sir Edward, upon his reception by the Parliament forces, was stricken with a loathly disease, "Whereby his nose by God's mercy is now clene gon", we take the following lines, in which all point seems to be sacrificed to heavy ferocity and dirtyness:

> "That part which holds his wit and grace
>   Is Morvan's only pride;
> Lest we might think it was his face,
>   He shewed us his backside."

The best of them perhaps is a long catch called "Morvan's—," written, it is alleged, by "A Person of Honour now with his Ma... tie." It is too gross to repeat. The reader, we are sure, has been holding his nose over this noisome paragraph, which nothing but a scrupulousness to present this narrative impartially could have persuaded us to pen.

But Mr. Verschoyle himself with equal fervour, if more decorously, drew a grave and sober pen against Sir Edward, writing, as soon as he was possessed of the particulars, with great secrecy to Sir Edward Nicholas who had long stood his friend:—

MUCH HONORED FREND,

The Pleasure I gain from writing to You is dulled and tarnished by the heavy Matter I treat of wch a poysonous wind hath presently blown into mine eares. Sr. the newes of Sir Edward Morvan's defection, who was my Neighbour, with Tyes of kindred to my Wife, has panged those Hid and Vital Parts wch truely I did think naught but the Cold Hand of Death himself could reach to. For I do conceive that those who from the first stirring of these troubles have stood with the Parliament, should end by rangeing openly in the Field against the King, is what our sad Occasions (though bitterly) have learned us to endure: But that One who did enlist himselfe under the King's Standard, and as it were under the very shado and countenance of Maiestie, should now unsheath the Sword against his Anointed Lord and Sovraine, is what I can find no mate of in Blacknesse since this most Cruel Unnatural War, and doth Drap in herse-like weeds the Pen of, Sir,

YOUR MOST AFFECTIONAT FREND

AND HUMBLEST SERVAUNT

SIMON VERSCHOYLE.

And when he considered his neighbourhood and familiarity with Sir Edward, and how that one had unhinged all his cunningly laid plans by stepping over to the Roundheads, instead of being taken and killed in his own house; when he reflected upon Morvan's constant visits of late, and how promptly and terribly the King's troops had come down; he thought it wisest to allay any suspicion which might be reflected from Morvan on himself, and to nullify any pretext the Royalists might seize from this affair to plunder him in the same way. Accordingly he departed from the neutral and temporizing policy he had hitherto pursued so far as to add to the foregoing letter this postscript:—

"Sir, I ask you to represent to His Maiestie's Favour (tho' God knows I am not beforehand in my Fortune) that 3 sound hors goe with these to the Army, and Monyes for the Comfort and Maintenance of the Cause: Also 3 lusty Fellowes goe. S^r. I pray your Frendship to stand me in a Fayre light before His Maiestie."

But he had favourable relations with both parties: raging as he was at Morvan's escape, he thought it convenient to throw a plank between the knight's legs in the camp of his new friends; and so within a few days he wrote as follows to the Speaker of the House of Commons:—

RIGHT HONOURABLE,

One I am ashamed to call my Cosen and Neighbour, Sir Ed. Morvan I meane, hath of late so insinuated himself as to be carried to Your Armies. Sir, be vigilant lest Ye be by him Ensnared. Truely I doe think he is a spye. He hath been entertained in Yorks by Mr. Perigal, a most fierce Papist and Malignant, who is his Oncle, and careth not for staid Company, but lewd and roaring boys. I confesse I would be loath to see you receive a foyle by this deboshed drinking Cavalier, who for all his white eies and feignings is a true Castilian at hart. S^r. he strangely loves the Bottle, and I misdoubt me will join in your army with certain Merrie Roysterers (being a prime Favourite among Such, the same who have contrived his putting over to the Parliament) and thus sow poysonous tares of unrighteousness among the Godly Field of Your Army.—Were my occasions to serve you matcht with my Desires, I must be even more than now I am

YOUR HONOUR'S TRUELY
GRATEFUL HUMBLE SERVAUNT
SIMON VERSCHOYLE.

VII

What precise effect these letters had, or if they had any, cannot now be determined. But it is certain that Morvan was regarded unamiably by many of the Puritans: there are two letters of Whalley's, for instance, in which he is unmistakeably aimed at in bitter and discrediting terms. Still, for all that, he continued to serve with the New Model, and appears to have more than once distinguished himself, till the flight of the King and the capitulation of Oxford put an end to the war. In the troubled times that followed he took an active, though of course very subordinate part, and made himself useful to that party in the State with which certain of his friends, Sir Harry Vane amongst others, were identified. But he had never influence enough to get himself compensated out of the sequestered estates for the loss of his house, or—what he wanted much more—to obtain legal authority for the rooting out of old Verschoyle. In those days he lived very hard and meanly; for the King's troops had not only burned his house, but had ruined many holdings on the estate, and the tenants, being encouraged by Mr. Verschoyle, who worked among them with a thousand wiles, gladly availed themselves of the excuse, which the unsettled state of the country made a sufficient one, that having been forbidden by the King to pay rent to Sir Edward Morvan they were no longer sure to whom rent should be paid.

They ended by paying nobody. And it is doubtless on account of his extreme poverty that the movements of Sir Edward about this time are so clouded. We lose sight of him more than once in the months that passed between the surrender of the King by the Scots and the outbreak of the second war. He seems to have had a lodging, or at least an address, in Milk Street, over against Maudlin Church; but we do not find in his obscure and tormented history any fact worth noticing till near the end of 1647, when he was a principal in a peculiarly unhappy sort of duel, the circumstances of which seem odd enough to deserve some particular relation in this place.

As he was seated one evening in an Ordinary, there entered a young gentleman who had been his greatest friend at the University, and who was now become one of those wild and dissolute spirits in the King's party whose exploits left that party as a whole accessible to the worst accusations of its enemies. This gentleman, perceiving Morvan, planted himself directly in face, called for wine, and began staring insolently, and making a thousand offensive gestures studied to affront the other opposite, who for his part paid but little heed to these antics. When the wine was brought, the newcomer turns to a precise serious clergyman near him who was attentively reading in some papers, and "By your leave, Doctor," he calls out, "determine me by the Synod of Dort whether it is the greater sin to sit in a room colloguing with Judas Iscariot, or to... ... ..." The clergyman, seeing that a disturbance was in the air, answered drily, and gathering up his papers left the house. Upon this the Cavalier, not to be baulked of his quarrel, rose with a clatter so as to draw the eyes of all men in the room, and strolling over to where Morvan was seated, he cocks his hat at him, calls him a cuckoldy ass, and asked him what he meant by sitting down while his betters were standing? Without waiting for more, Morvan got slowly to his feet and hit the speaker a damned blow in the mouth. And in their frenzy they were going to a bout of fisticuffs on the spot; but the drawers and some of the company pulling them apart, they caught up their cloaks and swords and stepped into the street, none offering to stay them, though all guessed the fierceness of the business they went upon.

Once outside, the two made their way doggedly and sullenly to the fields beyond the Pest-house. It was a rainy night, with a tearing wind, and a full moon, which shining forth at intervals through the tumultuous clouds gleamed on the pools and wet grass of the place. And, in effect, it was probably owing to the condition of the ground that the contest after all was so brief, which otherwise might have been prolonged and hardly fought, for Morvan was no better at sword play than his opponent; who, however, unhappily slipping in the mud, almost fell on Morvan's point which pierced him through. When he found himself down, with Morvan clumsily bending over him, the wounded man raised himself on his hands and looked at the other very tenderly. "Buss me, Ned", says the poor heedless wretch, "for I think thou hast hurt me, lad, and I swear to God I loved thee better than any one all the time." Whereupon Morvan, weeping like a silly big child, careless of the danger he ran, took his friend up on his shoulders intending to make for his own lodging; but ere he had covered half the distance he was arrested with his dismal burthen. Whether the stricken cavalier recovered is uncertain; but from the somewhat considerable efforts which St. John, who was Morvan's friend over this matter, apparently had to make, notwithstanding his influence, ere he could extricate his client, it is to be feared that the poor foolish gentleman died. Still it is evident that this affair, however rigorously it may have been judged by some of the Puritans, did not stand in the way of Morvan's employment when the war broke out afresh, for he was undeniably in the field as a horse-captain under his old leader Fairfax at the capture of Maidstone.

Meanwhile, during those broken times, Mr. Verschoyle had dwelt on his lands perfectly unmolested. He gathered his rents as usual; he was regular in paying his taxes; he had taken the Covenant, and laboriously improved his relations with the Parliament. Sheltered by the Presbyterians, and looked on with a certain favour even by the Independents in London, at home he grew more close, more mysterious, and on occasions more truculent than ever. To his wife he would guard a moody taciturnity for weeks together; though he did not choose to spare her his company at these seasons, but would sit with her sometimes for hours, glowering, and frowning, and mumbling, and harshly rebuking her if she tried to leave the chamber. At other times, with that fury which always possessed him because of his foiled vengeance upon Morvan, he would turn against his wife and cover her with insults which were no less stinging because they were indirect and veiled. He had a favourite song, beginning "I am a cuckold bold," full of low jests, and this he and his one-eyed steward would sit together bawling solemnly for half-an-hour on end, shewing a wonderful ingenuity in twisting Sir Edward's name into the verses, and appealing to Paola to applaud, as it were, the hits. The unfortunate lady gradually became such a slave to her fears that she was never able to pass a moment with him free from trepidation. If he spoke she awaited some reproach; every morsel that she ate she knew not but it was poisoned. One day when he had been extremely violent and sour, wishing at length to draw his watch from his pocket to regulate his time, his wife thought he was going to pull out a pistol to kill her, and fell from her chair fainting. When he was abroad she could only sit for hours with a book on her lap which she would not even open, so discouraged was she!—wan, motionless, gazing afar off with a blank stare, holding a quaint flower to her cheek languidly. She went no more into the garden, neither in summer nor at autumn-tide, shrinking plaintively from that scene of her intensest joys and bitter sorrow.

VIII

The extraordinary and lamentable situation of Paola was not known to Morvan in all its details, but he knew more about it than Mr. Verschoyle suspected. Though he could not come into the country himself, he had trusty spies and sure intelligence. But rage as he might at what he heard, he could compass nothing against his enemy: Mr. Verschoyle was too strongly supported in London for Sir Edward's necessarily vague charges to prevail, and such charges, advanced as they had to be without any direct proof, did Morvan more harm than good. He would have been sensible of this himself, had not every new report of Paola's sad condition put all else out of his head save an iron purpose to deliver her by a bloody and punitive deliverance, no matter what the consequences might be, so long as she was delivered. For he feared that Paola might even die between the cruel hands of her gaoler, like a young bird panting out its life in the clumsy grasp of a boy.

But at last, when despairing and maddened he had almost made up his mind to desert and attempt Verschoyle's house single-handed, he obtained, by a singular piece of good-luck, or rather, if we recollect the methods by which his own integrity had been blasted before the King, by a kind of wild justice, the very thing he needed to assist his aim. This was nothing less effective than the letter given some pages back which was written by Mr. Verschoyle to Sir Edward Nicholas, and which, having been sent by Nicholas to a certain nobleman, was again passed on, and was at last forgotten with other papers in a house in Wales, hurriedly abandoned, to fall into the hands of a Parliament troop commanded by a friend of Morvan's, who knew partly what Morvan had suffered from Verschoyle, his soreness and rancour, his restless impatience to be avenged. It was by the postscript of the letter that Verschoyle was undone: in face of such irrefutable evidence of malignancy there could be no more hesitation to prosecute the writer, who moreover added to his malignancy a particularly detestable kind of double-dealing. Nevertheless there was still some delay; for Morvan, who was bent upon attacking Verschoyle's house in person, could not be spared from the blockade of Colchester, where he was indefatigable during the sick and rainy summer; and at last, it was the day after the town fell that Fairfax, whose good opinion he had secured by various acts of gallantry and discipline, gave him leave to detach half a troop, at the head of which he set forth grimly on his errand. It so happened that although Morvan, like Fairfax himself, for the rest, was of a "rational" temper, as it was called, most of the soldiers riding with him were zealots and fanatics of one kind or another, transported by various wild fancies, seraphical and notional, and full of a stubborn religious arrogance and intolerance.

It was on the fine afternoon of one of the earliest days of September that he drew near the familiar, and in spite of all! well-loved place. He was ready to forget the stern work he had come to do, as he gazed from a turn of the road at the house he had always preferred to his own or any other, standing now russet-toned and grey, so venerable, so sweetly quiet, so ineffably serene in the clear thin light. Just at the moment that the troopers wheeled in at the gate, Mr. Verschoyle was sitting down to dinner, finding himself today in an excellent humour with the world. He was cordial, even conciliating to Paola, with debonair gracious manners, engaging enough when he chose to give them play; and he awed into cringing silence the one-eyed knave who usually at this hour had a loose rein. But scarcely had they begun the repast, than a young man, excited and panic-stricken, stood on the threshold.

Without interrupting himself in what he was saying to his wife, who attended dejectedly, Mr. Verschoyle made a sign to the steward to rise and learn the youth's message. The two whispered a minute at the end of the room, and then the steward came up to Verschoyle's chair, shewing a countenance perturbed and sallow.

"How now, whey-cheeks?" sang out his master, noticing his fearful look. "Why, what a troublesome thing is guilt! Have they come for thee at last?"

"May't please your honour", stammered the other, all of a shake, "'tis the soldiers in your noble honour's gate. 'Tis the soldiers that— 'tis the soldiers—"

"'Tis the soldiers, 'tis the soldiers" repeated Mr. Verschoyle, mocking him. "They will surely hang thee, Abraham; that is in no doubt at all. Thou art the last of thy noble race. Sure (he went on scoffingly) I have heard thee talk sedition and hold most damnable invective speeches: I have heard them and I'll say them. I'll betray thee, Abraham,—yes, I'll give thee up. I have heard thee say thou didst hope to see the Roundheads tumbling in their blood, when some of their money should chink in thy pockets. Was it not so?— Nay, the truth is thou hast been at the wine. Where are these soldiers save in thy drunken fancy and yon fool's?"

"Nay, so please you sir, even as I speak you may hear them". And in effect the trampling of many horses and the clatter of accoutrements were coming in plainly through the open windows.

Perceiving that he was for some reason or other evidently besieged, Mr. Verschoyle rose gravely from the table. "Since the soldiers encompass us", he said, "let us go forth to meet them."

But as he was passing down the room the steward in a frenzy of terror flung himself at his master's feet.

"Save me, save me!" he yelled. "Only you can save me. I have been an evil man, I have collogued, I have had commerce with the devil, I have lain embraced by harlots. Here comes my last breathing hour, God ha' mercy! They will hang me if you'll not protect me, sir; they will tear out my bowels—yea, truly, they will rip me up."

Mr. Verschoyle spurned him with his foot as he might a whelp. "Get thee hence", he said contemptuously. And turning to Paola as they passed into the hall he added: "'Tis but an hour's madness in that poor mean fellow. He is no coward for the things of this world, but he sees hell-fire in a farthing rushlight. He was bred a Puritan."

By now some of the soldiers had entered the grassy court, and the great bell clanged harshly. This being followed by loud peremptory knocks, Mr. Verschoyle, who could not have offered any effectual resistance even if he had wished, ordered the doors to be thrown open. No sooner was this done, than Morvan at once stepped into the hall. Completely armed, he had his steel cap on his head, and it was easy to see he had come there to bring trouble. But Mr. Verschoyle, standing large and gaunt and black before the hearth, chose to ignore his implacable demeanour.

"Welcome, Ned!" he cried with an emphatic cordiality, "thou art returned home at last. We have heard of thy prowesses. No part of the earth but is full of thy labours. What battles thou hast seen, what signal victories!"

For all answer Morvan bowed low to Paola, noting with grief and anger as he did so her emaciated frame and the almost spectral paleness of her visage. She on her side spoke no word, but merely bent her head slightly in acknowledgement of his salutation, and remained seated in a high-backed chair, resting her head upon her fragile hand. Morvan then looked straight at Verschoyle.

"My business, sir", he observed coldly, "is of an unpleasant nature, at least for you. My orders are to inform you that you are suspected to be a dangerous malignant, and to search your house. For that, I warrant you," he added insultingly, for he could hardly control his rage, "I'll not ask your leave—only taking care", said he, again looking at Paola to reassure her, "that the innocent shall not be confounded with the guilty."

About half-a-dozen troopers had by this time followed their captain into the hall. Mr. Verschoyle stared at them a moment with a kind of bland wonder, rocking himself up and down in his big shoes. Then he blew a long whistling breath through his teeth.

"Hoity-toity, these be fine words", he said; "vastly fine words. I protest I do love a round speech, sonorous and musical. But thou hast improved thyself in the army, Ned; thou hast plied thy book, man! How have they transformed thee? The next ignorant, sottish, ill-licked, impudent cub that I meet who's no good but to shamble about and make eyes at the women, I'll send him to the army. Truly, 'tis a better school for dunces than a university,—that I see, that I see. Hast thy search-warrant, lad?"

Morvan, outraged and indignant, curtly handed him the document. Mr. Verschoyle glancing through it saw that he was accused of sending horses and money to the Royal army, and otherwise comforting those in arms against the Parliament; his servants and tenants too were said to be deeply engaged. He saw further, that he was charged circumstantially with playing the traitor to the Parliament, and that Morvan was empowered to bring him in custody to London. There could be no doubt that the warrant was genuine; and with a feeling of uneasiness which he disguised perfectly he gave the paper back to Morvan.

"I question your authority", he said boldly. "But that can stand over till later. There is naught of treachery here; no, nor hidden either. Begin your search; I am small afraid."

Paying little attention to what he said, Morvan gave a few sharp orders, and the troopers scattered about the house striking their swords and the butts of their pistols against the wainscotting to discover monies or compromising papers concealed. Morvan left the hall to control the search, for it was not in the least his intention to have the house wrecked and plundered. Mr. Verschoyle too mounted the stairs and sat himself in the embrasure of a great window on the wide landing where the staircase turned, keeping always on his face a smile false and terrible. And Paola still remained moveless in the hall, resting her head on her hand.

While matters were at this tension, suddenly there arose a doleful wail or ululation which drifted in from the terrace, and softened by the walls, filled the rooms and corridors with sobs and miserable cries. It seemed as if the spirit of the place, rudely disturbed after peaceful years, and presaging some tremendous misfortune and downfall, was wandering disconsolate through the building with laments and long moans. But as a matter of fact, the disquieting rumour was due to the soldiers stationed outside, who, finding the waiting heavy, had started a religious service. Most of these men were Straddlingites, or as they were more commonly named, "Oh-Ho's", one of those numberless petty sects which flourished at the period and found their most favourable ground in the army. Originally called by its popular name simply from a physical defect of the founder, Know-the-Lord Straddling, one of Harrison's captains a defect which forced him when he rose to preach or pray at first to emit certain involuntary ejaculations, and cry out many times "Oh-ho, oh-ho!" accompanied by uncouth writhings,—the popular name indicated in a measure the ritual of the sect; for the cries and contortions of the afflicted man would after a while so disturb the nerves of his listeners that they could not do otherwise than fall to imitating him sympathetically, and wail "Oh-ho, oh-ho!" in their turn with all their might. And this was the ominous and melancholy sound which was now wafted in and floated sadly through the house, while Morvan's troopers relentlessly searched, and Mr. Verschoyle sat smiling, smiling, gazing blankly out of the window.

After about half-an-hour, Sir Edward tramped down the stairs. He was ghastly pale, but his eyes gleamed, and on his face was a look of unshakeable resolution. Mr. Verschoyle rose to meet him, gathering together all his formidable powers of intimidation.

"Well, honest soldier," he began jeeringly, "gallant Hector, noble swashbuckler, runaway Ned, brave warrior on women and the aged, have you nosed out any treason lurking in my walls?"

"No", answered Morvan briefly, "we have found nothing". Then seeing that the other was going to speak, "You took good care of that", he added as an afterthought. "However, we know enough."

"All you can know, Edward", returned Mr. Verschoyle, speaking deliberately for the ears of the soldiers who now had gathered behind their leader up the stairs and on the first floor, "all you can know to my discredit is that I am a poor old man, bowed with age, who live here with no other wish than to finish out my few harmless dusty years in peace, far from all state tumults, and to be laid in a quiet grave."

"Ay, we'll give you that, brother", retorted Morvan grimly, "even as we gave it to Sir Charles Lucas a few days since. I mean to have you shot."

Mr. Verschoyle made a slight convulsive movement with his shoulder as if indeed a bullet had just struck him there, but otherwise he betrayed no surprise nor any emotion. "No, Edward", he said with sorrowful dignity, "you will not do that. You will not slay an unarmed, defenceless, and grey man, who has offered no resistance to your search. I knew your father, Edward, and your grandfather;

I knew you when you were a little boy. If you command this most bloodthirsty and unnatural act, I tell you solemnly you will rue it all the days of your life. Observe, the deed will not be on the heads of these honest fellows here whom you order to fire the shot (and I heartily forgive them!) but you will be the horrible murderer yourself—yea, as truly as if you sheathed your sword in my vitals. Think well on it, Edward; commit not this black and horrid murder of a helpless old man".

He might as well have called to the east wind to blow softlier. "You burned my house", answered Morvan sombrely; "you scandalized me before the King. You have betrayed the dearest pledges; you have fired and harried. You have hunted the poor man like a partridge on the mountains. You have brought about the ruin and loss of many lives. You are an execrable and satanical cozener. Your lusts stink, your magics and bedevilments cry to Heaven. My conscience is clear for what I now do, and God judge between you and me. Not this country only, but all England will bless me for ridding it of such a monster." And turning, he called the soldiers to attention.

But the corporal, leveller, fanatic, preacher and Straddlingite as he was, a man who had been some time before chosen an Agitator for his uncompromising root-and-branch principles, on this occasion took the freedom to interpose.

"Stay, sir", he said familiarly to Morvan, "balance well what you do. Our warrant goes not to the spilling of this blood. Sooth, I know that this greybeard is a son of Belial, spuing forth rottenness from his mouth, and given over pertinently to destruction; but oh, consider you that he is old, his sojournings with rogues and strumpets termed, his toyings with his painted young concubine below stairs soured, his days of iniquity nigh ended. For what says Paul? Paul says, That which decayeth and waxeth old is ready to vanish away. Not of all malignants do I speak as one who would spare them—nay, rather should they be smote with the edge of the sword, their kings utterly destroyed, and their hellish dunghill of filthy, beastly, Babylonish priests consumed by fire. But this malignant man is old, and old blood should have a dry death. Oh, if this man's days be evil, they are soon done; if his nights unruly, they are soon one black; and verily his latter end will be bitterness".

This harangue, cast in the language, and spoken, or rather preached, in the tone they delighted in, had a marked effect on the soldiers. Sir Edward, noticing this, and fearing the scruples of the soldiers might even provoke them to mutiny, and his prey escape after his careful toils, endeavoured with considerable readiness of wit to move them in a contrary sense by a vivid appeal to their prejudices.

"Seize the sorcerer!" he shouted, "he has bewitched our worthy corporal. Now he casts his Popish spells on us. The change is about to reach us all; soon we shall be turned into mice and rats if he be not presently slain. All the country knows this miscreant puts on the shape of a bloody beast at night, and has devoured two-and-twenty children in that form. Would you have the devil among you in the shape of a large wolf, raging and tearing? I tell you he is a wizard, and a Papist, and an atheist. Out into the courtyard with him ere worse befall! See!" yelled Morvan pointing excitedly, "Oh, God, see!—he is even now changing to a grey wolf."

The soldiers stared with dilated eyes, and thought they did really see some frightful transformation in process. Recklessly brave in the field, they were slaves to their terror of Popish spells, and witchcraft, and magical receipts. Willingly, and even eagerly, they formed up under Morvan's order to drag Mr. Verschoyle forth.

But he, stepping up to the corporal who stood between him and Morvan, laid his hand on the trooper's shoulder. "Stand by, friend", he said gently; "I am no drunkard and carnal man as thou dost fancy, but a precisian even as thyself, who follows sermons and prays in my family. The gentlewoman below stairs is indeed young, but of godly carriage, and truly my wife. I do set my face against the wicked railers and swearers and other lewd persons who persecute me for righteousness, even"—he said, raising his voice and pushing the corporal aside, "yea, even as this swearing, cursing, sottish knight of the blade here now".

And with that, fetching a spring swift and lithe as a tiger's, he leaped upon Morvan, with a force amazing in such an ancient man, and bore him to the ground—seizing him by the throat and face and throttling him with his great powerful hands. The soldiers threw themselves on him, and with immense difficulty mastered the terrible frantic creature who had now cast off all self-control and struggled with them, striking and ravening, to get once more at Morvan, the hatred of years boiling in his head.

"What!" he roared, "You would slay me, and then steal my house and marry my wife? Ah no!—before God, no! Not till I have torn the false tongue from your throat. What Verschoyle has Verschoyle holds. I will not leave the earth till I have seen you dead."

The soldiers dragged him downstairs, struggling furiously. But Morvan, gasping for breath, outraged and shamed, was taken with such a devilish frenzy of passion that he thought if he did not now kill Verschoyle with his own hand, he would be cheated after all of the sweets of revenge. He ran down the stairs, and reaching across the shoulders of the troopers, clapped the nose of his pistol against the old man's breast. But the weapon snapped without exploding, whereupon he brought the butt down with a smash on Verschoyle's face. "I will lie in Hell for all eternity to be even with you", he said.

A soldier threw open the door leading out from the hall; and there was the court, placidly green and silver in the kind afternoon sun. Mr. Verschoyle, since he had taken the blow, had ceased to struggle, and stood amid his guards gaunt, sinister and inscrutable, with his bleeding face raised to the sky, or perhaps only to a stone set high near the roof on which had been carved long ago the punning motto: *Verschoyle's Keep Verschoyle Keeps*. Sir Edward and another officer handed their carbines to a couple of troopers; and as it happened, Morvan being still too strangled with fury and excitement to get his voice, it was the cornet at last who gave the word. The soldiers fired and the old man fell lifeless.

How much of these dreadful scenes Paola had witnessed no one can tell. When Morvan went in search of her he found her still seated in the hall with her head resting on her hand, but she had swooned.

IX

In the event, when at length she was able to realize the sane wide spaces these harsh doings had opened about her life on all sides, it was not, astonishingly enough! relief that was her principal sensation. She felt gratefully, indeed, that the immediate stifling pressure of the tyrant was removed; that she was now able to breathe freely where before she had been suffocating; that she could go and come when she liked; that she was young and rich and free; but these pleasant impressions were blurred by the haunting conviction that her new state was unreal, that her terrible husband had but withdrawn himself for a little while, and would certainly come back whenever it suited his ends. This insensate fear invested all her actions with a certain indecision; upon everything she did there was an air of the makeshift and temporary; she recoiled from any step decided and permanent, shadowed as she was by the dread of that gaunt irresistible form returning to take possession, to demand an account. Her very sleep was afflicted by shocking dreams in which he was constantly before her: now in the clinging cerements of the grave; anon in his habit as he lived, but with a green wound in his breast still bleeding; and always towering, threatening, terrifying, standing over her with a diabolic majesty, then crushing her down with his hands; till at last she would start up strangling, covered with sweat, feeling even after she was broad awake that the old man was there actually in the room, at her bedside. Such dreams as these, the intensified prolongations of her waking reveries, took away from her all desire to stir abroad and see the world, or otherwise to taste the advantages of her freedom. Any attempt at pleasure, she felt, would not come off happily; would be cursed, so to speak, in advance. Far better to stay at home, to change nothing in her mode of life, to traverse none of the old orders and measures—not to beat, in fine, against that still powerful and implacable will, but just to rest quiet and wait.

Morvan tried to disengage her from these gloomy apprehensions, but it was long ere his exertions met with any response; and in fact it may be said that never at any time did he succeed in quelling them altogether. Although towards the spring of 1650 she at last consented to marry him, that too was still with the consciousness of an act provisional, desultory, an idle and temerarious catching at happiness which the unseen, horror-striking watcher did not approve of, and might at any time bring to a harrowing termination. It was not, either, that Paola regarded the circumstances of her husband's death with compunction, or instinctively shrank from Morvan as a guilty and blood-stained man. As far as her knowledge of the affair went, Mr. Verschoyle's house had been attacked by soldiery; he had resisted, perhaps slain one or two, and had been slain himself in turn. Such events were become too common in England of late years to cause any special wonder. She thought of her husband's end as she might have thought had he fallen in the field of battle, and of Morvan's part in it as if he had commanded a regiment which had but done its duty and come off victorious. Sir Edward took every precaution not to disabuse her mind in its imperfect apprehension of those events, and never spoke with any particularity of the attack on the house.

Abating these clouds, which were wont indeed since their marriage to dwindle to a thin sun-coloured haze, the wedded pair ought to have been happy; the world smiled before them almost genially. Young, and lovers who, long separated, were now fortunately joined in the suavity of wedded love, rich, seated in one of the fairest estates in England, truly it seemed as if Fortune, having plagued them so long, had of late grown ashamed of her persecutions, and turning benignant, was remorsefully loading them with compensating favours. The troubles which were shaking the country passed them by. Sir Edward was looked upon with favour by the leading spirits of the Republic, and was outside of all suspicion because of his prowesses against the Royalist armies, and his signal unkennelling of that notorious malignant and plotter old Mr. Verschoyle, of whose death he had rendered an acceptable account, which was perhaps the more eagerly received as there were more than one or two in the House who would have found themselves strangely embarrassed and uneasy if the old schemer had been carried alive to London. Vane the younger and Haslerig were special friends to Morvan, and willingly looked after his interests. To be sure he had his enemies, and he was disliked, among others, by Cromwell, who, it is said, distrusted him for changing his coat and gulping down the Covenant with such suspicious readiness, and who, after he became supreme, persistently refused to employ him in business of state; but for all that his credit was so good at the Protector's Council-table, that when, in time, the Major-Generals were let loose to fine and otherwise harass the country gentlemen whose loyalty to the government was questionable, he was left unmolested.

Yes, they had every reason to be happy, and no doubt in a measure they were so. The husband certainly was happier than he had ever been in his life. And Paola too would throw herself desperately on waves of love for days and days together, letting herself be drifted and swayed and lulled till her obsession, waning then and almost dying out, seemed to her as foolish as it did to her husband, and she arrived almost to forget the old man in his grave. For whatever her fancy might suggest, he *was* in his grave, deep down in the cold earth; of that there could be no question at all. The huge ugly body had been buried as that of a Popish and atheistical villain, not in the churchyard, but by Morvan's orders under a tree which stood at some distance from the consecrated plot. And at present inside the house there was little to remind one of its former owner. All those servants employed indoors and out who had clung to Mr. Verschoyle, and who had even borne a kind of love for him, or at least took a sort of low pride and delight in his brutalities and powers of chicane— and strangely enough! they made a good number—had fled to the four winds on that day of their master's downfall. None offered to stay these panic-stricken wretches; but Sir Edward beat the country relentlessly for the one-eyed steward whom he would have hanged up with pleasure had he caught him.

That one, however, had taken to his heels at the first bruit of violence, and by the time Mr. Verschoyle had been laid in earth, and the soldiers began to look round for the fugitive, he had put a good many miles betwixt himself and the house. After various and surprising adventures, which probably would not interest and certainly would not edify the reader, he came at last to a town in Berkshire, where he settled ostensibly to the trade of a tailor, under the name of Everard. Now in the town where he found himself dwelt one Dr. Pordage, a man of beard and severity, the chiefest then in England of that sect known as the Behmenists. Into the sober family of the Doctor did our Everard force himself, pretending that he desired to be of their communion, and setting up a claim to rival Dr. Pordage himself in discerning spirits by the smell, with divers other deceptions of the sort. But in the end he embroiled the Doctor most lamentably by his pranks, bringing the reverend man to be accused of wantonness and familiarity with devils. For in truth, as the Doctor soon found to his dismay, Everard was nothing less than a most wily speller and sorcerer, who held active conversation with extremely savage dragons and devils. Besides that, he most heinously endeavoured to seduce and terrify the good Doctor by his damnable arts, appearing to him, it is credibly related, at one time as a fiery dragon as big as a room, and then suddenly changing to a pernicious fly or gnat which buzzed about the Doctor's face for above an hour, thus constraining him from learned meditations. Nor was this all. One morning the Pordage family were horrified to discover on the chimney-piece of their parlour the impression of a coach drawn by tigers and lions, and seated in the coach a figure, a very lively image of the reverend Doctor himself, taking tobacco and embracing a madam; all obviously the handiwork of Satan. This, though alarming enough, might yet have been endured; but what was far graver, by his magic and snares Everard gradually turned the good Doctor to all manner of abominations, so that the excellent man's house became, while the spell worked, a harbourage for many of the deboshed sort to sit tippling, while he himself turned into an ordinary gamester at cards, sitting up and burning lights in the company of this Everard till two or three o'clock in the morning, to the intense scandal of the township. And one night in particular, the Doctor, having sat many hours with the nigromancer engaged in drinking wine, and playing mine host and the good fellow in a very beastly and disgusting fashion which suited not at all with his reverend hairs, must now, if you please, when the night was near done, begin to roar most lewdly, singing carnal songs and setting up to be one of your blades, which brought upon him a remarkable and fearful judgment. For he suddenly found himself in his bed without any knowledge of how he got there, all clothed, and having on a pair of boots with spurs which belonged to no one else but Everard; whose face, the light being now come, the Doctor, as he afterwards testified, descried nine times at his window, which was raised many feet from the ground, pulling his forelock at him, and making various low and disparaging signs with his fingers. Upon these monstrous events, and the consequent indignation of the Doctor's wife, Everard was driven forth from the town, none heeding his contention that the Doctor in his cups had insisted upon trying on the boots and could not get them off again; and it is attested that after his departure the excellent Doctor at once regained the ways of decorum, to the great contentment of his pious family. As for the steward, his subsequent fortunes are uncertain; one can only form the blackest conjectures touching his occupations; but there is reason to believe he was among the riff-raff who joined the expedition of Venables to the West Indies and died of a flux in Jamaica.

But though Morvan had the luck to find his house itself cleared of those servants who might have proved hostile, or by their presence recalled unhappy memories, the peasants, on the other hand, rapidly became very irregular and troublesome. By a singular piece of misfortune, the death of Mr. Verschoyle was followed within a few weeks by an outbreak of fever in the cottages, by mortality among the cattle, by all those ills from which for years the estate had been free. In face of this distress the peasants turned mulish and unruly, and fervently wished their old landlord back again, whose death they confounded with that of King Charles, and held Sir Edward Morvan responsible for both. They would lounge in the ale-house, or hang about the churchyard on Sundays, telling over with a sheepish pride Mr. Verschoyle's most dastardly exploits, and drawing malevolent and disloyal comparisons with the present owner. And the legend, the inevitable legend, began to gather about the old man's name. It was reported that on the night of his death, and for some nights after, the moon was covered with a shroud of a dismal and fearful texture, while a pool near the house where he used to be seen at twilight in converse with spirits stood three days the colour of blood to the amazement and terror of many. The sober and godly minister who (upheld by Morvan) now performed the duties of that parish, had a most difficult time of it. In vain he preached elaborate and learned discourses against Antinomianism; in vain he uprose searchingly against astrologers and witchcraft: his hearty words fell against stubborn and preoccupied ears. His parishioners had got it into their heads that old Mr. Verschoyle had been opposed to all clergy, and they had done better by following his ways than they ever expected to do again. As a matter of fact, Morvan was a far more liberal and easy landlord than Mr. Verschoyle had ever been; he had them tended in their sickness; he sent them wine and food and fire; but when all was done he found that his charities were accepted more as a compensation than a benefaction. The more he did for them the more they hated him. It would seem as if there were a secret method to govern these people, and having that secret you might trample on them, you might treat them like dogs, and yet preserve their respect, obedience, and perhaps their affection; whereas, lacking the secret, though you lowered their rents, though you improved their holdings, though you covered them with favours, you would find in the end the same ingratitude, derision, and sullen implacability. For some time after his marriage Morvan used to make kindly visits to his tenants, bringing them gifts, and sitting patiently with those in pain. But he was not wanted; the sickness and misery increasing, notwithstanding his efforts, he was supposed to bring bad luck; and as he rode through the villages he was met with scowls and mutters, while a few of the most desperate would threateningly lay stones in their hands. And as frequently happens, those people, especially those women, who had been the worst treated by Mr. Verschoyle were now his boldest partizans. Even the gentle Paola, whose heart was wrung by the sufferings of these poor folk, going abroad on an errand of mercy, was not spared some insults; and a strapping black-eyed wench called Lizzie Mend, who was said to have lent herself to the old man's embraces, and—as Heaven knows Mr. Verschoyle never made any scruple of defrauding the labourer of the wages of sin—had gained little more by her complaisance than a rough mouth and a wet jacket,—well, what must this quean do but frighten Paola almost to death by daringly calling out in her pillory voice the words "Murderess" and "Adulteress". The groom rode back and laid about him with his heavy whip which soon brought Lizzie Mend to her tears; and upon his return, being closely questioned by his master who had noticed his wife's perturbed air, the man with many apologies and begging-of-pardons told the whole story. Morvan was naturally enraged, and the happy-go-lucky damsel would have been dragged before the justice and whipped almost to death, had not this measure reached Paola's ears, who commanded that nothing of the kind should be done. But she went forth among the tenantry no more. Lizzie Mend, on the other hand, became a sort of popular heroine, and perambulated the country shewing her weals, which she maintained my lady herself had inflicted on her with a foreign-like scourge simply for calling out "God's rest to Mr. Verschoyle!" This lie took all the more because it had by this time become one of the grievances of the common people that Mr. Verschoyle's body had been cast rudely under a tree by soldiers instead of being laid in consecrated ground, and the unredressed injury to his corpse was reckoned against his widow.

The idol of a people is sometimes made out of the most unpromising materials: it would have astonished Mr. Verschoyle himself more than any one else to learn the reverence and affection with which his memory was cherished. His name was now become a defiant banner, which rallied the most various and extravagant complaints. Had the silly people but known it, they might have done far better, they could have been far happier, with brighter opportunities and encouragement, under the government of Morvan than under their old landlord; but they would make no effort. Believing themselves under a curse, they became churlish and slovenly and unclean, and thus aggravated the evils which pressed upon them so sorely. All their energies were spent in railing against the present family; and if we make due allowance for the narrow circle of his fame, it can truly be said that in that age of unpopular men there was not a more unpopular man in England than Sir Edward Morvan. And what made the situation immensely worse, Morvan's own estate, the estate he had inherited from his father, having lacked for some years the direction of his own hand and lain open to Mr. Verschoyle's potent wiles and cajoleries, was become infected with the heresies of the neighbouring one. Often Sir Edward longed to go away and leave these perverse and ungrateful people to the unchained mercies of bailiff and steward; but since Cromwell's troopers had plucked the Parliament men out of their House, and especially after Cromwell himself became Protector, Morvan's hopes of state employment were shattered, and from a political point of view it became in the highest degree expedient for him to rest quietly on his lands.

To these grievous annoyances, and to the unnatural narrowness of life, the restrictions and seclusion which grew out of them, should doubtless be ascribed the singular mental condition which Sir Edward Morvan developed about this time—manifesting itself by an inclination to choose for his favourite resting-place out of doors the tree just out of the churchyard at the roots of which Mr. Verschoyle's body had been laid. This habit, adopted at first perhaps in a mere angry spirit of bravado, provoked in him by hearing his old enemy's name and powers dinned constantly in his ears, and by the widespread belief that the dead man would not be content to rest there quietly and cold on his back while another sat in his place and watched his fire, became ere many months an uncontrollable impulse, a necessity of his very being; and he would linger for hours under the tree strangely entranced. It really seemed sometimes as if he were drawn there against his will, and even without his knowledge; for he would often start up from his meals, or in the middle of cheerful talk with his wife, and wander dreamily to the door; but no sooner did Paola lay her hand gently on his arm, and ask him with her fond smile on what business he went, than he would turn round with a sigh, apparently shake himself free from some hallucination, and forthwith returning to his place continue the talk as though it had not been broken off. But as time went on this melancholy obsession grew more and more marked, and the unhappy lady could not fail to consider it now with the greatest distress. He would steal from her side at night, and go forth to stand by that unblessed grave for hours of wind and storm.

What strange fascination led him there? It broke his sleep; he ate but little; he would answer vaguely with far-away looks: his spirit, one might think, was always by the tree even when his body was elsewhere. From a practical, healthy man, a soldier and sportsman, a man of good spirits and the open air, he had turned in a few months into a hesitating, haunted-looking dreamer, moody and distracted.

Oddly enough, the tree itself, sere and thunder-blasted as it was, quite dead long since as all supposed, began about this time to put forth blossoms and leaves, flourishing at first indeed only at the top; but as Morvan yielded more and more to his mournful fancy, and lengthened his stations by its side, it felt increasingly life slipping through all its boughs, and in less than six months it was completely robed with a dense and poisonous-looking foliage which fell not when the autumn winds stripped the other trees near by. Of course there must always have been some life remaining in the tree which the disturbance of the earth at its roots when the grave was dug had invigorated; but what had the worst effect on the superstitious peasants, and what is indeed inexplicable, was the uncommon—nay, unknown species of leaves wherewith it had covered itself in this resuscitation. Large, round, spongy, velvety leaves, thick, clammy and soft to the touch, and when pressed or broken giving forth a putrid odour—such was the unfamiliar vesture of the tree, at which the peasants standing at a distance would gaze as long as they dared, and at the lonely figure so often beneath it. And the terrors daily increased. Zilpah Green, a woman of conduct, reported that she had seen between lights a huge unmistakable hand reach out of the clay and move gropingly, as if it searched for some one whom it meant to pull down with it into the grave. Ere long the opinion grew that the tree was bewitched and brought the direst misfortunes upon those who loitered near it; and once that opinion had taken hold,

Sir Edward's sad musings were no longer spied upon even by the hardiest. But he, careless whether he were observed or not, used to stand by that ominous tree for hours in all weathers, till his patient wife, shaken with anxiety, would at length go out and lead him in from the damps of the graveside and the dank umbrage of the tree, to the warm house and her warm embrace.

On top of all this there fell out towards the autumn of 1655 an extraordinary incident, which might well have been taken for a warning of the immense evils in store for that house. It chanced one evening as Sir Edward and his wife were at supper that her glance fell on his hand, whereupon she recoiled in horror.

"Where did you find that ring?" she exclaimed breathlessly, moved to the soul.

"What ring?"—Even as he spoke he looked down carelessly and incuriously at his fingers, and turned very pale.

There was a ring on his finger, and it was old Mr. Verschoyle's signet-ring. The ring was unmistakable. It was an unusual stone, carven with magical symbols, and had been given to Mr. Verschoyle by his "son", the youthful Elias Ashmole, out of gratitude for some instruction in divining by the Mosaical rods, and especially for the communication of secrets in the Rosycrucian faculty. Morvan gazed in a stupor at the ring for a minute, and then tried to pull it off; but it was as fast to his finger as though it had been moulded there.

"It must have been lying about the house and I slipped it on unawares", he said at last.

Paola assented, but neither of them believed this explanation. She knew that Mr. Verschoyle never laid by that ring, attributing to it various potent influences; while he remembered that it was still on the dead man's hand when he was laid in the grave, for a soldier had offered to remove it and had by Morvan himself been forbidden. Besides, how came it that a ring which fitted the thick finger of Verschoyle clung so tight to the slim finger of Morvan? The two looked heavily into each other's eyes with these unuttered thoughts, shaken by terror of the unknown, the inevitable.

"O my love, whatever happens I have you—you, your own self"! cried Paola at length with a burst of tears, and they clasped each other in a long embrace of intolerable sadness and anguish. Nevertheless, even in face of this ghastly and harrowing accident, he could not resist stealing forth in the course of the night to keep his station by the grave.

The next day, after many trials, he found that the ring was so deeply imbedded in the flesh that if he would have it displaced the finger itself must be sacrificed. Henceforward he concealed his hand as if it bore some disgraceful stain, and he and his wife in their talks together were sedulous to avoid all allusion to the ring. But it fell out with them as may be observed in an affectionate family whereof one of the members is stricken with a lingering and fatal disease, when, although each takes infinite care to shun that subject, still the conversation against the will of all is constantly circling about the forbidden topic: each knows what the other is thinking as if he were speaking aloud, the sick person as well as the rest, and she and all are oppressed by abominable dolours, the more poignant because they are stifled.

But though the ring was ever in their thoughts, giving them the disquieting sensation that they were watched and threatened, and perhaps at the mercy of some pitiless invisible spirit, still, in the two or three months which followed its appearance they tasted intenser joys than any they had known since their marriage. The offence which was common to both, and assured them that the menace hung over both alike; the conviction that if one were struck the other would fall too; the fear always lurking in their breasts when they sought their bed that they would never again see the day, or else see it in incalculable conditions of misery and prostration:—all this induced in them a pathetic mutual dependence, a dread of being separated or distinguished even in their sufferings; as two prisoners who have been taken and tried and sentenced together might come at last to feel, as they were being carted to the place of execution, all other hopes and fears swamped now in the ultimate great fear that ere their agony was ended one of them might be reprieved in spite of himself, and they would be cheated of dying together. These feelings, and an instinct which told them that their lives were blighted, that such happiness as they might snatch would be of the briefest, and some tremendous price of despair and tears exacted for it, led them to open their hearts to the transports of love with an abandon hardly to be understood by those whose lives are regular and content. Though it is true that Morvan still persisted in his visits to the grave, and that by the tyranny of this habit they were for some precious hours of each day necessarily separated, yet it falls to be remarked, that once his dismal watch completed, he emerged so to speak out of a cloud, shook off the morbid ugly fancies with the damp from his hair, and came to Paola with the utterance and smile of a lover. The two grew so enhardied by this enduring tranquillity that they no longer thought seriously of going away: they were almost quite happy where they had always dreamed of being happy. The calamitous ring, even, lost some of its terrors in this time of passion and caress, and Morvan no longer troubled to conceal his hand when he was with Paola.—One lingers with complaisance over the last peaceable moments which were granted to this unhappy pair, and contemplates with especial assuagement any feeble and transient gleams of light which lay across the dusky life of the gentle and kind Paola, whose sufferings were so out of proportion to any faults she had committed during her brief, joyless, and baffled existence. The last days of the winter saw burst forth the germ of the evils which remain to be related, and in the procession of which there was never to be another interval of ease.

On a bleak and desolate evening in the beginning of March 1656, Paola was standing by the fire in that little wainscotted parlour where Sir Edward long ago had sung to her his love-song. The snow had been falling heavily for two days, and when her husband, whom she awaited, at last came in, his clothes and hair were covered with snow. He had been standing knee-deep by the grave; his eyes were not yet steady in the shine of the room; and there was a certain trembling indecision in his step. Warm and beautiful in the soft glow, Paola, glancing but carelessly from where she stood, laughed out some gay reproof for his tardiness, and with her wonderfully graceful gesture held out her arms. Upon this, all snowy as he was, he drew near and bent over her, but just as he did that, he saw the smile swept out of her eyes and face, and leaping up in its place an unmistakable look of repulsion and terror.

Morvan drew back, stung to the heart. "I should have shaken off the snow—" And he was going on.

"Oh, no, no!" cried his wife. She rested her elbow on the chimney-piece and covered her eyes with her hand. "It is nothing, nothing at all", she said, breathing hard. "A stupid fancy. I thought—I was reminded—O God!" she broke off, slapping her hand down on the wood, "why am I so tormented?"

He thought she was unreasonable and capricious and rather child-ish; and as the look still rankled, he turned on his heel and left the room without more words, and mounted the stairs to his own closet. This chamber had two steps down to it placed inside the door, the door itself not being so high as some other ones in the house, but still quite high enough for a man of the average height to pass through it without stooping. Morvan himself had always gone in and out without taking heed, but tonight his forehead struck against the lintel.

"How extraordinary!" he thought, rubbing his forehead ruefully, yet with some amusement. "I must be growing taller."

And as soon as he had shifted his habit—his little flick of ill-temper now quite gone—he hastened downstairs, eager to relate this comical accident to his wife, and promising himself they would laugh merrily upon it. So, standing in the hall, he called with cheery intention: "Paola, Paola, come hither, sweetheart."

Something in the sound of his voice sent the blood running cold through his veins. Whose voice was that? Where had he heard it before?

Into the hall came his wife slowly and wearily, supporting herself as she moved against the wall, and shewing a countenance deadly white and panic-stricken. She gave a quick oblique glance at her husband, and then drew from her heart a sigh or rather groan of relief, though the suspicious and terrified look still clouded in her eyes.

"I thought I heard *him* call", she said faintly, almost in a whisper.

"Whose voice did you think you heard, dearest one?" He meant to ask this question soothingly, as you might question a feverish child about its fancies, but it came out so harsh, so arrogant, with such a note of devilish raillery comprehended in the sound of it, that he stood thunderstruck.

"Ah, I knew, I knew! Yes, it is his voice!" cried Paola, and with that she flung herself down at full length in a perfect ecstasy of fear and despair, and beat her head against the floor.

Morvan heard a servant stirring at his work in a room near at hand, and hastening there, while he was still in the little dark passage which led to it, he called to the man to run for my lady's waiting-woman.

With a clang, the servant dropped the vessel he was holding, and stared in the wildest amazement towards the passage whence the voice had come. Thereupon Morvan stepped out into the light, and the servant, recognizing the well-known figure, hastened away.

"I saw Sir Edward right enough", he said to the others when he had given his message, "but I could have sworn to God it was old Mr. Verschoyle that called me".

X

Alas, the change thus observed in the master of the house was no delusion of the senses, but the bitterest reality, miserable and appalling, and that night only at its beginning. As the months ran, the features and presence of the fated Morvan gradually changed by slow, but salient and terrible stages, to the appearance of the dead old man. Morvan's handsome face became sallow and leathery and wrinkled; his hair fell, leaving only some grey locks straggling to his shoulders; his hands grew large and coarse, and his frame increased in size. And what was infinitely disquieting, and even disgusting, these loathsome changes attacked his body sporadically: for several weeks he carried one hand large and thick, and the other his own slender hand,—watching this day by day as it inflated; for over two months he stood on his own well-shaped foot, and on another much larger and broader; for nearly a year he found when he undressed himself, on one side of the body from the neck to the waist the flesh sane and firm, while on the other it was dry and shrivelled, coated with white hairs. Picture his emotions as he studied day by day the stealthy progress of his affliction! Perhaps the most perturbing detail of all, was the long white beard which swept over his breast. At first

Morvan, loathing this abominable ensign more than almost all other changes, used to shave his face closely many times a day; but in a few hours, in the course of sleep, the white thing would grow and again be hanging down, till at last the punished man resigned himself to let it grow as might.

Indeed, the struggles of the poor stricken wretch against his fate were as terrible and pathetic as the fate itself. By a refinement of torture, his character and mental attributes were not altered with his body; his soul was mercilessly enabled to stand by, as it were, and mark the ravages of the change; and Morvan would sit for hours, leaning Verschoyle's face on Verschoyle's hands and moaning in Verschoyle's voice that he was still Morvan. No, he was not Verschoyle, he would insist to himself vehemently all day—he was utterly different; he was not domineering, rapacious, tyrannical; he had no dealings with the devil; he was cheerful, merciful, eager for love and light, willing to give men their dues. And perhaps his character did in truth assert itself, and his mind regain somewhat of its health under its shameful housing; for when the bodily transformation declared itself more rigorously, he relinquished his visits to the graveside. Strangely enough, about this time too the tree began to die, as if that which nourished it was passing elsewhere—perishing slowly in its rank luxuriance from the top.

He took the custom to go to Paola's room when it was dark, when his figure would be obscured, although he knew that she shrank from his presence in excruciating anguish and dismay; and there he would utter to the half-fainting woman in Verschoyle's voice words which came from his own soul—making passionate appeals, begging her not to flee from him, to let him stay near her, for he was cold and lonely; imploring her to believe that, sick and weary and bewitched as he was, her lover was still there; endeavouring, in fact, to make the true accents of his soul heard from out of its monstrous prison of flesh. But for her, only that dread figure remained from which she recoiled in unutterable horror and woe, as she witnessed it speaking her husband's thoughts and particular phrases with the voice, the inflexion, the gesture of the dead. No, this was not her brave kind husband who sat now in the room, but a phantom agenced by the powers of evil: those old bones long buried had disinterred themselves and stolen from their sepulchre. The sickness and revolts she experienced at his appearance would throw her into long fits, from which she would emerge haggard-eyed, undone, with flecks of blood upon her lips. The afflicted Morvan, fearing for her life, was fain at last to bend his head under the scourge, and perceiving that it was the will of the inexorable Fates that in his calamities he should be desolate, he put himself in her presence no more.

From that accursed house the servants aghast stole away on various pretences, and never returned. There were left but an Italian woman who had nursed the lady Paola and loved her as her own child, and an old, half-witted, dumb man who shuffled about the sinister corridors till nightfall, and then betook himself to the stable;—for even he rebelled when it came to a question of sleeping in the house. And the beautiful place, sorely neglected, took gradually an air of isolation and ruin. The stalls stood empty, for there was no one to care for the horses; the garden was become a wilderness; while within doors the rooms where the sun never entered waxed dusty and dank and sombre. For by this time neither Morvan nor his wife could bear the glare of day, and the few rooms in use had lights burning in them at all hours. A waft of decay and anxiety, of death—nay, of a death beyond the familiar corporal death, as if Death himself had come to preside and be housekeeper there, exuded from the walls and tainted the atmosphere. For hours long a heavy stillness weighed on the house which seemed uninfluenced by sense or space or time, an illimitable stillness to which sound was not merely an antithesis, but in which any chance sound seemed indescribably single, alien, arising out of nothing, and having neither origin nor consequence in that underworld; and instead of falling, as sounds do, disturbingly through stillness, seemed here outside, beating against a burnished wall. If you can imagine a tower which has never a bell, standing in an arid, void, and sterile plain uninhabited for centuries, and that suddenly, in a minute lying amid the centuries, a bell tolls slowly thrice in the tower, reverberates, and expires in the waste; if you can imagine a ship moving through an enchanted sea which washes round her keel and bows and deck without wetting them; if you can imagine how the voices of the living sound to the listening dead: then you can form some idea of the suddenness, distinctness, the isolation of any noise in the vacant air of that house. So at intervals would strike dully against the silence a symptom of life, as detached from the general vacuity as to a man suspended by vindictive gods just outside this globe of earth might come the cries of those at work or play upon it—a pathetic ditty crooned in a voice that vainly tried to be steady: it was the nurse who thus endeavoured to soothe Paola with a song she used to sing to her little child in the cradle. And one who might have wandered about the house day and night would have seen in a lower chamber, dusty and unkept, a white-bearded man, gloomy, and muttering to himself a crazy litany of curses and prayers, or resting his old wrinkled head exhausted and throbbing in his arms on the table; and above stairs a pale lady lying spent and still and nearly lifeless, or else torn with a passion of weeping.

Why did she tarry in that doomed, forsaken dwelling? Surely there were still for her, if not for the scourged and hedged-in man, the air, the birds, the sea; and far from here, Italy lay flowery and basking in the pleasant sun. Ah, pity her! She ever longed for her dear lost husband, and hoped the magic spells might yet be broken, and that suddenly, all in a minute! he would be there once more with his brave face to love her and to assuage her after these intolerable sorrows. And that old man who sat always in the house, who infected the house, and whose hand she felt as a physical weight on her breast, would be hurried out into the night and tempest and cold. No, she could not travel away and forget: how could she forget, wherever she might wander, that the old man was seated in the house poisoning the sweet familiar chambers, while her poor lonely husband was creeping outside in the chill airs, longing to be at home by her side, and beating with vain hands at the doors. In the feverish dreams which thronged her broken sleep he would resurge, and solemnly enjoin her to wait for him. Therefore she lay there courageously and patiently, settled in her vague hopes, which after all kept her from dying of mere heart-break, and that chill sense of finality, of termination, of the outlets to life unredeemably beset and barred, which kills so many finely tempered spirits, so lamentably! And her hopes, after all, were not more monstrous and unreasonable than the calamity which gave them cause.—There came one night when as she lay on her bed she was so sure she heard his hands on the casements, and his voice outside crying to her to let him in, that she flung a white robe about her and descended. But as she entered the hall, suddenly she descried lurking in the shadows that gaunt black figure of the old man, whom she had escaped now for some months, and who began to cry out, "O Paola, my wife Paola, have pity—listen to me!"—words obviously of tenderness, but so deformed in the speaking that they seemed a mockery and jeer. The figure drew nearer, and Paola, sick and faint to the soul, frantically alarmed, dropped the lamp she held and fled away in the darkness with an unutterable panic and loathing, hearing as she regained her apartment a long, desolate, heart-rending wail from below which filled her ears for many a day afterwards, and spoiled her few pauses of perfectly restful sleep. And she realized that there were things in life more fearful and unnerving than death: the dead, after all, might hope to lie untroubled in their desolate places. But if *That* came loverly to her bedside?

Meanwhile, out in the sun-coloured world Oliver Protector ruled and died, and his battle-worn corpse was at length entombed with sumptuous if unimpressive pageantry. Now, his son carried without conviction an uneasy sovereignty. Already the clanging echoes of the war were dying out of earshot; already by alert listeners the bright scoffing laughter and gaillardise of the next court might be heard faintly chiming in the distance. But intelligence of these events hardly penetrated the walls of that house, which once would have been so patently stirred by the like; neither could stirring rumours lift the heavy shadows which encompassed the building, wafting out from their folds a cold noxious breath of mortality.

However, one visitor forced a way through those repelling shadows. In the beginning of 1659 that sickness known as the New Disease, which had been prowling for some time to and fro in England, came at last into that part of the country, broke into the house, and laid its blighting hand upon Paola's tired brow. Tended only by her loving nurse, she lay in a kind of trance, wasting away, longing exceedingly for death. Her few years had been so bitter for the young, gentle soul, and she was miserable, and haunted, and weary. Her hold on life, so frail already and uncertain, she felt now soothingly—by what blessed drowsy physic?—becoming as the hours passed looser and more nerveless.

About the same time, the old creature who lived hidden among the shadows, and wandered from room to room at the other side of the house, was likewise stricken, and kept his bed.

The chamber he occupied had long ago been put into deep mourning, to compliment, as the usage was, a certain honourable guest bereaved of a wife or child; and by some insouciance this melancholy furniture had never been changed. The walls were hung with black draperies which fell from the ceiling to the oaken floor, and as they vacillated in the gusts of wind seemed agitated by hands behind them. The bed was an immense construction of ebony, with black covers and hangings—a lugubrious funeral couch of a kind common enough at the period among families of importance; and the chairs, antique, outworn, and incommode, were shrouded in black. The sombre effect was increased by the almost complete exclusion of daylight, which filtered with difficulty through a window of stained glass. All these dismal trappings had been left to rot, and some of them were falling to pieces from long neglect; and it was doubtless owing to this, and to the absence of wholesome light, that there lingered in the room a sickening odour of decay and corruption.

Here, then, the old man lay suffering and forlorn. He was abandoned by all. Lacking Morvan's bodily features he could not attract, excite sympathy; lacking Verschoyle's brutal, indomitable spirit, he could not compel attendance through terror. The dumb servitor would come in the morning and cast down a parcel of faggots on the hearth; and then, as if the sadness and harrowing chill of the room struck intolerably even into his dull senses, he would shuffle away and return no more. And tossing wearily from dawn till evening, and through the long night waiting anxiously for the comfortless dawn, the friendless Morvan lay alone there in his loathed and hideous casing, lost and forsaken, with what thoughts to pass the hours! Feeble and racked with cough, he supplied the needs of his old body as he could, but most of the time he lay covered in the dark bed.

One night about eleven o'clock, when he had been sick like this for four days, with increasing weakness every day, he was sitting up gaunt and wretched in his bed supping a posset he had made shift to warm. As he sat there holding the bowl in his shrivelled hands, his ear caught the tramp of a horse on the terrace, and then the court bell rang with a loud reverberating peal, as bells are wont to echo in empty houses. By whose hand? To that silent accursed house, where no one ever came, what visitor had the hardihood to venture at that dead hour? Now the hands were on the great door; he could hear it creak open on its long disused hinges; and presently he distinguished a footstep on the stairs coming in the direction of his room. Yes, there could be no doubt of that; and the old man lay with wildly beating heart, marking the steps draw nearer and nearer. They moved slowly and as if with difficulty; now and then there would be a pause, and then they would come on again; and to the old man there was something strangely familiar in the tread. At last the steps came up to the very door, and there was another pause. But not for long! The door opened, and into that hearse-like chamber, in front of the old man watching the door with dilated eyes, there stepped the young Sir Edward Morvan. He carried a short riding-sword, and was dressed very elegantly, wearing a deep lace collar over which his fair hair fell in curls; but his eyes were hollow, his visage cadaverous, and on his breast was a great stain of blood as though he had been shot there. Watching this visitor from his bed in terror and bewilderment, Morvan (as we must call him) when his eyes lighted on the crimson splash, recalled from all the wounds he had seen where he had seen a stain just like that before: it was on Mr. Verschoyle's black robe, the day when he lay dead in the sunlight with his face to the sky.

The apparition glided noiselessly to the foot of the bed and stood there looking at the old man, not in anger, but rather with compassion and a great yearning. After they had regarded each other a little space,—"What brings you to this fatal house after so many years?" asked the old man; and if his accents had indicated the turmoil of his mind the words would have come out tremblingly and broken. But the voice, as usual, travestied the mental state, and the question actually sounded sardonic, unfriendly, and combative.

The figure stretched out his arm. "Mr. Verschoyle", he said, "I have come for my soul". His tone was soft and mournful and even appealing, and stayed a little on the air after the words had fallen, like the vibration of a harp when the musician is departed.

"I am not Verschoyle", clamoured the other frantically; "I tell you I am not Verschoyle. Do you not know? Verschoyle was shot to death and laid beneath the tree. I know it—I know it—I saw him put in the ground—I have said it to myself a thousand times. I am not Verschoyle. Why do you vex the night with your unhallowed pacings? 'Tis you who are Verschoyle, and you stole my body and hid it away in the earth. I am Edward Morvan."

Again his voice belied his heart, turning these eager feverish words to derision and the bitterest irony. But the figure neither assented nor denied, nor shewed surprise or any emotion; only again raised his hand and repeated in his gentle tones:

"Mr. Verschoyle, I have come for my soul".

As these words were spoken, there was heard a little noise of hands feebly groping about the door of the chamber and striving to open it. The two in the room appeared to be listening intently, but neither stirred. On the young face was a look of tranquil, even happy expectation; on the old, an indefinable minglement of hope, trepidation, and despair. Then the heavy door slowly fell open, and on the threshold stood Paola, holding a small carven silver lamp above her head. She was clothed in white, and her face, which bore the marks of long illness, gleamed strange and pale amid the black hair rolling loosely over her shoulders to her waist. No sooner did her eyes fall on the figure of the young man, than she put down the lamp and held out her hands with a wide amiable gesture, as if welcoming a long desired and long expected friend and lover, harnessed for her enlargement; and like a sudden light flashing across her shadowed and wasted features, came a look of wonder and content. She hastened her faltering steps through the wide room, till she stood by the side of the young man at the foot of the bed. But he, though his look upon her was kind and friendly, did not respond to her welcome otherwise than by a quaint frail smile, as people sometimes smile in dreams.

The old man on the bed regarded them meanwhile with a perturbed and lowering countenance. He was breathing hard, as the dying are seen to do in the supreme hour when the soul is struggling to go forth. And he began to speak.

"Stay with me, Paola", he said. "Go not down with yon dead man. Can you not see that he is dead? Ay, he has been long dead, long in the mould, ever since the old King's time. He exists no more. 'Tis I who shelter under time, and marshal the order of existence. I have the hours and years at my beck. But he—his limbs have been buried and are powerless; time and the agitation of the world are but like water poured over his hands. He is naught and gone, but I live—I am I", he repeated, and peered at her with his tired and blunted eyes.

"Ah, not you!" she answered, weeping dreadfully. "You have pressed too hard on me. Life has been too wretched!" And thereupon she turned to the young man with the air of making at that minute a deliberate and final choice, and threw her arms about him, and shadowed him with her hair. But that one responded to her caress in no wise, save with the same thin and friendly smile.

"You are cold, my dear", she murmured, "and we have been apart a long time. The day is at hand. Let us hasten to be gone, while yet the moon shines."

And with a countenance wrapped in dream, not quite happy, indeed, and yet far from grief-stricken and hopeless, she drew gently her companion towards a little door in the wainscot which opened upon a flight of steps built, just there, into the outside wall. But even as they moved, the form on the bed was shaken with an appalling convulsion, as if it were spending itself in a struggle with the spirit it held imprisoned; and then the old body rolled out of the bed and stood there confronting them. It seemed as if those three were a last time in presence, and engaged in an ultimate wrestle for mastery. For a minute they stood and gazed: then the old man, his face trembling with evil, advanced upon the two. But even as he came, they passed through the door out of his sight; and he was left staring with haggard eyes, triumphant, yet somehow broken and defeated, from the top of the steps into the darkness below.

*

The next morning the body of Paola, half covered with snow, was found by her faithful nurse at the foot of the steps. It was supposed that she had wandered to the dark room in her delirium, and having opened the little door, her senseless eyes had not noticed the void, and she had fallen headlong. But the woman was astonished to find, clasped tightly in the small dead hand, a lock of gold-like hair which she had never seen among the trinkets and keepsakes of her mistress.

By the orders of him who was called her husband, whose sickness, as it appeared, had suddenly left him, her grave was dug underneath the tree; for it was comely, he said, that she should be buried in the same enclosure as her husband, Sir Edward Morvan. Those who heard him—the waiting woman and the dumb man—refrained from questioning this curious speech, judging it to be some folded utterance of one who was scarcely human and who spoke to them out of another world. With some difficulty a certain reckless man who lived far off was found to assist the old servant: in the twilight, between a crimson winter sun and the moon already up in the penitential evening sky, they bore her quickly; and at length the thin piteous body, which had been so vexed and tormented, was hidden out of sight in the earth,—her hard fate, in the end, relenting so far as to spare her the vanity of mourners' tears, and the grisly pomps of sepulture.

Sir Edward Morvan—or Mr. Verschoyle, as some in that country, seeing the terror he inspired, preferred to call him—survived in great seclusion till near the end of Charles the Second's reign, disappearing at last with his house in one of those frequent devastating fires which swept away so many stately houses of the Seventeenth century.

THE BLACK REAPER

Bernard Capes

In a posthumous introduction to Bernard Capes's 1919 mystery novel *The Skeleton Key*, G. K. Chesterton called attention to a markedly poetic quality in the author's prose, one which, he felt, seemed almost wasted given the "sensational" genres—mystery, historical adventure, romance, supernatural fiction—in which Capes worked: "It may seem a paradox to say that he was insufficiently appreciated because he did popular things well. But it is true to say that he always gave a touch of distinction to a detective story or a tale of adventure; and so gave it where it was not valued, because it was not expected." "The Black Reaper," from the 1899 collection *At a Winter's Fire*, is a good example of Capes at his most "poetic," yet despite the story's fabulistic, almost parable-like nature, it is precisely situated historically as well: it is a tale of the Great Plague of 1665, which devastated London (as immortalized in Daniel Defoe's 1722 quasi-fiction *A Journal of the Plague Year*) before spreading out from the confines of the city into the English countryside, where Capes's story is set. Sadly, Capes's own life would be cut short by the reaper's blade of another famous pandemic, as he succumbed to heart failure after contracting influenza in 1918.

I

ow I am to tell you of a thing that befell in the year 1665 of the Great Plague, when the hearts of certain amongst men, grown callous in wickedness upon that rebound from an inhuman austerity, were opened to the vision of a terror that moved and spoke not in the silent places of the fields. Forasmuch as, however, in the recovery from delirium a patient may marvel over the incredulity of neighbours who refuse to give credence to the presentments that have been *ipso facto* to him, so, the nation being sound again, and its constitution hale, I expect little but a laugh for my piety in relating of the following incident; which, nevertheless, is as essential true as that he who shall look through the knot-hole in the plank of a coffin shall acquire the evil eye.

For, indeed, in those days of a wild fear and confusion, when every condition that maketh for reason was set wandering by a devious path, and all men sitting as in a theatre of death looked to see the curtain rise upon God knows what horrors, it was vouchsafed to many to witness sights and sounds beyond the compass of Nature, and that as if the devil and his minions had profited by the anarchy to slip unobserved into the world. And I know that this is so, for all the insolence of a recovered scepticism; and, as to the unseen, we are like one that traverseth the dark with a lanthorn, himself the skipper of a little moving blot of light, but a positive mark for any secret foe without the circumference of its radiance.

Be that as it may, and whether it was our particular ill-fortune, or, as some asserted, our particular wickedness, that made of our village an inviting back-door of entrance to the Prince of Darkness, I know not; but so it is that disease and contagion are ever inclined to penetrate by way of flaws or humours where the veil of the flesh is already perforated, as a kite circleth round its quarry, looking for the weak place to strike: and, without doubt, in that land of corruption we were a very foul blot indeed.

How this came about it were idle to speculate; yet no man shall have the hardihood to affirm that it was otherwise. Nor do I seek to extenuate myself, who was in truth no better than my neighbours in most that made us a community of drunkards and forswearers both lewd and abominable. For in that village a depravity that was like madness had come to possess the heads of the people, and no man durst take his stand on honesty or even common decency, for fear he should be set upon by his comrades and drummed out of his government on a pint pot. Yet for myself I will say was one only redeeming quality, and that was the pure love I bore to my solitary orphaned child, the little Margery.

Now, our Vicar—a patient and God-fearing man, for all his predial tithes were impropriated by his lord, that was an absentee and a sheriff in London—did little to stem that current of lewdness that had set in strong with the Restoration. And this was from no lack of virtue in himself, but rather from a natural invertebracy, as one may say, and an order of mind that, yet being no order, is made the sport of any sophister with a wit for paragram. Thus it always is that mere example is of little avail without precept,—of which, however, it is an important condition,—and that the successful directors of men be not those who go to the van and lead, unconscious of the gibes and mockery in their rear, but such rather as drive the mob before them with a smiting hand and no infirmity of purpose. So, if a certain affection for our pastor dwelt in our hearts, no title of respect was there to leaven it and justify his high office before Him that consigned the trust; and ever deeper and deeper we sank in the slough of corruption, until was brought about this pass—that naught but some scourging despotism of the Church should acquit us of the fate of Sodom. That such, at the eleventh hour, was vouchsafed us of God's mercy, it is my purpose to show; and, doubtless, this offering of a loop-hole was to account by reason of the devil's having debarked his reserves, as it were, in our port; and so quartering upon us a soldiery that we were, at no invitation of our own, to maintain, stood us a certain extenuation.

It was late in the order of things before in our village so much as a rumour of the plague reached us. Newspapers were not in those days, and reports, being by word of mouth, travelled slowly, and were often spent bullets by the time they fell amongst us. Yet, by May, some gossip there was of the distemper having gotten a hold in certain quarters of London and increasing, and this alarmed our people, though it made no abatement of their profligacy. But presently the reports coming thicker, with confirmation of the terror and panic that was enlarging on all sides, we must take measures for our safety; though into June and July, when the pestilence was raging, none infected had come our way, and that from our remote and isolated position. Yet it needs but fear for the crown to that wickedness that is self-indulgence; and forasmuch as this fear fattens like a toadstool on the decomposition it springs from, it grew with us to the proportions that we were set to kill or destroy any that should approach us from the stricken districts.

And then suddenly there appeared in our midst *he* that was appointed to be our scourge and our cautery.

Whence he came, or how, no man of us could say. Only one day we were a community of roysterers and scoffers, impious and abominable, and the next he was amongst us smiting and thundering.

Some would have it that he was an old collegiate of our Vicar's, but at last one of those wandering Dissenters that found never as now the times opportune to their teachings—a theory to which our minister's treatment of the stranger gave colour. For from the moment of his appearance he took the reins of government, as it were, appropriating the pulpit and launching his bolts therefrom, with the full consent and encouragement of the other. There were those, again, who were resolved that his commission was from a high place, whither news of our infamy had reached, and that we had best give him a respectful hearing, lest we should run a chance of having our hearing stopped altogether. A few were convinced he was no man at all, but rather a fiend sent to thresh us with the scourge of our own contriving, that we might be tender, like steak, for the cooking; and yet other few regarded him with terror, as an actual figure or embodiment of the distemper.

But, generally, after the first surprise, the feeling of resentment at his intrusion woke and gained ground, and we were much put about that he should have thus assumed the pastorship without invitation, quartering with our Vicar; who kept himself aloof and was little seen, and seeking to drive us by terror, and amazement, and a great menace of retribution. For, in truth, this was not the method to which we were wont, and it both angered and disturbed us.

This feeling would have enlarged the sooner, perhaps, were it not for a certain restraining influence possessed of the newcomer, which neighboured him with darkness and mystery. For he was above the common tall, and ever appeared in public with a slouched hat, that concealed all the upper part of his face and showed little otherwise but the dense black beard that dropped upon his breast like a shadow.

Now with August came a fresh burst of panic, how the desolation increased and the land was overrun with swarms of infected persons seeking an asylum from the city; and our anger rose high against the stranger, who yet dwelt with us and encouraged the distemper of our minds by furious denunciations of our guilt.

Thus far, for all the corruption of our hearts, we had maintained the practice of church-going, thinking, maybe, poor fools! to hoodwink the Almighty with a show of reverence; but now, as by a common consent, we neglected the observances and loitered of a Sabbath in the fields, and thither at the last the strange man pursued us and ended the matter.

For so it fell that at the time of the harvest's ripening a goodish body of us males was gathered one Sunday for coolness about the neighbourhood of the dripping well, whose waters were a tradition, for they had long gone dry. This well was situate in a sort of cave or deep scoop at the foot of a cliff of limestone, to which the cultivated ground that led up to it fell somewhat. High above, the cliff broke away into a wide stretch of pasture land, but the face of the rock itself was all patched with bramble and little starved birch-trees clutching for foothold; and in like manner the excavation beneath was half-stifled and gloomed over with undergrowth, so that it looked a place very dismal and uninviting, save in the ardour of the dog-days.

Within, where had been the basin, was a great shattered hole going down to unknown depths; and this no man had thought to explore, for a mystery held about the spot that was doubtless the foster-child of ignorance.

But to the front of the well and of the cliff stretched a noble field of corn, and this field was of an uncommon shape, being, roughly, a vast circle and a little one joined by a neck and in suggestion not unlike an hour-glass; and into the crop thereof, which was of goodly weight and condition, were the first sickles to be put on the morrow.

Now as we stood or lay around, idly discussing of the news, and congratulating ourselves that we were featly quit of our incubus, to us along the meadow path, his shadow jumping on the corn, came the very subject of our gossip.

He strode up, looking neither to right nor left, and with the first word that fell, low and damnatory, from his lips, we knew that the moment had come when, whether for good or evil, he intended to cast us from him and acquit himself of further responsibility in our direction.

"Behold!" he cried, pausing over against us, "I go from among ye! Behold, ye that have not obeyed nor inclined your ear, but have walked every one in the imagination of his evil heart! Saith the Lord, 'I will bring evil upon them, which they shall not be able to escape; and though they shall cry unto Me, I will not hearken unto them.'"

His voice rang out, and a dark silence fell among us. It was pregnant, but with little of humility. We had had enough of this interloper and his abuse. Then, like Jeremiah, he went to prophesy:—

"I read ye, men of Anathoth, and the murder in your hearts. Ye that have worshipped the shameful thing and burned incense to Baal—shall I cringe that ye devise against me, or not rather pray to the Lord of Hosts, 'Let me see Thy vengeance on them'? And He answereth, 'I will bring evil upon the men of Anathoth, even the year of their visitation.'"

Now, though I was no participator in that direful thing that followed, I stood by, nor interfered, and so must share the blame.

For there were men risen all about, and their faces lowering, and it seemed that it would go hard with the stranger were he not more particular.

But he moved forward, with a stately and commanding gesture, and stood with his back to the well-scoop and threatened us and spoke.

"Lo!" he shrieked, "your hour is upon you! Ye shall be mowed down like ripe corn, and the shadow of your name shall be swept from the earth! The glass of your iniquity is turned, and when its sand is run through, not a man of ye shall be!"

He raised his arm aloft, and in a moment he was overborne. Even then, as all say, none got sight of his face; but he fought with lowered head, and his black beard flapped like a wounded crow. But suddenly a boy-child ran forward of the bystanders, crying and screaming,—

"Hurt him not! They are hurting him—oh, me! oh, me!"

And from the sweat and struggle came his voice, gasping, "I spare the little children!"

Then only I know of the surge and the crash towards the well-mouth, of an instant cessation of motion, and immediately of men toiling hither and thither with boulders and huge blocks, which they piled over the rent, and so sealed it with a cromlech of stone.

II

That, in the heat of rage and of terror, we had gone farther than we had at first designed, our gloom and our silence on the morrow attested. True we were quit of our incubus, but on such terms as not even the severity of the times could excuse. For the man had but chastised us to our improvement; and to destroy the scourge is not to condone the offence. For myself, as I bore up the little Margery to my shoulder on my way to the reaping, I felt the burden of guilt so great as that I found myself muttering of an apology to the Lord that I durst put myself into touch with innocence. "But the walk would fatigue her otherwise," I murmured; and, when we were come to the field, I took and carried her into the upper or little meadow, out of reach of the scythes, and placed her to sleep amongst the corn, and so left her with a groan.

But when I was come anew to my comrades, who stood at the lower extremity of the field—and this was the bottom of the hour-glass, so to speak—I was aware of a stir amongst them, and, advancing closer, that they were all intent upon the neighbourhood of the field I had left, staring like distraught creatures, and holding well together, as if in a panic. Therefore, following the direction of their eyes, and of one that pointed with rigid finger, I turned me about, and looked whence I had come; and my heart went with a somersault, and in a moment I was all sick and dazed.

For I saw, at the upper curve of the meadow, where the well lay in gloom, that a man had sprung out of the earth, as it seemed, and was started reaping; and the face of this man was all in shadow, from which his beard ran out and down like a stream of gall.

He reaped swiftly and steadily, swinging like a pendulum; but, though the sheaves fell to him right and left, no swish of the scythe came to us, nor any sound but the beating of our own hearts.

Now, from the first moment of my looking, no doubt was in my lost soul but that this was him we had destroyed come back to verify his prophecy in ministering to the vengeance of the Lord of Hosts; and at the thought a deep groan rent my bosom, and was echoed by those about me. But scarcely was it issued when a second terror smote me as that I near reeled. Margery—my babe! put to sleep there in the path of the Black Reaper!

At that, though they called to me, I sprang forward like a madman, and running along the meadow, through the neck of the glass, reached the little thing, and stooped and snatched her into my arms. She was sound and unfrighted, as I felt with a burst of thankfulness; but, looking about me, as I turned again to fly, I had near dropped in my tracks for the sickness and horror I experienced in the nearer neighbourhood of the apparition. For, though it never raised its head, or changed the steady swing of its shoulders, I knew that it was aware of and was *reaping at me*. Now, I tell you, it was ten yards away, yet the point of the scythe came gliding upon me silently, like a snake, through the stalks, and at that I screamed out and ran for my life.

I escaped, sweating with terror; but when I was sped back to the men, there was all the village collected, and our Vicar to the front, praying from a throat that rattled like a dead leaf in a draught. I know not what he said, for the low cries of the women filled the air; but his face was white as a smock, and his fingers writhed in one another like a knot of worms.

"The plague is upon us!" they wailed. "We shall be mowed down like ripe corn!"

And even as they shrieked the Black Reaper paused, and, putting away his scythe, stooped and gathered up a sheaf in his arms and stood it on end. And, with the very act, a man—one that had been forward in yesterday's business—fell down amongst us yelling and foaming; and he rent his breast in his frenzy, revealing the purple blot thereon, and he passed blaspheming. And the reaper stooped and stooped again, and with every sheaf he gathered together one of us fell stricken and rolled in his agony, while the rest stood by palsied.

But, when at length all that was cut was accounted for, and a dozen of us were gone each to his judgment, and he had taken up his scythe to reap anew, a wild fury woke in the breasts of some of the more abandoned and reckless amongst us.

"It is not to be tolerated!" they cried. "Let us at once fire the corn and burn this sorcerer!"

And with that, some five or six of them, emboldened by despair, ran up into the little field, and, separating, had out each his flint and fired the crop in his own place, and retreated to the narrow part for safety.

Now the reaper rested on his scythe, as if unexpectedly acquitted of a part of his labour; but the corn flamed up in these five or six directions, and was consumed in each to the compass of a single sheaf: whereat the fire died away. And with its dying the faces of those that had ventured went black as coal; and they flung up their arms, screaming, and fell prone where they stood, and were hidden from our view.

Then, indeed, despair seized upon all of us that survived, and we made no doubt but that we were to be exterminated and wiped from the earth for our sins, as were the men of Anathoth. And for an hour the Black Reaper mowed and trussed, till he had cut all from the little upper field and was approached to the neck of juncture with the lower and larger. And before us that remained, and who were drawn back amongst the trees, weeping and praying, a fifth of our comrades lay foul, and dead, and sweltering, and all blotched over with the dreadful mark of the pestilence.

Now, as I say, the reaper was nearing the neck of juncture; and so we knew that if he should once pass into the great field towards us and continue his mowing, not one of us should be left to give earnest of our repentance.

Then, as it seemed, our Vicar came to a resolution, moving forward with a face all wrapt and entranced; and he strode up the meadow path and approached the apparition, and stretched out his arms to it entreating. And we saw the other pause, awaiting him; and, as he came near, put forth his hand, and so, gently, on the good old head. But as we looked, catching at our breaths with a little pathos of hope, the priestly face was thrown back radiant, and the figure of him that would give his life for us sank amongst the yet standing corn and disappeared from our sight.

So at last we yielded ourselves fully to our despair; for if our pastor should find no mercy, what possibility of it could be for us!

It was in this moment of an uttermost grief and horror, when each stood apart from his neighbour, fearing the contamination of his presence, that there was vouchsafed to me, of God's pity, a wild and sudden inspiration. Still to my neck fastened the little Margery—not frighted, it seemed, but mazed—and other babes there were in plenty, that clung to their mothers' skirts and peeped out, wondering at the strange show.

I ran to the front and shrieked: "The children! the children! He will not touch the little children! Bring them and set them in his path!" And so crying I sped to the neck of meadow, and loosened the soft arms from my throat, and put the little one down within the corn.

Now at once the women saw what I would be at, and full a score of them snatched up their babes and followed me. And here we were reckless for ourselves; but we knelt the innocents in one close line across the neck of land, so that the Black Reaper should not find space between any of them to swing his scythe. And having done this, we fell back with our hearts bubbling in our breasts, and we stood panting and watched.

He had paused over that one full sheaf of his reaping; but now, with the sound of the women's running, he seized his weapon again and set to upon the narrow belt of corn that yet separated him from the children. But presently, coming out upon the tender array, his scythe stopped and trailed in his hand, and for a full minute he stood like a figure of stone. Then thrice he walked slowly backwards and forwards along the line, seeking for an interval whereby he might pass; and the children laughed at him like silver bells, showing no fear, and perchance meeting that of love in his eyes that was hidden from us.

Then of a sudden he came to before the midmost of the line, and, while we drew our breath like dying souls, stooped and snapped his blade across his knee, and, holding the two parts in his hand, turned and strode back into the shadow of the dripping well. There arrived, he paused once more, and, twisting him about, waved his hand once to us and vanished into the blackness. But there were those who affirmed that in that instant of his turning, his face was revealed, and that it was a face radiant and beautiful as an angel's.

Such is the history of the wild judgment that befell us, and by grace of the little children was foregone; and such was the stranger whose name no man ever heard tell, but whom many have since sought to identify with that spirit of the pestilence that entered into men's hearts and confounded them, so that they saw visions and were afterwards confused in their memories.

But this I may say, that when at last our courage would fetch us to that little field of death, we found it to be all blackened and blasted, so as nothing would take root there then or ever since; and it was as if, after all the golden sand of the hour-glass was run away and the lives of the most impious with it, the destroyer saw fit to stay his hand for sake of the babes that he had pronounced innocent, and for such as were spared to witness to His judgment. And this I do here, with a heart as contrite as if it were the morrow of the visitation, the which with me it ever has remained.

THE WITCH-FINDER

Frederick Cowles

Alongside numerous works of travel, folklore, and other subjects, Cambridge-born librarian Frederick Cowles (1900–1949) also wrote enough macabre tales to fill three collections—*The Horror of Abbot's Grange*, *The Night Wind Howls*, and *Fear Walks the Night*—though the last of these was only published years after his death. Cowles's antiquarian interests suggest natural parallels with the work of M. R. James, with whom he was sometimes compared, though his best stories possess a special quality of ghastliness that is very much his own.

Here Cowles brings the reader back in time to the witch-hunting craze that swept through Great Britain and Europe in the early modern period, reaching a peak in the century or so between the second half of the sixteenth century and the second half of the seventeenth century. The most notorious instigator of this mania in Britain was of course Matthew Hopkins, the self-styled "Witch Finder Generall" who caused some 230 women and (to a far lesser extent) men to be judicially murdered during the turbulent Civil War years (fans of British period horror will recall the 1968 film *Witchfinder General*, with Vincent Price in the role of Hopkins). Cowles's fictitious witch-finder Hugh Murray, while looking down socially on "the fellow Hopkins," closely resembles him in other respects: both ply their trade in East Anglia (with Murray here seen operating in Cowles's native Cambridgeshire) and favour the same sadistic methods for obtaining "confessions" from their victims. Murray and his mission apparently have the sanction of James II, placing the story during the years of his reign (1685–1688), by which time Hopkins would have been long dead—and witch-hunting itself in decline.

"The Witch-finder" is taken from Cowles's collection *The Night Wind Howls*.

he wind howled mournfully and the cold rain lashed the solitary rider whose weary horse stumbled along the muddy road. The night was dark and the man could hardly see a yard before him, but, with an impatient word, he urged his tired nag onwards.

At a shadowed corner something clanked dolefully, and the horse reared as a shapeless mass swung out over the road. The rider drew rein with a startled exclamation, and then chuckled as he realized he had reached Caxton gibbet. He lifted his hat in mocking salutation, and in a thin, reedy voice cried out, "Is it thou, old Mother Lane? How doth it feel to be so high up in the world?"

"And is it thou, Master Hugh Murray, witch-finder of East Anglia, Justice of the Peace, and murderer of women?" a hoarse voice answered him.

Master Hugh almost tumbled from his horse in fright. His hair literally stood on end, and he trembled as though he had ague. With an effort he made to dig spurs into his mount, but before he could do so a figure leapt from beneath the gibbet and seized the mare's bridle.

"God's soul!" screamed the witch-finder. "Who art thou?"

"Anthony Lane," the low voice replied. "Son of the poor creature who hangs on yonder tree, and grandson of that Margaret Bell whom thou didst burn a year ago."

"Unhand me, fool," ordered the man, recovering himself. "Loose the bridle or it will fare hardly with thee."

"When I have delivered my message, Master Hugh. I give thee

greetings from the dead, and the promise that all the torments they experienced thou also shalt know."

With a muttered curse Hugh Murray raised his whip to strike the youth who dared threaten him. But the fellow dropped the bridle and vanished into the night. His laughter, weird and mocking, died away in the distance as the infuriated justice drove spurs into his horse's flanks and galloped on.

Soon he came to a cross-road and paused to decide which path to take. It was still some miles to Cambridge, and in such a storm he had small hope of arriving there before the early hours of the morning. There was the direct way through Grantchester which would mean a ride through the Cambridge main street to get to his inn near Magdalene Bridge. The other road, crossing Madingley Hill necessitated a slight detour, but would bring him into the town almost at the door of the hostelry where he intended to lodge. On the whole, it would be better to take the Madingley Road. He was not popular in Cambridge and had no desire to risk an encounter with the townspeople or scholars who might recognize him.

Mr. Hugh Murray turned his horse's head to the left and rode on through the night. He recalled with a shudder how a Cambridge mob had once pelted him with garbage and broken his head. And all because he had gone there hunting witches in the name of His Majesty James of England. It was not as if he were an ordinary witch-finder like the fellow Hopkins. He, Hugh Murray, was a man of property, a Justice of the Peace, and in high favour at the Court. Witch hunting was his hobby, and he was determined to use every means to exterminate the foul brood of witches and warlocks from the counties of East Anglia. The road was bleak, with no village for miles, although he did see the lights of Childerley in the distance as he joined the main highway.

The storm increased in fury. Master Hugh was already soaked to the skin, and his horse was in a sorry plight. The gentle slope of Madingley Hill was before him, but the nag could hardly stumble onwards. The witch-finder looked for some place where he could shelter until the storm abated. Thick woods lined the road, but the trees afforded no protection. With a groan he dismounted and resigned himself to climbing the hill on foot. It was then he saw a cottage amongst the trees. A narrow path led up to it, but the window showed no light and the house appeared to be deserted. He knocked on the door with his riding crop, but a hollow echo was the only reply. He knocked louder, and this time thought he heard the sound of someone moving within. After an interval of some seconds the door opened slowly and a white face peered out at him. It was the countenance of an old woman, lined and wrinkled and vaguely familiar. Before he could utter a word the hag addressed him in a cracked, wheedling voice.

"Come inside, Master Hugh Murray. Come inside, my bonny witch-finder. Here is shelter for thee."

Without pausing to inquire how the woman knew his name the man tied his horse to the branch of a tree and entered the cottage. A peat fire was burning on the hearth, but no lamp or candle illuminated the hovel.

"All we can offer your honour is a bed," the cracked voice whispered, "just a bed to stretch your limbs upon—to stretch your limbs."

A cold hand grasped his arm and led him across the room towards a low couch which was dimly visible in the firelight. He removed his saturated coat, and flung himself down upon the bed. It was very hard—just a wide board with no mattress. But the witch-finder was tired, and even such a primitive resting-place was welcome. He stretched his limbs and closed his eyes.

The sound of soft laughter disturbed him. He endeavoured to raise his head and so became aware of the fact that, in some mysterious manner, he had become fastened to the bed. His feet and hands were secured by ropes and his body spread-eagled in a most uncomfortable way. And then he realized that it was no bed he was stretched upon, but the rack—the rack of torture. Master Hugh licked his dry lips and voiced a protest.

"What is the meaning of this foolery?" he cried.

"Not foolery, my brave witch-finder," answered the woman who had admitted him to the cottage. "Surely it is not foolery when Master Hugh Murray hath himself shown us how usefully this instrument may be employed?"

The hag laughed, and another joined in the mirth. There were two of them bending over him. He saw their white faces, their cruel eyes, their grey elfin locks.

"Who are thou?" he cried. "And what damnable mummery is this?"

"Softly, softly, Master Hugh," came the reply. "Little did you think to meet us again. I am that Alice Lane whose broken body yet hangs upon Caxton gibbet. With me is my mother, Margaret Bell, whom thou didst condemn to the fire a year ago this very day."

A cold sweat bathed the witch-finder's body. His lips essayed to mutter a prayer.

"Aye, pray, but it will avail thee nought," went on the lifeless voice. "The tortures we knew thou also shah experience. Death shall come slowly even as it came to us."

"He pricked me all over to find the witch mark," said the other voice.

The man felt cold hands unloose his clothes and expose his body. Then a pin was driven into his chest and another into his leg. He screamed and twisted in agony, but his torturers only withdrew the pins and inserted them in other places.

"Are the pincers hot?" the first voice inquired. "He drew my teeth with red hot pincers—drew them one by one until the flesh was burnt from my gums and my tongue but a charred stump."

"Mercy, mercy," cried the victim. "Have mercy, I implore you."

"Hast thou ever shown mercy?" asked the tired old voice.

He saw the glow of hot pincers and felt his mouth forced open. Then came the scorching pain as they touched his gums. The red-hot instrument tore at his teeth and dragged them from his jaws. His mouth was a well of fire, searing his throat and stinging his eyes. Warm blood spurted over his chest, and he was conscious of the reek of burning flesh. Another tooth was drawn, and then he fainted.

Cold water splashing on his face revived him, and he tried to articulate another plea for mercy. But his tongue was burnt to the roots and was incapable of functioning. He strained weakly at his bonds and writhed on the wooden frame.

"Daughter," croaked the elder woman, "he put needles under the nails of my fingers and toes—hot needles."

"He also shall know the agony of the needles," was the reply.

Master Hugh felt cold hands grip his fingers, and then the excruciating pain of a glowing needle being driven under a nail. He sobbed and twisted his body. Then another needle was forced beneath one of his toe nails. He prayed for death to release him from this torment.

"Mother, he had my nails torn from my fingers."

"Tear his nails, daughter. Here are the pincers. Break and tear his hands even as he tore thine."

The tortured wretch, almost unconscious with pain, felt the instrument grip a nail, and then it seemed that the whole top of a finger was torn away. He tried to scream, but no sound issued from his bleeding mouth.

The elder woman was speaking again. "When I reproached him with my eyes he ordered hot coals to be laid upon them."

Dimly he was aware of smouldering embers burning into his head—into his brain. Surely this must be the end? He could endure no more. And then, with a creaking and groaning, the rollers of the rack began to turn. His body was stretched until the joints were dislocated. With a gasp of agony Hugh Murray died, and the last sound he heard was the hellish laughter of the women he had tortured and killed.

*

A farmer, driving into Cambridge in the early hours of the morning, noticed the horse tethered to a tree near the cottage. Being an inquisitive fellow, he entered the building and discovered the witch-finder's body lying on the bed. Master Murray's face was twisted into a horrible grimace, but he seemed to have died a natural death, for there were no signs of violence on the body.

Only the people of Madingley noted the curious fact that Hugh Murray had died in the cottage formerly inhabited by two of the notorious witches he had condemned to death—Margaret Bell and her daughter Alice Lane.

THE CONFESSION OF BEAU SEKFORDE

Marjorie Bowen

The story appeared (as "The Housekeeper") in *The Crimes of Old London* (1919); Bowen later selected it for inclusion in *The Bishop of Hell* (1949), a collection of her own favourites among her weird stories. Here we are in the England of Queen Anne's time, and in the company of an ageing and unhappily married pair of rogues: "Beau" Sekforde, dissipated gambler and "damaged man of fashion," and his wife, a Countess who (it is all but explicitly stated) earned her title through having been the mistress of the "Merry Monarch," Charles II, a quarter of a century earlier. Both characters are good candidates for one of the cautionary pictorial sequences (e.g. *The Rake's Progress*, *The Harlot's Progress*, *Marriage A-la-Mode*) which the painter William Hogarth would create a couple of decades later.

r. Robert Sekforde, a rather damaged man of fashion, entered, with a lurching step, his mansion near the tavern of the Black Bull, High Holborn. He was still known as "Beau Sekforde", and was still dressed in the extreme of the fashion of this year 1710, with wide brocade skirts, an immense peruke, and a quantity of lace and paste ornaments that were nearly as brilliant as diamonds.

About Mr. Sekforde himself was a good deal of this spurious gorgeousness; from a little distance he still looked the magnificent man he once had been, but a closer view showed him raddled with powder and rouge like a woman, heavy about the eyes and jaw, livid in the cheeks; a handsome man yet, but one deeply marked by years of idleness, good living, and the cheap dissipations of a nature at once brutal and effeminate. In the well-shaped features and dark eyes there was not a contour or a shadow that did not help towards the presentment of a type vicious and worthless; yet he had an air of breeding, of gallantry and grace that had hitherto never failed to win him facile admiration and help him over awkward places in his career. This air was also spurious—spurious as the diamonds at his throat and in his shoe-buckles; he was not even of gentle birth; the obscurity that hung round his origin was proof of the shame he felt at the dismal beginning of a career that had been so brilliant.

He entered his mansion, that was modest but elegant, and called for candles to be brought into his study.

Taking off slowly his white, scented gloves, he stared thoughtfully at his plump, smooth hands, and then at the walnut desk scattered with silver and ebony stand dishes, pens and taper-holders, and a great number of little notes on gilt-edged and perfumed papers.

There were a great many others, neither gilt-edged nor perfumed; Mr. Sekforde knew that these last were bills as surely as he knew the first were insipid invitations to rather third-rate balls and routs.

Everything in Mr. Sekforde's world was becoming rather third-rate now.

He looked round the room desperately with that ugly glance of defiance which is not courage but cowardice brought to bay.

Nothing in the house was paid for; and his credit would not last much longer; this had been a last venture to float his shaky raft on the waters of London Society; he could foresee himself going very comfortably to the bottom.

Unless he could again carry off some successful "coup" at cards; and this was unlikely; he was too well-known now.

Every resource that could, at any pinch, afford means of livelihood to an unscrupulous rogue and yet permit him to move among the people on whom he preyed, had already been played by Mr. Sekforde.

The sound of the opening door caused him to look up; he dreaded duns, and was not sure of the unpaid servants.

But it was his wife who entered; at the sight of her, Beau Sekforde cursed in a fashion that would have surprised his genteel admirers, over whose tea-tables he languished so prettily.

"Oh, pray, keep civil," said the lady, in a mincing tone.

She trailed to the fireplace and looked discontentedly at the logs that were falling into ashes.

"The upholsterer came," she added, "with a bill for near a thousand guineas—I had difficulty in sending him away; is nothing in the house paid for?"

"Nothing."

She looked at him with a contempt that was more for herself than for him; she was quite callous and heartless; a sense of humour, a nice appreciation of men and things alone prevented her from being odious.

"Lord!" she smiled. "To live to be fooled by Beau Sekforde!"

She was a Countess in her own right; her patent was from Charles II and explained her career; she still had the air of a beauty, and wore the gowns usually affected by loveliness, but she was old with the terrible old age of a wanton, soulless woman.

Her reputation was bad even for her type; she had cheated at everything from love to cards, and no tenderness or regret had ever softened her ugly actions. At the end of her career as presiding goddess of a gambling saloon she had married Robert Sekforde, thinking he had money or at least the wits to get it, and a little betrayed by his glib tongue that had flattered her into thinking her beauty not lost, her charm not dead, only to find him an adventurer worse off than herself, who had not even paid for the clothes in which he had come to woo her; her sole satisfaction was that he had also been deceived.

He had thought her the prudent guardian of the spoils of a lifetime; instead, selfishness had caused her to scatter what greed had gained, and for her, too, this marriage had been seized as a chance to avert ruin.

Haggard and painted, a dark wig on her head, false pearls round her throat, and a dirty satin gown hanging gracefully round a figure still upright and elegant, she stared at the fire.

"We shall have to disappear," she remarked dryly.

He looked at her with eyes of hate.

"You must have some money," he said bluntly.

Avarice, the vice of old age, flashed in her glance as jealousy would have gleamed in that of a younger woman.

"What little I have I need," she retorted. "The man has turned simple." She grinned at her reflection in the glass above the fireplace.

"Well, leave me, then," he said bitterly; could he be rid of her, he felt it would gild his misfortune.

But my lady had come to the end of all her admirers; she could not even any longer dazzle boys with the wicked glory of her past; she had no one save Mr. Sekforde, and she meant to cling to him; he was a man, and twenty years younger than herself; he ought, she thought, to be useful.

Besides, this woman who had never had a friend of her own sex, shuddered to think of the last loneliness it would be to live without a man attached to her—little better the grave, and of that she had all the horror of the true atheist.

"You talk folly," she said with a dreadful ogle. "I shall remain."

"Then you will starve, my lady!" he flung out violently.

"Oh, fie, sir, one does not starve."

He could not endure to look at her, but staring at the desk began to tear up the notes before him.

"Will you not go to a mask tonight?" she asked querulously.

"I have no money to pay for a chair," he sneered.

"We might win something at cards."

"People are very wary."

"You were very clever at tricking me," remarked the Countess, "cannot you trick someone else, Mr. Sekforde?"

He wheeled round on her with concentrated venom.

"Ah, madam, if I were a bachelor—"

She quailed a little before his wrath, but rallied to reply with the spirit of the woman who had been spoilt by a king:

"You think you are so charming? Wealthy matches are particular. *Look in the glass, sir; your face is as ruined as your reputation.*"

He advanced on her and she began to shriek in a dreadful fashion; the town woman showed through the airs of the great lady.

"I'll call the watch!" she shrilled.

He fell back with a heavy step and stood glaring at her.

"A pair of fools," said my lady bitterly.

Then her cynical humour triumphed over her disgust.

"Your first wife would smile to see us now," she remarked.

Beau Sekforde turned to her a face suddenly livid.

"What do you know about my first wife?" he demanded fiercely.

"Nothing at all," replied my lady. "You kept her rather in the background, did you not? But one can guess."

Mr. Sekforde raged; he loathed any reference to the woman he had married in his obscurity, and who had been his drudge in the background through all his shifting fortunes; her worn face, her wagging tongue, her rude manners, had combined to make the thorn in the rose-bed of his softest days.

He had hated her, and believed that she had hated him; she was a Scotchwoman, a shrew, thrifty, honest, plain, and a good house-keeper; she had always made him very comfortable at home, though she had shamed him on the rare occasions when she had forced him to take her abroad.

She had died only a few months before his present marriage.

"One can guess," repeated the Countess, showing teeth dark in a ghastly grin behind rouged lips, "that you made her life very pleasant."

He sprang up and faced her, a big, heavy bully for all his satins and French peruke.

"Oh," she shrilled, frightened but defiant, "you look like murder!"

He turned away sharply and muttered some hideous words under his breath.

"What are you going to do?" asked my lady, with a quizzical gaze round the tawdry splendour that had been hired to lure her into marriage, and that now would be so shortly rent away.

Beau Sekforde controlled his wrath against the terrible woman who had deceived him into losing his last chance of retrieving ruin.

"Where are the servants?" he asked.

"All gone. I think they have taken some of the plate and all the wine. There is some food downstairs."

Mr. Sekforde had seen it as he came up; a hacked piece of fat ham on a dirty dish, a stained cloth, and a jagged loaf had been laid out on the dining-room table.

"I have had my dinner," remarked the Countess.

Her husband rudely left the room; he was hungry and forced to search for food, but the remembrance of the meal waiting nauseated him; he was delicate in his habits, and as he descended the stairs he thought of his late wife—she had been a wonderful housekeeper—even in poverty she had never failed to secure comfort.

As he opened the door of the dining-room he was agreeably surprised.

Evidently one of the servants had remained after all.

The hearth had been swept and a neat fire burnt pleasantly; a clean cloth was on the table, and the service was set out exactly; a fresh loaf, butter, fruit, a dish of hot meat, of cheese, of eggs stood ready; there was wine and brightly polished glasses.

"I did not know," Mr. Sekforde muttered, "that any of the hussies in this house could work like this."

He admired the spotless linen, the brilliant china, the gleaming glasses, the fresh and appetizing food, and ate and drank with a pleasure that made him forget for the moment his troubles.

One thing only slightly disturbed his meal; among the dishes was a plate of goblin scones; they were of a peculiar shape and taste, and he had never known anyone make them but the late Jane Sekforde.

When he had finished he rang the bell for candles, for the short November day was closing in.

There was no answer.

Surprised and slightly curious to see the servant who had been so deft, Mr. Sekforde went to the head of the basement stairs and shouted lustily; still there was no reply.

He returned to the dining-room; the candles were lit and set precisely on the table. Mr. Sekforde ran upstairs to his wife.

"Who is in this house?" he asked in a tone of some agitation.

The Countess was by the fire, seated on a low chair; before her on the floor was a wheel of playing cards from which she was telling her fortune.

"Who is in the house?" she sneered. "A drunken ruffian."

Misery was wearing thin the courtier-like manner from both of them.

"You old, wicked jade," he replied, "there is someone hiding in this house."

She rose, scattering the cards with the worn toe of her little satin shoe.

"There is no one in the house," she said, "not a baggage of them all would stay. I am going out. I want lights and amusement. Your house is too dull, Mr. Sekforde."

With this speech and an air that was a caricature of the graces of a young and beautiful woman she swept out of the room.

Even her own maid, a disreputable Frenchwoman, had left her, having moved out of the impending crash; but my lady had never lacked spirit; she attired herself, put all the money she had in her bosom, and left the house to pass the evening with one of her cronies, who kept an establishment similar to that which she had been forced to abandon.

Even the departure of her vindictive presence did not sweeten for Beau Sekforde the house that was the temple of his failure.

He glared at the furniture that should have been paid for by bills on his wife's fortune, and went to his chamber.

He, too, knew haunts, dark and gloomy, where health and money, wits and time might be steadily consumed, and where one who was bankrupt in all these things might be for the time tolerated if he had a flattering and servile tongue and an appearance that lent some dignity to mean vices and ignoble sins.

He found a fire in his bedchamber, the curtains drawn, his cloak, evening rapier, and gloves put ready for him, the candles lit on his dressing-table.

He dressed himself rather soberly and went downstairs.

The meal was cleared away in the dining-room, the fire covered, the chairs put back in their places.

Beau Sekforde swore.

"If I had not seen her fastened down in her coffin I should have sworn that Jane was in this house," he muttered, and his bloodshot eyes winced a little from the gloom of the empty house.

Again he went to the head of the basement stairs and listened.

He could hear faintly the sound of someone moving about—the sound of dishes, of brisk footsteps, of clattering irons.

"Some wench *has* remained," he said uneasily, but he did not offer to investigate those concealed kitchen premises.

That evening his companions found him changed—a quiet sullen, dangerous mood was on him; they could easily understand this, as tales of the disaster of his marriage had already leaked abroad.

But something deeper and more terrible even than his almost accomplished ruin was troubling Robert Sekforde.

He returned very late to the mansion in High Holborn; he had drunk as much wine as his friends would pay for, and there was little of the elegant gallant about the heavy figure in the stained coat with wig awry, and the flushed, swollen face, who stumbled into the wretched place he named home with unconscious sarcasm.

A light stood ready for him in the hall; he took this up and staggered upstairs, spilling the candle-grease over his lace ruffles.

Half-way up he paused, suddenly wondering who had thought to leave the light.

"Not my lady wife—not my royal Countess," he grinned.

Then a sudden pang of horror almost sobered him. Jane had never forgotten to put a candle in the hall.

He paused, as if expecting to hear her shrill, nagging voice.

"You're drunk," he said to himself fiercely; "she is dead, dead, dead."

He went upstairs.

The fire in his room was bright, the bed stood ready, his slippers and bedgown were warming, a cup of posset stood steaming on the side-table.

Mr. Sekforde snatched up his candle and hurried to the room of the Countess.

He violently entered and stood confronting her great bed with the red damask hangings.

With a shriek she sat up; her cheeks were still rouged, the false pearls dangled in her ears, the laced gown was open on her skinny throat; a cap with pink ribbons concealed her scant grey hair.

She flung herself with claw-like hands on an embroidered purse on the quilt, and thrust it under her pillow; it contained her night's winnings at cards.

"Have you come to rob me?" she screamed.

Terror robbed her of all dignity; she crouched in the shadows of the huge bed, away from the red light cast on her dreadful face by the candle her husband held.

Beau Sekforde was not thinking of money now, and her words passed unheeded.

"Who is in this house?" he demanded.

"You are mad," she said, a little recovering her composure, but keeping her hands very firmly on the purse beneath the pillow; "there is no one in this house."

"Did *you* put a candle for me and prepare my room and light the fire and place the posset?"

He spoke thickly and leant against the bedpost; the candle, now almost guttered away, sent a spill of grease on the heavy quilt.

"You are drunk, you monstrous man!" screamed my lady. "If you are not away instantly I'll put my head out of the window and screech the neighbourhood up!"

Beau Sekforde, regarding her with dull eyes, remained at his original point.

"There was someone in the kitchen this afternoon," he insisted. "I heard sounds—"

"Rats," said my lady; "the house is full of 'em."

A look of relief passed over the man's sodden features.

"Of course, rats," he muttered.

"What else could it be?" asked the Countess, sufficiently

impressed by his strange manner momentarily to forget her griev-
ance against him.

"What else?" he repeated; then suddenly turned on her with
fury, lurching the candle into her face.

"Could rats have sent this for me?" he shouted.

The Countess shrank back; when agitated her head trembled with
incipient palsy, and now it trembled so that the false pearls rattled
hollow against her bony neck.

"You will fire the bed-curtains!" she shrilled desperately.

He trembled with a loathing of her that was like a panic fear of fury.

"You time-foundered creature!" he cried. "You bitter horror!
And 'twas for *you* I did it!"

She sprang to her knees in the bed, her hands crooked as if ready
for his face; there was nothing left now of the fine dame nurtured
in courts, the beauty nursed in the laps of princes. She had reverted
to the wench of Drury Lane, screaming abuse from alley to alley.

"If you are disappointed, what about me?" she shrieked. "Have
I not tied myself to a low, ugly fool?"

He stepped back from her as if he did not understand her, and,
muttering, staggered back into his own room.

There he lit all the candles, piled up the fire with more fuel,
glanced with horror at the bed, flung off his coat and wig, and settled
himself in the chair with arms before the fire to sleep.

The Countess, roused and angered, could sleep no more.

She rose, flung on a chamber-robe of yellow satin lined with
marten's fur, that was a relic of her court days and threadbare and
moth-eaten in places, though giving the effect of much splendour.

Without striking a light she went cautiously out into the corridor,
saw the door of her husband's room ajar, a bright glow from it failing
across the darkness, and crept steadily in.

He was, as she had supposed, in an intoxicated stupor of sleep by the fire.

His head had sunk forward on the stained and untied lace cravat on his breast; his wigless head showed fat and shaven and grey over the temples; his face was a dull purple, and his mouth hung open.

His great frame was almost as loose as that of a man newly dead, his hands hung slack, and his chest heaved with his noisy breathing. My lady was herself a horrid object, but that did not prevent her giving him a glance of genuine disgust.

"Beau Sekforde indeed!" she muttered.

She put out all the candles save two on the dressing-table, found the coat her husband had flung off, and began going swiftly through the pockets.

He had been, as she had hoped, fortunate at cards that night; he was indeed, like herself, of a type who seldom was unfortunate, since he only played with fools or honest men, neither of whom had any chance against the peculiar talents of the sharper.

The Countess found sundry pieces of gold and silver, which she knotted up in her handkerchief with much satisfaction.

She knew that nothing but money would ever be able to be of any service to her in this world.

Pleased with her success, she looked round to see if there were anything else of which she could despoil her husband.

Keeping her cunning old eyes constantly on him, she crept to the dressing-table and went over the drawers and boxes.

Most of the ornaments that she turned out glittered and gleamed heavily in the candlelight. But she knew that they were as false as the pearls trembling in her own ears; one or two things, however, she added to the money in the handkerchief, and she was about to investigate further when a little sound, like a cough, caused her to look sharply round.

The room was full of warm shadows, the fire was sinking low and only cast a dim light on the heavy, sleeping figure on the hearth, while the candlesticks on the dressing-table served only to illuminate the bent figure of the Countess in her brilliant wrap.

As she looked round she found herself staring straight at the figure of a woman, who was observing her from the other side of the bed.

This woman was dressed in a grey tabinet fashioned like the dress of an upper servant. Her hair was smoothly banded, and her features were pale and sharp; her hands, that she held rather awkwardly in front of her, were rough and work-worn.

Across one cheek was a long scratch.

The Countess dropped her spoils; she remembered her husband's words that she had taken for the babbling of a drunkard.

So there *was* someone in the house.

"How dare you?" she quavered, and in a low tone, for she did not wish to rouse her husband. "How dare you come here?"

Without replying, the woman moved across to the sleeping man and looked down at him with an extraordinary expression of mingled malice and protection, as if she would defend him from any evil save that she chose to deal herself.

So sinister was this expression and the woman's whole attitude that the Countess was frightened as she never had been in the course of her wicked life.

She stood staring; the handkerchief, full of money and ornaments, dropped on the dressing-table unheeded.

Beau Sekforde moved in his sleep and fetched a deep groan.

"You impertinent creature!" whispered the Countess, taking courage. "Will you not go before I wake my husband?"

At these last words the woman raised her head; she did not seem to speak, yet, as if there were an echo in the room, the Countess distinctly heard the words "My husband!" repeated after her in a tone of bitter mockery.

A sense of unreality such as she had never known before touched the Countess; she felt as if her sight were growing dim and her hearing failing her; she made a movement as if to brush something from before her eyes.

When she looked again at Beau Sekforde he was alone; no one was beside him.

In dreaming, tortured sleep he groaned and tossed.

"The baggage has slipped off," muttered the Countess; "belike it is some ancient dear of his own. I will send her packing in the morning."

She crept back to her own room, forgetting her spoils.

She did not sleep, and Mr. Sekforde did not wake till the pale winter dawn showed between the curtains.

The Countess looked round on a chamber in disorder, but for Beau Sekforde everything was arranged, shaving water ready, his breakfast hot and tempting on a tray, his clothes laid out.

When he had dressed and come downstairs he found his wife yawning over a copy of the *Gazette*.

She remembered last night quite clearly, and considerably regretted what she had in her confusion left behind in Beau Sekforde's room.

She gave him a glance, vicious with the sense of an opportunity lost.

He flung at her the question he had shouted last night:

"Who is in this house?"

"Some woman has stayed," she answered. "I think it was Joanna the housekeeper, but I did not see very clearly. She must be out now, as I have rung the bell and there has been no answer."

"My breakfast was brought up to me," said Mr. Sekforde. "So it is Joanna Mills, is it?"

The Countess was angry; she had had to go to the kitchen and pick among yesterday's scraps for her own food.

"And who is she?"

"You said, madam, the housekeeper."

"She must be very fond of you," sneered my lady.

He started at that and turned on her with a ghastly look.

"Oh, don't think I am jealous!" she grinned cynically.

"It was the word you used," he muttered. "I do not think anyone has been *fond* of me save one—"

He paused and passed his hand over his weary, heavy eyes.

"I dreamt of her last night."

"Who?"

"Jane, my wife."

The Countess remembered the ugly echo of her words last night.

"Your wife—do you forget that I and no other am your wife?"

"I do," he replied sullenly; "to me, Jane is always my wife."

"A pity," said my lady sarcastically, "that she did not live longer."

He gave her a queer look.

"And now we have got to think of ourselves," he said abruptly. "I cannot keep these things much longer—you had better go."

"Where?"

"What do I care?" he answered cruelly.

"I stay here," she replied. "Is the rent paid?"

"No."

"Well, they will not disturb us till quarter-day," said my lady calmly. "You do not want to be parted from your loving wife, do you, dear?"

He stared at her as if her words had a double meaning.

"Cannot you be quiet about my wife?" he exclaimed.

"La! The man is off his head!" shrilled my lady. "Jane Sekforde is dead!"

"That is why I think about her," he retorted grimly.

"A model husband," jeered the Countess, eyeing him viciously. "I am sorry I never knew the sweet creature you regret so keenly and so touchingly."

He raged at her like a man whose nerves are overwrought.

"Will you not let the matter be? Think of yourself, you monstrous horror! You will soon be in the Fleet!"

This picture was sufficiently realistic to make the Countess shiver.

"What are you going to do?" she asked with sudden feebleness.

He did not know; brooding and black-browed, he withdrew to the window-place and stared out at the leaden November sky that hung so heavily over the London streets.

"I suppose if you were free of me you would take your handsome face to market again?" added my lady, with a sudden lash of new fury.

He gave her a red look, at which she shrank away.

"Well, still we do not decide on anything," she quavered.

He would not answer her, but flung out of the house.

His unsteady steps were directed to St. Andrew's Church.

It was a long time since Beau Sekforde had been near a church.

Even when his wife had been buried here he had not attended the service.

He stood now in the porch, biting his thumb; then presently he entered.

Hesitating and furtive he went round the walls until he came to the new, cheap tablet with the badly-cut, draped urn and the florid Latin setting forth the virtues of Jane Sekforde.

"They don't say anything about her being a good housekeeper," he found himself saying aloud. "Why, she told me once she would come back from the grave to set her house in order."

He looked round as if to seek the answer of some companion, then laughed sullenly, drew his hat over his eyes, and left the church.

Towards dusk he wandered home.

The dining-room was neat and clean, the fire attended to, the dinner on the table. He managed to eat some of the food, but without appetite. The Countess was out; there was no trace anywhere of her slovenly splendour.

The whole house was as clean and precise as it had been when that neglected drudge, Jane Sekforde, had ruled over it.

When the Countess returned he was almost glad to see her—he had been thinking so much, too much, of Jane.

He had thought of her as he had seen her last, cold in her bed, clothed in her best grey gown, and how he had stared at her and hung over her and drawn suddenly away, so sharply that the button of cut steel on his cuff had left a scratch on her dead cheek.

"Where is Joanna Mills?" he abruptly asked his wife.

She stared at him; in such a moment as this could he think of nothing but the housekeeper? Was he losing his wits?

But she did not now much care; she had found a crony willing to shelter her and exploit her ancient glories.

"I am going away," she said. "I do not know who is in the house—I have seen no one."

He seemed to pay no attention at all to her first remark.

"What was that woman you saw last night like?"

"A very plain, shrewish-looking creature," replied my lady, with some bitterness, as she recalled how she had been startled into dropping the filched money.

"Are you sure it was a woman?" asked Beau Sekforde, with a ghastly grin.

"Why, what else could it have been?" she replied curiously.

"I do not think it has been a woman for—some months," he said.

"Why, do you imagine there is a spectre in the place?"

He would not, could not, answer; he left her, and went from room to room throwing everything into disorder, taking a horrid pleasure in making a confusion in the neatness of the house.

And then he flung himself away from the dreary mansion, leaving the Countess, like an old, weary bird of prey, wandering among the untidy rooms to see if there were anything worth taking away.

When he returned in the dark hours before the dawn he found the candle on the hall-table.

"Curse you!" he screamed. "Cannot you let me alone?"

He hastened upstairs; everything was neat, his bed, his fire, his posset ready, his shoes warming, his candles lit.

His terrified eyes cast a horrid glance round the room.

"The medicine cupboard—has she tidied that?" he muttered.

He crossed to where it hung in one corner, opened the door, and looked at the rows of pots and bottles.

One he knew well had been stained—had been left with a broken stopper... a bottle of peculiar, ugly look, holding a yellow liquid that stained linen purple.

Such a stain, very tiny, had been on Jane Sekforde's pillow.

As he stared into the cupboard he saw that the bottle had been cleaned and set in its place, while a new, neat label had been pasted on the front.

The writing was the writing of Jane Sekforde—it said in clear letters: "Poison".

Beau Sekforde dropped the candle and ran into the Countess's room.

"Wake up!" he shouted. "Wake up and hear me! She has come back. I want to confess. I murdered her! Let them take me away— somewhere where—where she cannot tidy for me."

The room was empty; the Countess had fled; an unnatural light came from the unshuttered windows and showed a woman sitting up in the great bed.

She had a pale, shrewish face, wore a grey garment, and had a scratch across her cheek.

As the shrieks of Beau Sekforde's confession echoed into the night and drew the watch to thunder on the door, the woman smiled.

1936

THE PINK COLUMBINE

Frederick Cowles

The bloody years of the French Revolutionary period have long been a favourite setting for writers of weird and macabre stories, from Washington Irving's classic "The Adventure of the German Student" to tales by Wilkie Collins, Alexandre Dumas, Marjorie Bowen, and many others. In this story Cowles takes us away some little distance from the tumult of Paris—though the sanguinary harvest of "Lady Guillotine" in that city is referenced—to the fictitious village and Château of Chantal-Claire. We are told that, exactly one year before the events of the tale, "The storm of the Revolution was already threatening"; this would seem to refer, however, to the coming of the Reign of Terror rather than the beginning of the Revolution itself, as the bloodthirsty Jacques Poisson is a member of the Committee for Public Safety, which was founded in 1793. "The Pink Columbine" was published in *The Horror of Abbot's Grange*.

acques Poisson finished his wine with a contented grunt. More would have been acceptable but he must keep a clear head as behooved a Commissioner of the Committee of Public Safety with important work to do.

He fingered his cockade lovingly. The tricolour meant the day of the people at last, and he, Jacques Poisson, the miller of Chantal-Claire, was now a leader of men, an officer of the new Republic. He was very much like a pig, this Citizen Poisson. His body was round and sleek, his eyes small and very evil, his clothes filthy and torn.

His wife sat by the fire plying her knitting needles. She was a tall, gaunt woman with a hard mouth, and a harder heart. She also wore the badge of the reign of terror.

The miller spat into the fire.

"Bah!" he said. "Tonight they may feast and dance, but ere morn they shall tremble."

He spat again. The woman said nothing.

"How I have waited for this day," the heavy voice went on. "Did she not call me dog, and strike me with her riding whip!"

He showed his yellow teeth in a wicked grin.

"As I am a dog she cannot blame me if I bite now that I am unmuzzled."

His wife laughed shrilly, but there was no humour in the sound.

"Curse them all," she cried, and knitted faster.

"Yesterday in Paris," the man went on, "I saw the heads of aristocrats rolling into the basket under the Lady Guillotine, like apples falling from a tree in autumn."

The woman laughed again.

"Would I had been there to see the sight," she said.

The miller rose from the table and passed over to the open doorway. From there he gazed up at the great, grey outline of the Château de Chantal-Claire towering on the hillside above the village. The gardens and vineyards were gay with the bright hues of late summer. Above them a terrace was built into the rock, and this encircled the house.

Jacques Poisson shook his fist at the weather-worn towers.

"*Mon Dieu*," he cried in a voice shrill with hate. "Soon I will chase the rats from their nest, and pull every stone to the ground."

On the terrace of the Château the Marquis Jean Marie Gabriel de Chantal-Claire paced up and down with his wife on his arm. The sun was already low in the sky, and there was a hint of storm in the air.

"How much longer, dearest?" whispered the Marquise.

Her husband laughed mirthlessly.

"Tonight, maybe," he answered. "They will not leave us alone much longer. You are not afraid?"

She raised her head proudly, and the light of battle shone in her eyes.

"Never," she cried. "But what of our guests?"

"They too are ready," was the reply. "Death awaits them wherever they are. The coast is carefully watched, and all the roads are patrolled. None is afraid of what must come sooner or later."

"Then we shall die in good company," whispered the little Marquise.

"Tonight," the man went on, "we may dance together for the last time, and I should like you to be, once again, the pink columbine of a year ago."

The Marquise nodded silently, and the tears came into her hazel eyes. Could it be only a year ago, at a ball given by her mother, she had danced as a pink columbine, and the Marquis had seen her for the first time? The storm of the Revolution was already threatening, and the wooing had been swift.

In the peace of Chantal-Claire they had been very happy, but now the full flurry of hatred had broken loose, and they could not hope for continued security.

So, on this night, the anniversary of their first meeting, they were giving a ball to those of their friends who were not afraid of capture and death.

The Marquis stooped and kissed his lady's fingers.

"At midnight," he said softly, "I shall look for the pink columbine."

As they parted a sudden gust of wind shook the roses on the walls, and the petals fell around them like drops of red blood. The Marquise trembled as she entered the house.

Down in the village Citizen Poisson spat yet again.

"I must give my orders," he grunted as he moved slowly along the street. "We will let the guests arrive in safety, then, at midnight, we will surprise them all."

II

Soon after sunset the storm broke over the village, and the rain fell in torrents.

Jacques Poisson swore loudly as he issued his final instructions to the band of men under his charge. It was a mixed company composed of Republican troopers from Paris, and a few villagers.

Women hung about in doorways, whispering half fearfully, and looking up at the lights in the windows of the château on the hillside. Years of toil and oppression had hardened their faces. Even the storm of the Revolution seemed unreal. They had lived so long under the rule of the Lords of Chantal-Claire that any change was regarded doubtfully.

With the men it was different. Some of them had been in Paris, and had seen the tribunals at work condemning and beheading the hated aristocrats. They had returned to their native haunts with wild tales of liberty, and a terrible thirst for blood. Many of them were more like wild beasts than men.

Citizen Poisson cursed again. He bellowed an order, and the company moved off.

In the Château de Chantal-Claire bright lights shone in every room, and soft perfumes stole in from the rain-drenched garden.

Flickering candles, in sparkling chandeliers, illuminated the ballroom where, to the strains of lively music, dancing feet tripped lightly over the polished floor. Laughing couples moved in stately minuet or gay gavotte. These were the flower of the chivalry of old France.

Jests were freely exchanged, yet all knew that death was watching near at hand. Such a meeting of aristocrats could not be disregarded by the revolutionary authorities.

Just one night of the old beauty and romance, one short dream of the old days of security, and they were ready for whatever the morning might bring. Some even, in contemptuous mockery, wore red silk bands or necklaces of rubies tightly clasped at their throats, as if to mark the place where the knife of the guillotine would soon sever their heads from their bodies.

In alcoves round the room lovers forgot the shadow that hung over them, and lived only in the romance of the evening. Soft lips met soft lips, and loving words were spoken.

Near the doorway the Marquis stood alone. His eyes were sad, for he saw the gay, beautiful France he had known since boyhood, and knew that he was watching its death struggles. During his one short year of married life he had witnessed the complete overthrow of the old régime.

He could have taken his young wife to England and joined other exiles, but she refused to go. Death would be more welcome and honourable than a hurried flight from their native land.

A clock chimed softly, and through the dancers came the figure of a pink columbine. The Marquis smiled. He was living in the past. It was a year ago, and he was falling in love again.

A space was soon cleared in the centre of the room, and the Marquise began to dance. Her little feet twinkled to and fro, and she swayed like a pink rosebud in the breeze. The Marquis trembled a little. How he loved this young girl who was his wife!

A low voice whispered in his ear. He turned. It was a servant.

"Monseigneur," said the man, "they are here."

Almost at once the sound of a hoarsely shouted order came from the terrace, and the coarse figure of Jacques Poisson entered through the French windows.

In the ballroom rapiers were drawn, and the pink columbine stole over to her husband's side.

The miller advanced boldly.

"Citizen Chantal-Claire, I arrest you as a traitor, in the name of the Republic," he thundered.

The Marquis lifted his glass to his eye.

"Citizen Chantal-Claire!" he repeated, with the slightest inflexion on the first word. "I know no one of that title. I am the Marquis Jean Marie Gabriel de Chantal-Claire."

"Marquis or Citizen," growled the little man, "it is all the same, as you will soon discover."

His sword flashed. "Arrest the traitors," he shouted to his men.

Only a few members of the company were armed, but those who were made a gallant fight for freedom. The struggle was brief. A few were wounded, one or two escaped through the windows, but the majority were quickly overpowered.

Jacques Poisson looked at the Marquis. "This time I win," he said. Then, for the first time, he noticed the pink columbine. "Madame la Marquise"—he bowed in mock courtesy—"we meet again."

The Marquise regarded him scornfully.

"How different is this meeting from our last," the man went on. "Then you called me dog, and struck at me. Now, you see, the dog has teeth, and knows how to bite."

She lifted her head, and her voice was very low. "Would to God I had my whip now that I might strike you and call you dog again," she said.

A wave of anger crimsoned the miller's face, but the harsh retort that came to his lips was suddenly checked. A new look came into his face, and a terrible gleam crept into the little evil eyes. Jacques Poisson realized that this little pink-clad dancer, be she Marquise or commoner, was the most desirable thing he had ever encountered. A fierce eagerness to kiss those red lips and caress those white limbs filled his soul.

The Marquis saw that look and he was afraid.

Another change came over the miller's face. He rapped out an order, and his party formed up with their prisoners.

"I will attend to the woman," the man went on. "I suspect that she knows secrets against the safety of the Republic."

The Marquis stepped forward. His face was white and drawn.

"Man," he cried, "you cannot take her from me!"

It was his first sign of fear. The miller laughed, but before he could reply the voice of the Marquise broke in.

"Monseigneur," she said to her husband, "you forget yourself. You cannot stoop so low as to bandy words with a dog."

Then her voice sank to a whisper.

"It will be all right, beloved. I am yours for ever and nothing can part us."

Jacques Poisson had turned away. He picked three men from his band to guard the château, the rest he ordered to remove the prisoners to the village. He would remain at the house awhile to examine the woman, and would conduct the party to Paris early in the morning.

"He has something worse than death in mind for you, dearest," the Marquis whispered.

The answer came quickly. "Death is always near at hand and he will not fail me now," and the Marquise smiled at her husband through tear-dimmed eyes as he was dragged from her side and she was left with Jacques Poisson.

"Come," said the miller. "There is no rank in France today, and, if you are kind to me, perhaps I may be kind to you."

The pink columbine raised her head, and her eyes were hard as she replied: "Do you think I should ever accept kindness from such as you?"

The man laughed. "Yet I will be kind," he cried. "Those white arms were made for loving, those red lips for kissing."

He strode towards her, and, filled with a nameless dread, the little

Marquise turned and fled. Along the ballroom she ran, and up the wide staircase, and the miller lumbered after her.

It was to her own room she went—the great stateroom with the furniture of rose and gold.

Jacques Poisson followed, but on the threshold of the room he paused. The magnificence dazzled and maddened him. How he hated these aristocrats who had lived in such luxury whilst he had laboured in misery and want.

Another thought came to him. The servants had fled away, or had been removed to the village, and the three men downstairs would be taking advantage of his absence to fill their pockets with spoil. They might even be taking his share.

The Marquise shivered in a shadowed corner. She could wait. A key was on the inside of the door. He transferred it to the outside, and, with a chuckle, turned it in the lock.

"I shall soon return to your loving arms, so be ready for me," he shouted, and tramped away from downstairs.

The Marquise was alone… Yet, ere long, he would return—this beast of the Revolution. She shuddered.

The moon was shining and the storm was over. In a corner two long tapers flickered before a silver crucifix. She crossed the room and knelt before the image.

Only a year ago… Her thoughts were wandering back to that happy day when the Marquis had come to her with love that was to make all the rough ways smooth. Now her husband had been taken from her to certain death, and worse than death awaited her at the hands of a gross devil in the likeness of a man.

She looked round the room again. Everything in it spoke of that one short year of perfect love. The tears came into her eyes, and she prayed softly.

When she arose from her knees a new courage was in her heart, and she hummed the air of a little song. From a drawer in a cabinet she took a tiny phial, and, with this in her hand, returned to the crucifix. Her lips moved in prayer again.

"O God of love," she whispered, "you will understand, and let my husband come to me soon."

III

In the great hall of the château Citizen Poisson made merry. The wine from the cellars of the Marquis was very good and Jacques and his men were thirsty.

They were a wicked-looking lot, these newly freed slaves, these sons of liberty. There was Antoine Lambal, the cobbler; Charles Godeau, the miller's cousin; and Henri Martel, who had been a soldier in the old army. All were drinking heavily. This Revolution was a great time for them. All the old, age-long hatred was let loose, and the smell of blood in the streets of Paris had created a desire to kill. This capture at the château would bring great glory to them, and other pickings would follow.

Jacques Poisson crossed to a window and looked out into the night. The moon was shining brightly, and lights were still burning in the village. He saw the gleam of a lantern in the window of his mill. His wife was waiting for him. Poor fool! Let her wait.

He looked towards Paris. What further honours awaited him there? He had already been of some service to the Republic, and had been suitably rewarded. He would aim higher yet. There were many aristocrats still to be caught, and dragged before the tribunals. He spat deliberately.

"Curse them all," he muttered.

Meanwhile there was the Marquise de Chantal-Claire awaiting him upstairs. He returned to the fire and kicked the logs into a blaze. He snapped the neck off a bottle, and, with an oath, lifted it to his lips.

The candles were burning very low; some were already out. A little breeze brought a heavy perfume of roses in from the garden. In spite of the rain the air seemed hot and oppressive.

Jacques Poisson wiped the sleeve of his coat over his face, and, as he did so, he fancied he saw a gleam of pink on the stairs. He looked again. Yes! It was certainly there. It moved, it flitted softly downwards, it paused in fear, then glided onwards—it was the marquise, the pink columbine.

He rose in anger. He was very unsteady, for the wine was strong.

"How did she come here?" he screamed, pointing at the figure. "I locked her in."

"Who, Citizen?" queried Antoine.

"Fool!" cried the other. "Use your eyes... There, on the staircase."

The men looked again. Certainly there was a little gleam of colour, but it was only a pink moth fluttering lazily in the candlelight.

"It's only a moth," said Henri.

A terrible oath was his captain's answer.

"Moth! Are you mad? It's the woman, I tell you," he yelled.

Charles Godeau winked at the others. It was certainly the wine. It had gone to the head of Citizen Poisson.

The miller rushed to the foot of the stairs. As he did so the figure in pink tripped lightly past him, through the hall, and stood framed in the doorway.

"Come here!" he shouted. "You cannot escape me."

The other men laughed heartily. Certainly the Citizen Poisson was drunk.

Another candle flickered and died, and a log, falling into the hearth, cast up a shower of sparks.

Jacques Poisson trembled with rage. He strode towards the door, and, just as he reached it, the figure glided away with a low laugh.

Out on to the terrace he went. The dawn was breaking in the east, and the cool breeze swirled the rose petals around him. The pink form was standing in the shadows. He hurried towards it, and it flitted away again. Faster he went, and faster went the figure. He ran, and it ran also. It paused a moment. He stretched out his arms to catch it, but again it eluded him. He turned and tried once more.

They were now at the end of the terrace, and the steep flight of steps to the garden was near at hand.

The dancer stayed again, and remained poised above the steps. This time he could not miss her. He made another effort, but only embraced the air. He slipped, tried to steady himself and slipped again, then fell, with a sickening thud, and rolled over and over down the steps.

From the château came the sound of voices raised in a drunken song, and the tinkle of glass as the soldiers of the Republic broke the neck of another bottle.

In the rose and gold bedroom the figure of the pink columbine lay dead before the great silver crucifix, and the candles flickered fitfully.

At the bottom of the terrace steps, ghastly in the light of early dawn, lay the thing that was once Jacques Poisson.

Down in the village of Chantal-Claire a weary, heavy-eyed woman knitted hose for a man who would never wear hose again.

THE TRANSLATION OF AQBAR

Aaron Worth

It was with extreme diffidence that I approached my editor at British Library Publishing with the idea of including my own weird fiction in this collection; I was, and am, deeply grateful for (also, of course, disconcerted, confused, and terrified by) his enthusiastic response. This tale of late-Victorian London (we are, I believe, in the early 90s here) incorporates several aspects of nineteenth-century British culture which have long obsessed me: the (so often sinister) figure of the stage conjuror (one of the great archetypes of modernity), the spectre of Darwinian retrogression, and even, in a small way, the now-superannuated media technologies of the day.

"The Translation of Aqbar" first appeared in the December 2017 edition of *Cemetery Dance* magazine.

he famous conjurer, Ugolini, was coming to their house in Islington to perform, in less than a fortnight.

This was what Harry's older brother Willy had told him, in a whisper, as they lay in their room one night, supposedly asleep. And Harry, who nearly always believed what his brother told him without question, had sat bolt upright in his bed, with an incredulous snort.

"What' d'you mean, *our house*," he'd cried, and Willy had *shh*'d him angrily, throwing a pillow at his head for good measure.

"What d'you mean, *our house*," Harry had repeated, in a quieter yet no less disbelieving voice. "Don't be daft, Willy. Next, you'll be telling me Father Christmas isn't fairy tale, after all." He snorted again. "Our *house*, indeed!"

All of London had heard of Ugolini, and most of it had seen him perform at Assyrian Hall: the great building of reddish stone in Piccadilly, the one with the curious friezes and the pair of carved bulls glaring down from the roof. In less than a year, his illusions had become household names—and this in an age when titans like Maskelyne, Lynn, and Booth disputed amongst themselves the title of king of the wizards. No lesser a personage than Queen Victoria, it was said, had invited Ugolini to perform at Osborne House.

Harry and Willy had themselves been three times to Assyrian Hall to see Ugolini, and had gasped and oohed and applauded with the rest of London as he had vanished caged canaries, inexplicably enlarged playing cards to lunatic sizes, and smashed borrowed pocket-watches to smithereens with a hammer, only to produce them again, quite undamaged, from a borrowed silk hat.

In short, Ugolini was a celebrity of the first order—perhaps, just then, the most talked-about man in London.

So the idea that he would come to perform at their *house*…

"I know it sounds mad," Willy had gone on to explain, "but I heard cook telling her beau all about it, at the servant's door. Said she wouldn't be needed Saturday fortnight, on account of the 'show in the parlour.' And then he asks, 'What show?' and she says, very quiet but very distinct, 'Why, *Ugolini's* coming!' ('cept she says it '*Hugo*-lini,' like you'd expect).

"'It's to be a *special* performance,' she says. 'Tricks as he don't put on for the *oy-balloy*'—which is to say, the common folk. That's what dad told mum. To that lot, *this* set of tricks'd be, how'd he put it, caviar for the generals.

"Apparently, cook says, he's become quite the thing in certain circles—a private show, for those who can afford it. 'Not for the kiddies, though,' is what she says."

In the days that followed, Harry, still somewhat skeptical, watched their parents for signs of unusual behavior; and sure enough, he was soon able to confirm the truth of Willy's improbable assertion for himself.

One morning, after the boys had been sent from the breakfast table to get ready for school, Harry lingered behind, standing just out of sight in the next room, where he could see and hear his mum and dad without being observed.

His father took a sip of coffee, then said to his mother: "Ugolini's agent will expect the check tomorrow. It is a substantial sum, so I shall have to make certain arrangements at the bank before going to Whitehall. Oh, and do be sure, my darling, to confirm that Captain Wilkins will be one of our party that evening."

"Of course, dear," replied Harry's mum. "I, shall send Thomson 'round later this morning." Then she got up to clear the table, and as she passed by his dad's chair he reached out suddenly and snaked an arm around her slender waist.

His little round spectacles glittered above a wicked smile, the likes of which Harry had never seen on his father's placid face before.

Harry watched in surprise as his other hand violently crushed his mother's breast, whilst a hiss like that of a teakettle escaped from between her clenched teeth.

At this Harry ran upstairs, his face burning.

From that morning to the night scheduled for the performance there remained nine days, and for Harry and Willy those nine days crawled by as slowly as treacle pouring: for of course the two boys were determined secretly to see the show for themselves. There was a long and heavily-draped table at the back of the parlor, on which a couple of seldom-used decanters rested. They reckoned that, with the grown-ups' attention directed towards the front of the parlor, they would be able to scuttle underneath without being detected.

At last the much-anticipated evening came, and after pretending to go to bed the boys waited a decent interval, then snuck down in their pajamas to the kitchen. A few minutes later they heard the sound of applause, which they took for their cue. On all fours they crept to their hiding-place, and peeped out through the gaps in the tablecloth.

Harry first cast a quick look at the audience, which included their parents, as well as some dozen or so guests. Harry recognized two or three men who worked with his father at Whitehall, as well as his banker and solicitor, along with their wives.

Then he turned his attention to the front of the parlor, where (Harry saw) the furniture had been cleared away.

Instead of the usual chairs, sofa, card table, and bookcase, a large Chinese screen of black satin stood to the left, covered all over with very queerly-colored dragonflies. To the right stretched a long table of black, ancient wood, its surface littered with a myriad of props: Harry saw silver cups and crystal goblets, an ormolu table clock surmounted with a grinning sphinx, a vase of cream-colored lilies, and a tarnished arquebus, among other objects.

In the center stood Ugolini himself, in evening dress, with a red carnation in his button-hole. His shining black hair was brushed back, and his hands, the fingers covered with glittering rings, were clasped together in a gesture of acknowledgement.

Nearby stood an assistant, a tall Indian with a badly scarred face and a mulberry-colored turban. Harry did not remember having seen him at Assyrian Hall, but then there were so many colorful figures on the stage there.

For half an hour Ugolini performed a series of tricks not dissimilar in kind from those Harry and his brother had already witnessed at Assyrian Hall: he produced doves from an empty cigar box, did miraculous things with half-crowns and shillings, and broke half a dozen eggs into a hat, only to lift out, moments later, a cooked omelet, smoking in a pan.

The boys enjoyed the show greatly: certainly it was a thrill simply to have the great Ugolini *in their own parlor*.

But apart from a trick he did with giant playing cards whose backs displayed photographs of half-naked ladies, there was nothing really *new* about the show. Not, that is, until after a rather conventional illusion involving a knotted rope.

At the conclusion of this last trick Ugolini acknowledged the polite applause with a gracious wave of the hand, at the same time wiping his forehead with a cloth-of-gold handkerchief. He then made a sign to his assistant, who bowed and withdrew.

The Indian returned a few moments later, pushing into the parlor a queer glass cabinet, which glided across the Turkey-carpets on little wheels of silver. It was rather taller than a man, and fitted together with brass.

"And now, my friends," said Ugolini with a slight bow, gesturing at the cabinet, "with your kind permission, and the aid of my faithful assistant Aqbar, we shall essay something quite novel: an illusion never before attempted upon the London stage, though—" (here he lay a ring-bright finger alongside his aquiline nose) "—not entirely unknown in certain *Parisian* circles..." (A knowing titter raced through the parlor.)

"The illusion has no name. Or rather, it is known by many names. Tonight, my friends, shall we term it—The Translation of Aqbar?"

With a dazzling smile, Ugolini again indicated the cabinet.

"Aqbar, if you please?"

The Indian, whose scarred countenance had remained stoically grim to this point, now directed a pleading look at Ugolini—a look of which the great man took no notice whatever.

And so, with a trembling brown hand, the Indian turned a golden key that protruded from the front of the cabinet, and it swung silently open, as if eager to receive him. Shakily he stepped inside and shut himself in, a piteous look upon his disfigured face, now the color of ashes.

Ugolini locked him in with a flourish, held up his hands to show that they were empty, then plucked a silken scarf out of thin air, to appreciative coos and murmurs. Then, delicately pinching it by two corners, Ugolini shook out the scarf, and (before their very eyes) it grew larger and larger, until it was the size of a tablecloth. It was a deep cerulean blue, and embroidered all over with sly, knowing eyes of gold, like those painted on Egyptian tombs.

A sprinkling of applause followed.

Ugolini walked slowly around all sides of the cabinet, at one point tipping a slow, deliberate wink at Harry (or so it seemed to him).

"There is, you perceive," he crooned to the rapt audience, "no hidden means of communication between the cabinet and the outside world—no way for even a mouse to enter or escape the cabinet without being detected."

Then he draped the great silken cloth over the cabinet, and waved an imperious hand in the air, at the same time murmuring something inaudible. Dramatically he tore the covering away, and the audience gasped as one.

Inside the cabinet now squatted a large and loathsome ape, its hide sparsely covered with bristly, reddish fur. Harry's own hair stirred upon his scalp and arms as he stared at it. He reached for his brother's hand and gave it a squeeze.

Harry had looked into many lavishly illustrated books of natural history, but the thing in the cabinet, while unmistakably an ape, was like no ape he had ever seen, or heard of.

It pressed the blue-black, rubbery pads of its fore-paws against the front of the cabinet and slowly dragged its claws across the glass with a soul-thrilling rasp. It leered at the audience, a hideous intelligence gleaming in its red eyes.

Someone murmured "Good Lord," and Harry became aware of a hateful odor in the parlor.

Still looking at the audience, and showing a mouthful of large, discoloured teeth, the ape-thing now began slowly to hop up and down, in a kind of odious, flopping dance. At this the cabinet creaked and swayed alarmingly, and swiftly Ugolini stepped forward and cast the silken covering over the cabinet once more, and it was still.

Another series of mystic passes followed, and another muttered string of words, and the covering was whisked away once more, to a collective hiss of surprise and shock.

Now the cabinet held a giant spider-crab, as big as a dog. It stood motionless as a painting: a congeries of long, jointed legs, supporting a mottled carapace.

"Don't be afraid," said Willy in Harry's ear. "It's—it's only a statue, I'm sure."

Then the thing moved, with a frightful clicking sound, as the thin, stalk-like legs scrabbled for purchase on the glass floor. Clackingly it blundered against the glass sides of the cabinet. More gasps from the audience, and Harry heard his brother moan softly.

"I reckon," Harry whispered, trying to reassure himself as much as his brother. "I reckon it's one of those auto—auto—what-d'ye-call-ems?—automa-things. Like we saw at the Crystal Palace, remember? The dummy organ-player, and the tin soldier that bowed, and saluted."

Meanwhile the conjurer, working more quickly now, had already effected another transformation, tearing the Argus-eyed cloth away again to reveal a great grey worm—or was it a slug?—which lay, coiled and glistening, on the floor of the cabinet.

"My God," someone croaked hoarsely.

Then it stirred, and a woman stifled a scream.

Ugolini, his face now shining with perspiration, had taken off his jacket, and stood in shirt-sleeves and waistcoat.

Again he covered the cabinet; again he uncovered it.

Harry caught a brief glimpse of something black and viscous, before he felt Willy's ice-cold hand pressing against his eyes, and he saw nothing more.

"Don't look, Harry," said his brother in a tremulous whisper, and Harry did not argue.

There were a few faint moans from the audience, and then a kind of electric silence seemed to grip the room. *Something*, Harry understood, was happening, but he had no desire to see.

He felt Willy's hand, cold and damp, begin to shake.

"No, no, *no*," he was muttering, and then: "Don't look, Harry, don't look, Harry, for God's sake don't *look*—"

This went on for nearly a minute, until Willy's pleas decayed into a vague unmeaning yammer, and his hand slid nervelessly away. Harry, however, kept his eyes shut tight, and so he could only guess at what appeared next, as he heard the conjurer's scarf snap and whisper again... and again... and again...

*

With a slight frown, Dr. Russel stretched out a finger to stop the recording apparatus on his desk. For nearly a minute he sat, sipping at his whisky-and-water and drumming his fingers on the arm of his chair. He wanted to choose his words very carefully.

Finally, he turned the machine back on, and the cylinder began to rotate again, with a faint whispering sound. Dr. Russel cleared his throat and leaned forward so that his beard-fringed lips nearly touched the rim of the phonograph machine's horn.

"But I should not wish," he continued, "to convey the impression that the boy presents any *special* danger.

"Even the—incisions William Pike made in his brother's body, which resulted in the poor lad's death (and these incisions, let me concede at once, were indeed of the most appalling character) appear to have been motivated, not by anger or any malicious *intent*, but by an insane desire to *locate*, and to *remove*, something he believed to have been *concealed within his brother's body*, some pernicious organ or entity with whose precise location he was not sufficiently well acquainted.

"This I infer, from certain wild, broken phrases the boy uttered upon his admission to my asylum. He has not, unfortunately, uttered a single word since.

"That his actions, fatal though their issue may have been, were not fueled by a homicidal mania, properly understood, is further argued by the fact that young William was engaged in performing *an identical series of incisions upon his own flesh*, with the same kitchen-knife he had used upon his brother, when his parents managed at last to force their way into the boys' shared bedroom. (The boy had pushed several heavy pieces of furniture against the door, to retard ingress.)

"These self-directed mutilations were, mercifully, arrested before he could do himself permanent injury; sadly, however, the child *did* succeed entirely in... er..."

Dr. Russel coughed into his fist.

"In—depriving himself of sight, an object to which he immediately transferred his efforts, upon finding his primary goal frustrated..."

Dr. Russel switched off the phonograph again, and gazed at a window set in one wall of his office, a window covered with Venetian blinds, which did not look out of doors. He sipped at his whisky-and-water for a while, then switched the machine back on.

"The parents, alas, can dispel no whit of this psychological mystery. The youth, they tell me, never before displayed any signs of violent behavior. Indeed, he appears to have been quite an ordinary boy, in every respect. On the night of this tragic... occurrence, they were engaged in hosting a dinner party for some few friends, when they heard the younger child's shrieks, and rushed upstairs, to find..."

Dr. Russel scratched at his beard for a minute.

"In sum," he went on, "the boy does not, in my professional opinion, present any *exceptional* degree of danger to staff, provided of course that he is closely watched, and the usual protocols observed with respect to sharp implements, et cetera.

"No, my request that he be transferred to your care stems from a simple conviction that Hartwell is (I admit without rancor)" (here Dr. Russel managed a brief, self-deprecating chuckle) "much better equipped for the treatment of juvenile lunatics (in which respect it has acquired a national reputation, as you well know). Coupled with this is the fact that, within my own institution, I find that cell space is, at present, at an absolute premium, owing to, er, over-crowding."

He took another sip of his whisky-and-water.

"Finally, sir, I hope that you will forgive my own idiosyncratic preference for phonographic correspondence, and feel free to send a simple (and, as I hope, affirmative) reply by wire or post, at your earliest convenience.

"Very truly yours, et cetera, Wilfrid Russel."

Dr. Russel turned off the machine and removed the cylinder, which he dropped into a large envelope, already addressed to the director of an asylum in Kent. This he carefully sealed.

Then Dr. Russel rose from his chair, crossed to the window, and, as stealthily as he could, raised the blind.

What he saw did not surprise him, but he perceived, nevertheless, the prickling spread of gooseflesh (to put it in non-medical terms) across his arms...

The boy was standing, in the middle of his cell, staring directly at Dr. Russel.

Well—*staring* was not, perhaps, precisely the right word to employ, under the circumstances. But then, those two circles of gauze, with spokes of surgical tape radiating from them in all directions, *did* appear to gape up at him, in a grotesque caricature of innocent surprise.

Certainly, blind or not, the boy *knew* he was there, watching him. He always knew. No matter how careful Dr. Russel was to raise the blinds in perfect silence, the boy would always, and immediately, turn those terrible white discs in his direction.

Had Dr. Russel not been an absolute enemy of supernaturalism in all its forms, he would have admitted to himself that the thing was positively—uncanny.

In fact (not, of course, that Dr. Russel had breathed a hint of this into the horn of his phonograph), this... *uncanniness* was one of the *real* reasons it had been deemed desirable to seek the removal of William Pike, aged fourteen, to another asylum, one a good seventy-five English miles away, and that with all possible dispatch.

As for the *other* reason—the thing that had caused three of his best nurses to quit his employment within a single week, and compelled a fourth to take up residence in a cell of her own, in the female wing of the asylum...

Dr. Russel frowned and folded his arms.

Well, *that* reason was about to manifest itself, yet again, before his eyes.

As he watched, the boy, slouching forward and letting his arms dangle like an ape's, began to hop up and down, up and down, smiling all the time. He did this for about a minute.

Then he lay on the floor, splayed out his arms and legs, and raised himself up on his toes and fingers in the most bizarre fashion, so that he resembled a giant crab or arachnid. In this position he crept sideways, back and forth, for a while, still grinning and looking up at the window with those terrible eyes of gauze. It was really quite astonishing, Dr. Russel could not help reflecting even as he shuddered at the sight, how the boy managed to contort himself into such a position at all, let alone manage that horrid, lateral waddle...

Now the boy arranged his body into the coiled, prostrate figure which the staff had taken to calling, in hushed tones of disgust, "the Worm." As he began slowly to writhe and squirm, Dr. Russel hastily lowered the Venetian blind. He had no desire to watch this, or any of the further stages which comprised the boy's unvarying pantomime.

This dumb-show he had already witnessed once in its entirety, and in consequence understood perfectly the reactions of his nurses—the unfortunate Miss Gallagher's, perhaps, most of all...

Shaking his head vigorously, Dr. Russel finished his drink, put on hat and coat (the envelope tucked securely into one pocket), and switched off the electric lights in his office.

Then, turning up his collar against the chill evening drizzle, he hastened to the Central Post Office, where he sent the envelope speeding (figuratively at least) to his Kentish colleague.

Once this was done, Dr. Russel felt as though a substantial weight had been lifted from his shoulders.

Indeed, as he made his way to the chemist's shop (for he had one more errand to perform before he went home), he found himself actually *whistling*...

Goodness, he thought with a chuckle, pushing open the tinkling shop door. When had he last *whistled*, or indeed evinced any of the ordinary symptoms of a healthily equanimous mind? Not, at any rate, since before the Pike boy's arrival at the asylum.

No, since then, and particularly since the boy's first... *performance*, Dr. Russel's days had been most—harrowing indeed. Yes, that was the only word for it.

And yet, bad as his *days* had been (he reflected as he pointed out something on a high shelf to the chemist's boy), the *nights* had been even worse...

For he had been much troubled, of late, by the most frightful dreams.

In these dreams he found himself confronted by a host of morphologically unknown organic forms, forms whose lineaments he found both terrifying and exhilarating...

And when, upon waking, he looked at his own children's faces at the breakfast table, he could not help seeing ghostly eidolons of those same forms superimposed upon them, like projections from a kinematograph...

And as he looked at them, he would unconsciously grip the butter knife he held in his hand more tightly, till the knuckles went white...

He had no wish to endure another such breakfast.

The chemist was tying up the little parcel now, and repeating (Dr. Russel absently supposed) the usual cautions, and so he nodded and tried to look appropriately attentive.

But in fact his mind was, at that moment, occupied with quite another problem, to wit:

How, given the lateness of the hour, and the absence of any special occasion, might he best prevail upon his wife to prepare a nice glass of lemon-squash for the children, before bed?

COME, FOLLOW!

Sheila Hodgson

In addition to some three dozen or so ghostly tales, the English master of the genre, M. R. James, left us a short essay bearing the tantalizing title, "Stories I Have Tried to Write." Four decades after his death, Sheila Hodgson (1921–2001), a writer of radio plays, developed some of James's unrealized scenarios as scripts which were broadcast on BBC Radio Four (she had previously adapted several of Algernon Blackwood's stories featuring psychic detective John Silence):

> I used James himself as the principal character and narrator—for they were, after all, his scenarios—and pictured him telling the stories to friends at Christmas. Then I hit a snag. The programmes were popular—in fact, very successful—but when asked for more, I discovered there *were* no more. I had used up all the viable story lines. It seemed a pity to lose a well-liked formula, and by then James had become a powerful influence on me. I decided to continue with the series, inventing my own ghosts, and trying as far as possible to imitate James's style.

All told, Hodgson wrote eight radio plays, five of these being entirely original; subsequently these were turned into short stories for publication, and four additional tales were written. First published in the fourth issue of the Jamesian journal *Ghosts & Scholars*, and set "in this year of 1896," the present story, as far as I can determine, was not developed as a radio play despite being (it seems to me, and in apparent inconsistency with the above-quoted account) obviously inspired by one of James's scenarios (the one beginning, "Then there was quite a long one about two undergraduates spending Christmas in a country house that belonged to one of them. An uncle, next heir to the estate, lived near..."). In any case, the tale wonderfully captures the atmosphere of such early James tales as "Canon Alberic's Scrapbook" (first published in 1895).

t is a matter agreed upon among all right-thinking persons that Christmas should be spent in the bosom of the family; the picture conjured up by Mr. Charles Dickens has entered into the catalogue of English myths, a vision compounded of log fires, merry laughter and snow-bound countryside—all this despite the fact that the log fire may smoke, the snow prove non-existent, and the company be rendered speechless by indigestion. Moreover, it will rain.

"It will rain," said Mr. George Markham.

"What a dismal fellow you are, George!" His companion jerked on the bridle; they were riding in a light trap down the empty Sussex road. "My uncle is the only living relative I possess and I must, I positively must, call on him at Christmas."

"Why? The shops have a capital collection of greeting cards. Just send the old boy a robin. Or a picture of Santa Claus, signed Your Affectionate Nephew."

"That's ungenerous!" Paul Bernays laughed; they both laughed, for they were young men up at Cambridge in this year of 1896 and confident of their position. "He's got no money and no prospects, he lives with some dreary cleric of his own age."

"Worse and worse! My dear Paul, what are we going to say to a couple of elderly country bores?"

"Happy Christmas!" For some reason this struck both of them as an excellent joke; the barren hedgerows shook to their mirth, they slapped each other on the back and chortled with glee while the horse slowed to a walk and, yes, it began to rain. To either side the sepia downs curved against a wintry sky; a single bird rose above their heads and vanished over the hill.

"Confound it. Oh, let's go back!"

They might well have been tempted; the shower looked like developing into a steady downpour; but at that moment (seeking a place to manoeuvre the trap) Bernays turned his head and saw a most curious apparition approaching across the fields. A man of more than average height dressed in a flapping black cloak, he held a large umbrella high above his head and jumped over the furrows in a series of odd little skips; with each jump the umbrella jerked in the air while the rising wind tugged at his cloak, giving him the semblance of an old and agitated bat. He wore no headgear—and indeed would have found some difficulty in keeping anything upon his head by reason of the wind and the fact that both his hands were occupied in an attempt to restrain the umbrella handle. So, struggling against the malice of the elements, he contrived to gain the road where he stood peering at the travellers from under dark eyebrows; strangely hairy eyebrows which almost met over the bridge of his nose.

"Mr. Bernays?"

The words were swept away on a gust of rain. The young men stared at him; then Paul recovered sufficiently to shout:

"Hullo! Are you from the rectory?" And this was more than simple guesswork: at that distance the clerical collar could be plainly observed under the sodden cloak.

"My name is Alaric Halsey. You are welcome, sir, you are most welcome. Dear, dear, dear, what singularly inclement weather!" He smiled, a long grin which etched deep lines around his mouth and displayed a set of rather good teeth. He could have been some fifty years old, the hair still black and worn en brosse, the eyes luminous under those really very peculiar eyebrows. More might have ensued only at that moment there occurred a most unfortunate accident. Whether the wind, the rain, the flapping garments or a combination of all three alarmed the horse, suffice it to say that the animal bolted. It reared abruptly, backed—nearly upsetting the cart—and then set off at a tolerable gallop, causing the Reverend Alaric Halsey to leap into the ditch. His voice echoed thinly after them, the one distinguishable word being "uncle." It took Paul Bernays the better part of two miles to bring the horse under control. The creature then evinced a marked desire to go straight home, a point of view with which neither young man felt inclined to argue.

As they sat warming themselves before an excellent fire George Markham said: "So much for the clerical friend! We've shown seasonal good will, my dear chap. Do we really have to call on your uncle again?"

"Yes." Paul stretched his legs and reached for the decanter. "I'm sorry for the man, upon my word, he's been most shabbily treated."

"How?"

Rain spat against the window, the firelight made little amber gleams in the port. Bernays poured himself another glass before replying.

"Ancient history. He should have inherited this house. But he quarrelled with his father over certain companions, a pretty scandalous affair—don't ask me what!—and the whole West Farthing estate came to me. Uncle Nicholas went abroad; and didn't return to England till, oh, some time in 1895, I believe."

"Good Lord. Didn't he contest the will?"

"No."

"Lucky for you. Is the estate worth much...?" Markham drained his wine.

"I couldn't say. Yes, I suppose so. I've got the house and about two hundred acres of land. Mostly mixed farming, we passed the farm on the way up." Paul spoke with a genuine unconcern; he had a young man's easy contempt for money, a common attribute in those who have never had to do without it. They passed to other more congenial subjects such as women and horses, then went into dinner and gave the unlucky Mr. Nicholas Bernays only a passing thought and his friend the Reverend Alaric Halsey no thought at all.

It was therefore with a certain surprise on the following morning that—caught in the midst of his shaving—the owner of West Farthing looked out of the window and exclaimed:

"Good heavens. My uncle!"

A gentleman could be seen approaching the front door, a man below average height with thinning red hair and a faintly harassed expression. He glanced both right and left; seemingly troubled by something immediately behind him. Precisely what became apparent when a mongrel dog came round the corner of the outbuildings to join his master on the doorstep. Before Mr. Bernays senior could announce his arrival by the conventional rat-a-tat his nephew threw up the window and shouted:

"Uncle Nicholas! I'm delighted to see you, sir! We're spending Christmas here, I had intended to call on you—Come in, come in!"

Now it is entirely possible that the sight of a young man, his face covered in soap and one hand brandishing a cut-throat razor, startled the visitor; certainly he sprang backwards with an oath while the dog barked, leaping in the air and snapping with some display of viciousness. Both dog and master recovered their composure, however, and entered the house with haste. For the best part of an hour uncle and nephew exchanged the usual aimless remarks which pass for conversation amongst people who meet but seldom and have nothing in common when they do. If Mr. Nicholas Bernays bore any grudge against his relation he gave no sign of it. He was quite frankly a nondescript kind of fellow, he spoke in disconnected spasms and kept his eyes fixed on the carpet. The gaps in his speech grew more frequent, the undergraduates began to wonder how long he intended to stay and whether they should invite him to lunch—Paul being on the point of suggesting it when his uncle suddenly jerked round and cried, "Bless my soul! It's raining. And I—I—I have no raincoat!"

Well, that omission could speedily be remedied; he really was an odd uncomfortable kind of guest, and they would far rather lend him a raincoat than endure his company throughout a meal—besides, he had the strangest notions. George Markham's mackintosh fitted him tolerably neatly whereas Paul's was manifestly too big; yet Mr. Bernays showed a marked preference for the latter and departed with surprising haste, clutching the garment round him and babbling quite excessive gratitude. As they watched him hustle away through the drizzling rain, a curious point struck both young men simultaneously.

"Look!" exclaimed Markham. "What's the matter with the dog?"

The animal seemed to be following its master at a measured distance, it dodged and hung back and swerved almost as if leaving room for something else; moreover it kept its nose close to the ground, tracing the line of some invisible path. Forward. Sideways. Back a little. And always sniffing, sniffing. The rain dripping relentlessly off its coat made no impression on the creature; intent, it trotted on never once raising its head.

"Oh, there must be something running along under the ground. I feel sure I've seen that kind of behaviour before—yes, I'm certain I have. Probably a mole."

"In the middle of winter?"

But they were not country folk, either of them; and lacking any precise information they speedily lost interest in Mr. Bernays and his dog. Preparations for the Christmas feast occupied the next couple of days, they were expecting a group of young companions from London. It is doubtful whether Paul would have given the matter another thought save for one exasperating fact: it kept on raining. By the third day the lack of his raincoat became a serious inconvenience; taking an umbrella and thinking rather uncharitable things about his uncle, he set off across the fields to visit the rectory of St. Wilbrod's.

He had never been there before: the matter of the inheritance produced coldness on the one side and embarrassment on the other; it was impossible not to feel that he had deprived his relation (possibly unjustly) of a home. How fortunate that the Reverend Alaric stepped forward to provide Uncle Nicholas with a roof over his head. He must have known Uncle Nicholas pretty well—and even played a part in the long-forgotten quarrel between that gentleman and his father. Paul considered the matter as he walked; what had taken place, what could have persuaded a solid conventional pater familias to disinherit his son? Life's a rum business, thought Paul; with which solemn platitude he looked up and saw the rectory before him.

It was a great rambling building of quite remarkable ugliness. Remarkable, too, for it stood alone among ploughed fields, no other house appeared to be anywhere near and more oddly still, no church. He blinked. The rectory crouched like some grey animal against the wide curve of the sky, there were a couple of wind-torn elms beside it, a line of fencing badly in need of repair. There was no church.

"But where is St. Wilbrod's...?"

He had been made welcome by the rector, his uncle had, it seemed, gone out.

"St. Wilbrod's? A commonplace story, my dear sir. There used to be a thriving village here in the last century, oh yes, oh dear me yes, a sizable community. By some unlucky chance—failed crops, disease, bad husbandry, I cannot precisely identify the cause—the people moved away. What was the village of Barscombe has moved quite five miles to the east. A shift in the population which has, I fear, done nothing to enlarge my parish."

"Has the church gone too?"

"Good heavens, no." Alaric rose with a cold smile, and drew the young man toward the window. He had very soft white fingers, which stuck to Paul's arm like so manly enlarged slugs. "Some things are not easily destroyed, I assure you. There is my church."

It lay behind the house, invisible from the main path. It astonished by reason of its shape, for it was tiny, a tiny Norman building. A squat tower with a little spirelet or "Sussex cap"; surely incredible that such a miniature affair should have warranted this great barn of a rectory. Paul said as much. His host nodded, drawing hairy eyebrows together, dark eyes gazed at the boy.

"It has been a matter of some concern to the Church authorities. The ever-present question of finance! We live in difficult times, my son, singularly difficult times. Perhaps you would care to examine St. Wilbrod's? It has great historical though little artistic merit."

He led the way across a path made slippery by decayed leaves; the debris of autumn lay around them, there had been no attempt to clear the ground and an unpleasant musty smell contaminated the air. The rain had stopped, leaving a pervading dampness. As they went, Paul felt constrained to explain, to excuse himself—though he had done no wrong and merely chanced to benefit from a family quarrel.

"I trust my uncle keeps in good health, sir?"

"Tolerably." Again the wintry smile.

"I am very conscious he has been unfairly treated…"

"Life is not fair, Mr. Bernays. Fascinating. Complex. But not fair."

"Does he hold my good fortune against me?"

"Oh come, Mr. Bernays! You have the money. You really must not expect to be popular as well."

"Perhaps if I made him a small allowance, in recompense?"

"I think not," said the Reverend Alaric evenly; and motioned him inside the church.

It was bare to the point of emptiness; a simple altar, two Early English lancets in the chancel, a stained glass window of no merit whatsoever. Paul sat down. He was rehearsing a suitable comment when the priest murmured: "You must excuse me. I think I hear your uncle on the drive, he may not have a latch key." The next instant he had gone, fading noiselessly into the shadows. His guest remained seated, lost in a conflicting whirl of emotion; he did not wish to harm anybody, anybody in the world, and surely he could not be blamed for inheriting… He closed his eyes and composed a brief prayer. Dear Lord, bless this house and me and Uncle Nicholas.

He stiffened. There seemed to be a murmur, the dry patter of innumerable lips. Consciously he knew that he sat alone in a country church; yet he felt most powerfully that behind him opened a vast nave; a huge assembly of people were seated just out of sight behind his back. The very air opened up, he must be in the centre of a great cathedral…

Paul jerked round.

Bare walls, almost within touching distance. A few empty pews, stained and scratched with age. Dusty altar hangings. Needless to say, nobody was there. His bewilderment still lay strong upon him when the Reverend Alaric slipped from the gloom and, bending over him, whispered:

"Your uncle has returned and is most eager to see you. Come, follow."

The second encounter with Mr. Nicholas Bernays proved even more tedious than the first. He stammered his apologies, how monstrously careless to have forgotten the raincoat, and in this weather too! He seemed incapable of looking anybody in the face, his balding head twisted from side to side and when by chance Paul caught his eye the man blinked as if stung. By contrast, the Reverend Alaric Halsey appeared totally at his ease; he talked learnedly of St. Wilbrod's, its history and its architecture; he spoke of the Saxons and the influence Christianity had had on them.

"And vice versa, of course! You do know that Easter derives from the Saxon word Eostre, a festival celebrating the goddess of Spring? Our somewhat confusing habit of fixing Easter by the full moon must surely be pagan in origin; it is also linked to the Jewish Passover. As for Christmas—why, it seems tolerably certain that whenever Our Saviour was born, it was not in the middle of winter! You may remember that a decree went forth at the time of His birth that all the world should be taxed? In the ancient world taxes were levied at harvest time, therefore we can immediately discount December the twenty-fifth. But that date *is* the winter solstice, the Mithraic birthday of the Unconquered Sun. It would seem that the early Fathers of the Church found it paid them to be reasonably accommodating in the matter of dates. We have here a combination of Mithraism, Judaism, and who knows what pagan nature worship!" The Reverend Alaric smiled, he had a compelling manner and some degree of charm; after a while he proposed to show their visitor the Rectory, a tour which Paul had no desire to make and found himself quite incapable of refusing.

It proved a most embarrassing experience. Clearly the general exodus of its congregation had thrown the parish of St. Wilbrod's into a state of quite desperate poverty; room after room held nothing save a threadbare rug on the floor and two or three dilapidated chairs. It must once have been of some importance for the house boasted six bedrooms, three reception rooms, a library, a study, and a positive warren of kitchen and pantries. From these last Paul deduced that his host was in the habit of cooking for himself; various pots and pans lay on the table, uncleaned and smelling slightly of rancid fat. He wondered how in heaven's name the two men contrived to exist in such a penniless wreck of a home. The contrast between this squalor and the comfort of his own manor house, West Farthing, with its full complement of amiable Sussex maids and kindly gardeners, seemed too much for Paul altogether—he made his excuses and fled out into the wintry afternoon, taking his raincoat with him. Even as he pulled it on it struck him that Uncle Nicholas must have thrown the garment down in that abominable kitchen. It felt sticky.

The day had darkened, a discoloured sky fitted over the hills like a lid. Paul Bernays hurried on, conscious of a most irrational desire to escape.

From what?

The derelict rectory with its learned owner—his uncle, ducking that thin red head, avoiding all direct contact with the eyes? Absurd. His uncle was merely a nervous, unlucky man and the priest—why, the priest must be both charitable and kind to have offered him a home. Paul quickened his pace and nearly fell, the ground being pitted with disused rabbit holes and littered with stones. The strange depression, the mounting unease, could only be the result of bad weather and a bad conscience; he did indeed feel guilty, he must certainly do something to make life more tolerable for the ill-assorted pair he had just left. Meanwhile, home and tea!

He stepped out briskly. Thinking of the couple made him glance back over his shoulder, and he noticed a shadow at his heels. A second's thought made him look again, for there was no sun; how could he be casting... Yes, he had not been mistaken, it was there—a shapeless blur on the grass. Quite small; and eight or ten feet away. It moved when he moved, stopped when he stopped; it bore no resemblance to his own shape, so therefore something else must be causing the effect. Paul frowned, studying the landscape. There was nothing visible at all, nothing to account for the mark. Empty fields stretched to the foot of the downs, a most extraordinary silence, not even a bird sang—but it was the middle of winter, why should birds sing! He turned and put the matter from his mind. Yet the thing still puzzled him; after a few hundred yards he turned again. The shadow had moved closer and had grown in size, a formless grey stain wrinkling where it crossed the folds in the ground.

He could not say why it affected him so unpleasantly. Perhaps the scientific absurdity offended his intellect, for there must be some object between the light and the earth to account for...

"This is impossible!" said Paul out loud.

Close behind him something giggled.

He broke into a run; even as he went he told himself that his behaviour was no more than natural—it was cold, it might rain, he must get to West Farthing. As for the noise, that soft gurgle, some animal must have made it! Paul lengthened his stride. Yet he could not resist the urge, almost against his will, to twist round and glance behind him.

The shadow had swollen to twice its original size: as he watched, one corner elongated itself and slid across the ground in his direction. He let out a yell, and sprinted across the rough grass. Gasping for breath he made for the stile—unable to say what terror, what monstrous premonition of evil, impelled him forward. He clambered frantically over the wooden bar, and as he did so a voice shouted:

"My dear chap! Where on earth have you been? I've been waiting for you for hours."

George Markham stood in the yard, his face creased with anxiety.

Paul stopped. He forced himself to turn slowly, to look calmly back. The bleak winter fields lay motionless under the sky; barren acres extended to the foot of the downs. There was nothing there. He debated whether to mention the incident to his friend: really, it seemed too unlikely, too fanciful altogether! He muttered something to the effect of having been detained at the rectory; and hurried inside the house.

The temperature dropped during the night; they woke to find the air grown sharp and a thin coating of snow across the paths. From his window Bernays observed one of the farmers going by with a gun; the fellow seemed to be eyeing the ground, he stopped from time to time, peering and prodding at the frozen mud.

"Morning, Elliot!"

"Morning, sir." The man glanced up. "You haven't had any trouble over here, I don't suppose?"

"Trouble? Why, no."

"Thought you might have been visited by a fox. There's tracks running right round your house. There, see? And there again. Can't be a fox, I reckon; no, not a fox. I never did see a fox leave marks the like of that."

"What kind of marks?" asked Paul, refusing to acknowledge the very faint shiver of apprehension, no, not fear: he was cold, no more—he had the window open, and the weather had turned cold.

"Hanged if I know, sir." The farmer sniffed, blew his nose, and went out of sight behind the barn.

The moment passed. Those who live in the country must surely expect to find evidence of wild animals from time to time! Besides, there were preparations to be made, plans to be discussed, an entire Christmas programme to arrange. The owner of West Farthing slammed the shutter down and went in search of George Markham. They were seated in front of what may fairly be called a Dickensian log fire, happily arguing the relative merits of roast turkey and duck a l'orange, when the Reverend Halsey was announced. He had come, he said, to deliver an invitation—the residents at the rectory would count it a most particular blessing if Mr. Bernays would take dinner with them on Christmas Eve.

Strange are the complexities of civilization, the pressure exercised by society on even the most rational person. Paul Bernays did not want to dine at the rectory. He disliked the rector, and what he had seen of the kitchen caused him to entertain grave doubts as to the food. An older or more quick-witted man would have pleaded a previous engagement—pressure of work—the imminent arrival of a great many guests. There was, to be frank, no reason on earth why he should accept; save the horrid, the paralysing conviction that it would be bad manners to refuse.

"You have no other plans, I believe?" The clergyman smiled. "As I recall it, you told your uncle that your own festivities do not begin till Christmas Day."

Paul shifted miserably; for you see, it was true, his London companions did not arrive before then. If he told a direct lie he might be detected; a circumstance altogether too embarrassing. He toyed briefly with the notion of pleading illness; and that also was quite impracticable—he might be seen galloping across the downs.

Before his confused brain could handle the situation Paul heard his lips say:

"Thank you, sir, that's very kind of you." And then, as a desperate afterthought—"My friend and I will be happy to accept."

It became apparent from the clouding of the Reverend Alaric's face that his invitation had not included Paul's friend; but here, thankfully, the restraints of polite society worked in reverse. He could not bring himself to say he had excluded Mr. George Markham. So it came about that on Christmas Eve both young men sat down to dinner in St. Wilbrod's rectory.

The meal proved quite as excruciating as they had feared: a concoction of half-burnt meats and overdone vegetables served on cracked dishes, the entire menu redolent of frantic poverty and inefficient male cooking. Their host kept up a smooth flow of interesting, curious, and often amusing chatter; he had beyond question a most formidable charm—indeed, had it not been for those strange eyebrows he would have passed for a handsome man; the head well formed, the eyes darkly compulsive. He seemed completely at his ease. Uncle Nicholas, by contrast, appeared to be afflicted by a nervous tick, his speech impediment grew worse when thickened by wine, he seldom joined in the conversation and then only to defer to the rector. It came as a mild surprise when (the ordeal of eating mercifully finished) Alaric Halsey moved across the threadbare carpet, sat himself down at an old upright piano, and declared that his companion would entertain them with a song.

It emerged that Nicholas, in common with others who suffer his disability, could sing with no trace of a stammer; he produced a moderate tenor voice and the company joined in a variety of carols. That done, the pianist changed key and the singer moved on to ballads, folk tunes, old roundelays...

"Come, follow follow—follow follow—follow follow me!
Whither shall I follow—follow—follow, follow thee?"

The reedy notes echoed curiously in the gloom; only candles fought against the encroaching night, the rectory had not yet been equipped with gas. Melting wax splashed down onto the piano top.

"Come, follow follow—follow follow"

Paul turned abruptly; the high windows had no curtains and for one second he had an impression—the merest hint—of something peering through the glass.

"Whither shall I follow—follow"

A mistake of course. Black countryside lay all around the house.

"To the greenwood, to the greenwood, to the greenwood tree"

"Trees," said the Reverend Alaric, "trees figure prominently in the ancient Saxon religion. My dear Mr. Bernays, what is the matter?"

For Paul had leapt up: something, yes, positively Something, tapped on the window pane—a faint rattle as of drumming finger-tips, a staccato impatient knock. But now he had gained the window and now he stared out and it had gone. He stood there feeling very slightly ridiculous. His mind clutched at the notion of a tree, for there were trees, certainly; a couple of elms etched sharply against the sky. But too far away, surely, to account for the sound and the singular impression he had received of a figure, just beyond the glass, waiting.

269

"I thought I heard a noise," said Paul foolishly.

"Has it begun to snow?"

"I think not." And indeed the chill of the previous hours had passed off; not only was there no promise of the traditional Christmas white, but it had most disagreeably begun to rain again.

"Oh dear, dear, dear." The group round the piano broke up; Mr. Halsey crossed the room. "You heard a noise, you say? I do hope Elliot's horse hasn't broken out of the stables again."

His easy tone, and the natural-sounding explanation, calmed the visitor. We have already noted that Paul Bernays did not possess a remarkably quick mind; it did not strike him as monstrously unlikely that a horse should break out of a warm stable in the middle of a winter's night to go wandering abroad. He knew the animal in question; it did from time to time escape and had in the past been the subject of irritated complaint from other farmers. He was about to resume his seat, satisfied, when the priest took his arm.

"Shall we investigate, my dear boy? It might perhaps be prudent. I have no desire to see my fencing knocked down."

Again the fatal grip of good manners! A young man of sense had only to protest that it grew late, the countryside lay in inky blackness, and the pursuit of somebody's else's horse under such circumstances were mere folly. He did indeed open his mouth to remark on the rain; yet under the steely impact of Alaric Halsey's gaze, the smile that would not brook refusal, he heard himself answer:

"Yes, of course." And then—clutching once more at straws— "Will you come with us, George?"

It should have presented no problem. Clearly (given the improbable surmise that a farm animal was running loose outside) the more people to catch it the better. So much should have been self-evident;

yet somehow Paul found himself being drawn out into the hall, while behind him Uncle Nicholas cried: "You must stay with me, Mr. Markham! I—I—I feel sure the others can manage! I—I—I must ask you not to leave me alone..."

His voice rose to a plaintive yelp; and the door slammed shut. It must have been exasperated nerves which caused Paul to believe that, for a fraction before the door shut, Uncle Nicholas had looked to Alaric Halsey with frightened questioning eyes; and Alaric Halsey had almost imperceptibly nodded.

They passed through the dim hall and, pausing only to snatch up their raincoats, they hurried out of the main porch, into the rainswept night. It really was most horribly dark, an absolute blackness hung over the fields; a blackness so complete the eye could not determine the curve of the downs or see with any certainty where the horizon ended and the sky began. And the silence too held some quality positively unnatural: save for the drumming of rain on sodden grass there was no sound whatsoever.

"There's nothing there!" cried Paul; and as the words left him he knew he lied. Oh, most certainly *something* was there: within that black void Something waited, holding its breath.

"Beyond the gate, I imagine." His companion's hand fell on his shoulder, urging him forward. Paul stumbled against the wet shrubbery, precipitating a shower of cold drops; if only it were possible to see! He fumbled in the pocket of his raincoat for matches; they were not there! They should have been there, for he smoked a pipe and was in the habit of carrying...

"Hurry! Hurry!" The Reverend Alaric's voice, sharp with impatience, sounded behind him. "Come, come, you're a young man, I'm relying on you, don't loiter in the pathway! You're not, I take it, afraid of the dark?"

"Of course not!" yelled Bernays; he leapt forward and caught his foot against a stone. "It's just that—Confound it—which way are we supposed to be going?"

They were out of the garden by now. To the left lay a rising hill, to the right a flat stretch of meadow; this much he knew from memory—and memory was all he had to guide him; the land merged into an inky pool without form or definition. The rain appeared to be dropping in straight lines; the entire exercise seemed monstrously disagreeable and utterly pointless for there was no stray animal: no creature with a modicum of sense would be abroad in such abominable circumstances. Irritation began to replace alarm. What in the name of wonder were the two of them doing there? His dislike of Alaric Halsey hardened into a positive contempt. Blast the fellow, by what right did he drag a visitor from the house? He opened his mouth to protest, to voice his declared intention of returning indoors.

"Come," said Alaric in his ear. "Follow."

With fingers fastened onto Paul's wrist, he led the way across a grassy incline, moving forward with a very complete confidence as if perfectly aware of his destination. Walking became more hazardous; rough ground and darkness combined to make each step a risky business; the earth (rendered soft by the downpour) sucked at their shoes and left a coating of mud which smelt of farmyard refuse. Bernays glanced over his shoulder; he could see blurred patches of light behind them, the hazy outline of the rectory windows: as he watched, the lights went out. A curious effect. It must be an optical illusion, caused no doubt by some contour of the landscape. He turned to comment on it; thank goodness the Reverend Halsey had let go of his arm and moved a few paces on into the night.

"Did you notice that?" asked Paul; and then again, "I say, sir, did you notice that?"

Rain drummed steadily on the grass. He strained his eyes, for surely the man must be there; he had been there only a second before.

"Hullo!" He peered again—and yes, there he was, away on the left—No. That looked more like a tree; it was in fact a tree. Well, to the right, then, there had not been time for him to travel any great distance. "Mr. Halsey!"

He got no answer, and now concern swept over him: had his guide slipped and fallen, was he lying on the ground?

"Where are you, sir?"

The rain grew slower, spat, and stopped.

If there had been an accident he would have heard a cry, a shout for help. If his companion had gone on without him—unlikely in these difficult conditions—he should by now be aware of Paul's absence.

"I'm here!" cried Paul. The call was swallowed up in the surrounding darkness. "I'm here, where are you...?"

No reply; and still blackness defeated his eyes and still he could not find a trace. He hurried forward, which was unwise and led to a stumbling fall; he spent several minutes in agitated search before deciding that he would have to return to the house and get help. It seemed that some calamity had overtaken the Reverend Alaric Halsey. He straightened; then realized that with the disappearance of the lights, he had lost his bearings; he did not know in which direction to walk—quite simply, he did not know where he was. Paul Bernays possessed slow reactions yet a fair degree of common sense; he pulled himself up and stood completely still. To advance blindly might easily lead to his wandering miles out into the open countryside; the best hope lay in waiting, in hoping that his eyes would finally grow accustomed to the gloom and enable him to identify a landmark.

As he stood there a noise caught his attention: close at hand, close behind him, the sound of heavy breathing. Now there is no good reason why this should have alarmed him so extravagantly; it could have been a farm animal, a stray dog, a badger, a fox…

He knew it to be none of these.

The noise grew louder, a kind of panting followed by a hiss. It took all Paul's courage to remain where he stood, for an overwhelming presentiment of evil gripped him, a profound conviction that horror walked the night. Two things alone kept him in his place: the first, a very real fear that if he turned and ran he might all too easily lose his footing and crash to the ground; the second, a curious yet mounting impression that this invisible creature was not looking at him. He froze. Perhaps the darkness cloaked him? Yet surely an animal could smell; no animal would be hampered by… Something soft and faintly slimy bumped against his leg. Paul let out a yell; and still the Thing glided on indifferent, and now the breathing grew fainter and now it stopped.

"Dear heaven!" muttered Bernays, and he wiped his face with a handkerchief. Luckily there was a handkerchief in the pocket of his raincoat, although he could not remember putting it there. Relief swept over him; whatever the threat, it had gone. The next moment the sky above him split into groups of leaden clouds and the merest fragment of a moon slid through.

"That's better!"

The faint moonbeams did indeed throw some light across the country: the empty fields, the wide curve of the downs now came into view. Paul grimaced; he had been facing the wrong way; if he had continued he would have become most hopelessly lost. Thank goodness he had kept his head! He looked over toward the black outline of the rectory; and observed to his considerable annoyance a figure walking quite calmly up the path to the house. The Reverend Alaric.

"Confound the man!" Paul swore briefly. "Would he have left me, wandering about in the dark?" He ran forward, forming a protest in his mind; in pity's name, this lacked both hospitality and common sense.

And then he saw it; some twenty yards behind Alaric Halsey.

He took it at first to be a small rain puddle, and his eyes might have ignored it altogether but for one thing. It moved. As he watched, it heaved, swelling a little, and slid across the ground—it could have been a shadow but there was nothing there to account for a shadow; nothing between the wet earth and the moon. Heaving, pulsating, it moved with ever-increasing speed along the ground. The Reverend Alaric came to the gate and passed through; behind him the object swelled, sucked itself up, wobbled briefly on the top bar and dropped over. For no particular reason Bernays associated its movement with that panting, hissing breath. It had lessened the gap, a bare ten yards lay between it and the priest; it not only gathered speed as it went, but also seemed to grow, pushing outward in wide soft bulges.

"Halsey!" cried Paul. "Halsey! Halsey!"

The man looked round. The moonlight struck full on him and an expression that might have been surprise or rage or both showed in his face. Before the emotion could be identified he saw the Thing behind him and screamed.

He broke into a run and Paul ran too, leaping across the fields, driven on by a rising panic, for distance could not dim the terror in Alaric Halsey's voice. He fled around the corner of the rectory; the monstrous shadow gaining all the time. Paul had the advantage of youth; he cut round by the other side and caught up with him beyond the elm trees. The priest appeared to be in a state of advanced shock, his eyes stared blindly up and he shrieked:

"Deliver me! Deliver me! Deliver me from evil!"

Then he fell to the ground, senseless.

Bernays stooped over him. Fear still pulsed through the night. For the moment he had lost sight of that dark stain—it might be crouched slackly under the trees, it might have vanished altogether. He had abandoned all rational thought, all attempt to work out what in heaven's name it could be; his immediate concern was to get Halsey to safety. They were some little distance from the house; the church stood altogether more near, and there were practical considerations too; the elder man was above average height and heavy. Paul placed his arm around the unconscious figure and, half-pulling half-lifting, contrived to drag him through the stone porch and into the little Norman church. As he did so he got once more that extraordinary sensation. The tiny chapel seemed to open out around him, to change into a vast cathedral thronged with people whispering, muttering, praying—and high above them all a sudden triumphant laugh. He blinked; between them and the altar stood a formless Thing of towering height, growing larger even as he looked.

Oh God, thought Paul confusedly. *It lives here*. And fainted.

He came to his senses in the brightly lit bedroom of West Farthing; he had been ill, they told him, for three weeks. Out of concern for his health, another week passed before the doctor thought it proper to tell him that Alaric Halsey had died, presumably of a heart attack. The doctor (being a rational country physician) had no intention of repeating local gossip; the whispered story that the body had marks on it for all the world as if it had been trampled to death by a huge crowd. The marks were there; but must surely have been caused by something else, for the entire population of West Farthing village numbered no more than twenty people. Country folk were notorious for their imaginings, and the story struck the good doctor as a palpable absurdity.

Christmas had come and gone while Paul lay in his bed; and it was not until the end of January that he nerved himself to revisit the rectory. It seemed deserted. No one answered his repeated knock; and of his Uncle Nicholas there was no sign whatsoever. He considered examining the chapel—but became conscious of a repugnance so extreme he abandoned the attempt. The Spring term beckoned, he had work to do, examinations to sit; Paul Bernays tidied his house and prepared to return to Cambridge. Sorting through various papers belonging to the estate he came across a bundle of ancient correspondence; letters apparently written by Nicholas Bernays to his father, the squire of West Farthing. The ink had faded and the words (which seemed to have been written by someone in a violent rage) proved uncommonly hard to decipher. Ill-formed characters sprawled across the page at an angle; at one point the nib of the pen had actually gone straight through the document.

"... he is my friend! My friend! I do not care if you disinherit me! I shall devote my life to him! You have been listening to vile slanders, the babble of the village idiots who have all run away. He is a great man! It is not true that he worships the..."

Here followed a word which might have been Devil; but Paul could not be certain—besides, he was pressed for time, and so he threw the letters away.

Two events only remain to be told. On putting on his raincoat preparatory to leaving West Farthing, the young man discovered a pair of black leather gloves in the pocket; a curious circumstance as he did not possess any black leather gloves. Further consideration led him to the belief that he had in fact got the wrong raincoat—by some accident in the dim light of the rectory hall, he had picked up the Reverend Halsey's coat, and that gentleman had picked up his. The two garments were not dissimilar. (In passing it might be well if the manufacturers were to make these items of clothing more distinctive, thus avoiding possibly—*unfortunate*—mistakes.)

At Cambridge Paul resumed his studies, happily showing no ill effects from his disastrous adventure. But his friends did remark that from that date he evinced a marked dislike for the popular student song, "Come Follow"; and—on being present at a concert when the Glee Club performed that piece—he asked them to be good enough to desist.

THE THEATRE OF OVID

Aaron Worth

One last Victorian tale—though here we have travelled from London, the metropolitan heart of Empire, to the hinterlands (from the civilized Westerner's perspective) of Eastern Europe, specifically the port city of Constanța, Romania. It strikes me now that the story's Romanian setting and epistolary form both link it with Bram Stoker's *Dracula* (published in 1897, one year before this tale takes place); the reader is not, however, to expect any vampires here. Blood? Well, now. That's another story…

"The Theatre of Ovid" was first published in the first issue of *Vastarien: A Literary Journal*.

Y DEAR WILLIAM,

When, a fortnight ago, I helped my new bride into the Parisian railway carriage that was to whisk us away on the first leg of our Continental honey-moon, I fancied that I would be too much occupied with the pleasures of the connubial condition to write many letters to London, even to such an old and true friend as yourself.

I could hardly have then foreseen, however, that her illness, which I had believed to be entirely in remission, if not vanquished altogether, could return so suddenly to plague us, without my having the least suspicion of it.

It is the old delusion, you see, though poured, as it were, into new bottles. She now imagines—

But I must not run ahead of myself. I forget that you do not know all the details of her case. Let me fill in the background first.

The many tongues of Rumour being as loquacious today as in the Bard's time, you will have heard, I suppose, that Charlotte was briefly a patient of mine, at Thornton House. If I have not spoken openly with you before upon this subject, it was not, believe me, from any lack of affection for you, or of regard for our friendship, but rather from a certain reticence not entirely unallied with feelings of—*shame*; I cannot in conscience call it by a gentler name.

To put it very bluntly: one hardly expects to find a wife in a mad-house, particularly one's *own* mad-house.

Moreover, despite the great advances our civilization has made with regard to illnesses of the mind, no small degree of social *stigma* yet attaches, as you well know, to their sufferers. I have wished to spare Charlotte such embarrassment as I could.

So you may well believe that, if I broach the subject with you now, my dear friend, it is because I have very particular reasons for doing so.

I first met Charlotte in February of last year—then a girl of seventeen, and of remarkable beauty (as you have seen for yourself). I made her acquaintance, however, not in a drawing- or a ballroom, but in a well-padded cell. She was glaring at me, with a sullen and suspicious look which quite spoiled the effect of her lovely grey eyes.

The circumstances of her entry into my professional orbit were these.

She had possessed but a single relative in the world: an aged father (a classical scholar of some repute), with whom she had lived, near Oxford. Upon his death, Charlotte was left entirely alone, suffered a complete break-down of the nervous system, and was, shortly thereafter, admitted to my care.

The chief symptom of her condition was an extreme form of *grapho-mania*, i.e. an unnatural compulsion to write. The poor girl was found by a friend of the family, sitting, all alone, in the now deserted library of the house she had shared with her father. She was seated at his desk, bent over a very old and valuable edition of Sallust, in the margins of which she was scribbling. No, "scribbling" is unfair, as she was writing with great care, in a tiny yet precise hand. But the *matter* was the most utter nonsense. At first these rambling marginalia appeared to constitute an attempt at a scholarly essay, upon certain of the more obscure poetic *genres* practised in antiquity. But they proved upon closer inspection to be a hopeless farrago of the most bizarre phantasies, in which were mixed some few fragments of accepted history, rather like raisins in a Christmas pudding.

It was subsequently discovered that fully half of her father's books had been defaced in the same fashion!

In those vandalized margins, wholesale invention mingled with accepted fact to produce an unnatural hybrid, the whole clothed in the sober language of scholarship, and supported by a myriad of fictitious authorities. (The style was, no doubt, an apelike imitation of her father's writing.)

She seemed to believe herself to be a kind of feminine Tacitus or Gibbon, charged with the task of writing a vast history (or ought I to say, *counter*-history?) of ancient times, though one, again, which was about ninety per cent rubbish in its composition.

A singular feature of her pathology, I should here mention, lay in her obsessive delineation of a host of wholly fictitious *institutions*—i.e. churches, cults, libraries, equestrian orders, secret societies, senatorial bodies, and the like, organizations having no historical existence whatever, except in her own fevered imagination.

As she had no guardian living, a period of compulsory treatment at Thornton was decided upon, as the best course of action.

When she was first admitted, and for some weeks to follow, the poor girl rebelled—nay, it is hardly an exaggeration to say *raved*—against her involuntary confinement (as is by no means unusual in such cases, as you well know). Daily she railed against her keepers, myself above all (her "chief gaoler," she called me! how it stabs me to the very heart now to think of it!).

But, in the months that followed, I helped her to see that her true prison was one of her own making. Its bars were not of iron, but of ink; with every chimerical bit of quasi-history

Charlotte inscribed in the margins of her dead father's books, she immured herself more and more inescapably within a dungeon of delusion.

By slow stages, however, through long, patient talks—her slender, sylph-like hand in mine—I led her towards the light of sanity, until finally, the dear girl took the final step thither—quite of her own will, I rejoice to say.

This last step was, quite simply, fully and freely to *renounce* those mad, palimpsested volumes, and to consent to their destruction, which I am glad to say, she did without the least hesitation or equivocation. (The tomes in question had, in fact, already been consigned to the proverbial dust-heap long ago, on my orders; but the important thing was the mental *action* on her part.)

You will forgive me, I am sure, if I pass over in silence the period of transition during which an entirely professional relationship blossomed, most unexpectedly, into a courtship, complete with the most miraculous transformation of my own person, from mad-house doctor to husband!

Let it suffice to say, that the dear girl had developed strong feelings for me while under my care—feelings which were by no means unreciprocated.

What *is* important to the present account is some brief explanation of how bride and groom ended up in the backward waste-land of Roumania.

It began when I asked Charlotte where she would most wish to spend our honey-moon. The entire world, I declared with an histrionic flourish of my hand, was open to us. (This was perhaps a *little* disingenuous on my part, as I had dropped several broad hints in the weeks before our marriage, that I would greatly desire to see Wagner's *Parsifal* performed at Bayreuth.)

To my surprise, she mentioned the city of Constantza, in Roumania—which, she hastened to inform me (I am afraid I must have frowned), boasted a very picturesque setting, on the coast of the Black Sea.

When I asked her what in the world had put such a notion as that into her head, she looked timidly down at the carpet, and murmured something half-audible about the antiquarian attractions of the town, in particular some Roman remains she remembered her father speaking of once. But of course, she added quickly, looking up at me with earnest eyes, we should not go if I did not wish it, or if the distance rendered the journey impracticable.

At this I smiled and, taking her hands in mine, assured her that we should travel to Far Cathay, Timbuctoo, or the kingdom of Prester John himself, if it was her own heart's desire. The gratitude that shone then in her eyes was ample reward, as I thought, for my concession. (And besides, I realized, there was no earthly reason why we might not also stop in Bavaria upon our return home!)

After a seemingly endless journey, chiefly by rail, during which we seemed to leave modern civilization further and further behind with each passing hour, we arrived at last in Constantza. It does, indeed, look upon the Black Sea; but I can say little else in its favour. I must say, I don't know why the Romans bothered about the place at all.

But Charlotte was much taken with it. Indeed, from the moment we stepped out of the archaic, smoke-grimed vehicle in which we terminated our journey she has seemed—how shall I put it? *Radiant*, that is the word I want.

At first this puzzled me very much. But in the six days we have been here I have, I believe, uncovered the reason for her excitement (which has bordered, at times, on the unseemly), and it is one, my dear Will, which gives me much pain.

To begin with (and it is not, believe me, any idle egotism which motivates the observation, but simple concern for my wife's mental well-being), Charlotte has not paid me a twopence's worth of attention since our arrival here. Instead, she is in a state of almost constant distraction. Wherever we go in the town and its wooded environs, she looks about her in all directions, an occasional murmur or cry escaping her lips, sometimes pulling out a tiny notebook and pencil to record some thought or observation. Two or three times I have gently asked her what she was writing, but each time she has put me off with some casual remark about the *beauty* of the place (sic!).

Once, very soon after our arrival at the hotel here, I thought I observed Charlotte to slip some object into one of the drawers of her dresser, in a suspicious manner. In light of the curious behaviour she has subsequently exhibited in our walks about town, I have felt myself quite justified in taking the liberty of examining her possessions (I waited, of course, until she was in the bath.)

I told you, Will, that Charlotte had won her freedom from confinement, and (as I had thought) her very sanity, by agreeing to the destruction of those classical texts which she had ruined with her mad annotations.

Imagine, then, my surprise and deep sorrow, when I pulled from beneath a neat stack of her under-garments a smallish volume of Ovid, whose margins were filled with her tiny, careful script.

My heart sank as I paged through the book (it is called *Tristia*—do you know it? I have only read the *Metamorphoses*, and that in Dryden's English translation). Nearly four-fifths of its pages had been defaced. She must, I reflected, have begun her sad back-sliding immediately upon her release from Thornton.

Muttering a curse, I dropped into an arm-chair and began to read.

She had, I saw immediately, developed a new phantasy, though one quite consistent in general type with the others. She premises the existence of an ancient theatre, which—

But I shall let you read for yourself. Her "essay" begins thusly:

Regarding the precise *circumstances* of the Theatre's foundation, there remain to this day legitimate grounds for dispute; but we may assign a *date* to its origins with something very like precision. The key lies in an (undoubtedly symbolical) episode related in the fourth book of the poet's last work, the *Epistulae ex Ponto*, composed in the sixth or seventh year of his exile, shortly before his death.

After complaining for years about the barbarian population of remote Tomis (where he had been sent, by an implacable Emperor, for an unspecified "error," about which Mr. MacDonald has written what must be considered the most plausible account), Ovid now confesses to his friend and interlocutor that he has (as we should put it today) "gone native," becoming "almost a Getic bard" (*faciam paene poeta Getes*). He confesses that he has completed some new "work," marrying native and Roman elements.

But what was this hybrid creation?

The poet claims, of course, merely to have composed a conventional paean or encomium, in the Getic language, to the imperial family, forcing barbarian words, as with a shoe-horn, into Latin metres. Moreover, he would gull his readers into believing that he held a crowd of bellicose savages spell-bound with panegyrics to Augustus and Tiberius, their very quivers trembling in appreciation of his verse (*plenas omnes movere pharatras*)!

287

This supremely improbable scenario has been incontrovertibly (and mercifully) exploded long ago, *as a literal account* (see Nathanson, Gabriels, Roushkoff).

But this imaginary episode, as Dr. Schütz has established beyond all rational doubt in his magisterial *Ovidstheater*, conceals, or rather enciphers, an important truth.

The poet did indeed develop a close *rapport* with the natives of Tomis during his last years and may even have learned to speak with them in their own language (though this is hardly the place to add fresh fuel to that particular *querelle*). But this was not, surely, to compose insipid hymns of praise to those who had wronged him. No: Ovid spent the anguished conclusion of his life in continuing, or ought one rather to say *completing*, his life's master-work, the peerless *Metamorphoses*.

Ah! But here we come to a highly fraught question (for some an essential question), namely:

Did the poet oversee the founding of the Theatre himself, as a place to stage his new tales of transformation? (It must be remembered, of course, that the people of Tomis were entirely illiterate.)

Or did he simply relate these in Homeric fashion to his rough auditors, who after his death began to enact them, as a means (initially at least) of preserving them?

I incline towards the latter theory, but do not insist upon it. We have had, surely, useless polemics enough in recent years over puzzles which are at the present time insoluble; if and when fresh evidence may come to light, students of the Theatre and its history will hardly be found behindhand in reopening such questions!

In any event, however the Theatre came into being, we find that, in a relatively short time, it acquired something like fame.

The young Claudius is said to have made a secret journey to Tomis in 21 or 22 AD, for the express purpose of witnessing for himself the performance of Ovid's unpublished transformations. If this is so, then it may well have been he who wrote the sadly fragmentary account of the Theatre (now in private hands), of which only the following words survive (the translation is Meyersault's):

> ... the Tragic stage (as we have always known it) being generally inhospitable to transmutation *as such*. This is not to say that change is never pictured by Aeschylus, Euripides, and the like masters of the old art, but only as it were by *accident*. On the other hand, in the Theatre of Ovid, transformation is acted almost entirely for its own sake; as an end in itself, to which all other elements (narrative above all) are wholly subordinated...

Nor was this the only representative of the Julio-Claudian line to take an interest in the Theatre's productions. For it is surely one of history's crueller ironies that Tiberius, whose unremitting enmity had ensured the poet's death in exile, should, in the last year of his life, have summoned the Theatre—rather as if it were a pack of common strollers—to play for him at Capreae.

What transformation was acted upon this occasion is unknown, though the performance (as M. Renault has persuasively argued) was probably witnessed by the juvenile Gaius (or "Caligula," as he is known to history), upon whom it seems to have made a deep impression. The Emperor himself expired very shortly after this visit, though only a tiny minority of the Theatre's historians *openly* assert any connexion between the two events.

Such occasional peregrinations apart, however, the Theatre was not habitually or essentially peripatetic. Certainly it possessed a fixed *locus*, somewhere in or near the town whose soil held the poet's remains; i.e. an actual stage, with sophisticated apparatus for presenting miraculous and multifarious changes of bodily form; but precisely where this may have been is open to endless debate...

Do you see it now, William? Or perhaps you have already guessed, before this? Here is the explanation for her strange behaviour since we arrived here; nay, for her curious insistence that we travel to this wretched back-water in the first place, for our honey-moon! *For this is ancient Tomis*—something I might have surmised straightaway, had you and I pursued a classical education at "Oxbridge," rather than a practical one at Edinburgh! Yes, we are in the final resting-place of the Augustan poet, and poor Charlotte *is looking for her imaginary theatre*—searching the streets of Constantza for this phantom of her disordered mind, as if it were a real thing...

I do not even know, Will, whether I shall post these letters. For the moment, I am merely collecting them, between the pages of my day-book. Events, I suppose, will decide me: if our tale has a happy ending, I shall not, perhaps, feel the need to make these embarrassing disclosures to you. On the other hand, if it does *not*—

I do not like to think about it. But merely to write to you, Will, restores some of my equanimity of mind.

But I hear the gurgling of draining bath-water, from the next room. I must return the book to its hiding-place.

I shall write more later. My heart, dear Will, is quite broken...

*

18 MAY 1898

CONSTANTZA, ROUMANIA

DEAR WILLIAM,

I have two deeply troubling developments to tell of—both spring-ing, of course, from the same (sadly muddied) source.

The first, and most immediately alarming, is the fact that my wife, no longer content with making circumspect, diurnal investigations, appears to have begun searching *by night* for this chimera of her brain.

Let me tell you how I learned of this.

Very early this morning—three-forty-five, by my watch—I was awakened by the sound of our bedroom door opening (it creaks most damnably).

Blinking in confusion, I sat up in bed and listened intently as the door was slowly shut again—as stealthily and quietly as its ill-maintained hinges would allow.

I put out my hand for my wife, and finding that side of the bed quite empty, called out Charlotte's name in some surprise.

There was a silence of several seconds, and then came the sound of my wife's voice, timid and tremulous, from the darkness:

"John?" she said, seemingly much confused. "John, what am I doing out of bed, darling?"

I lit a candle (there seems to be no gas, much less electricity, to light this retrograde nation), fumblingly put on my glasses, and beheld poor Charlotte standing by the door, a coat thrown over her night-dress. Her eyes were wide and fearful, and her fingers plucked nervously at her throat.

"I must have been sleep-walking," she murmured, as I helped her to undress, "though I don't recall ever having done so before." A shiver shook her slender frame, as I put her to bed again. "Thank goodness you stopped me, dear, before I went any further than the door."

At this I frowned but said nothing, for besides the sounds I had heard, the testimony of her slippers and night-dress spoke loudly against such a transparent fiction, both being much coated with mud.

I cannot escape the conclusion that Charlotte was out for much of the night, God knows where, searching for a non-existent ruin—and, what is worse, lying to me about it.

(She is sleeping now, as I write this, by candlelight.)

I should hardly approve such nocturnal perambulations in the heart of London—who knows what additional perils the girl courts by pursuing them in a foreign land?

Yet I hesitate openly to remonstrate with her as yet, as there is no telling what the shock of such a confrontation might do to her, in her current, fragile state of mind.

I should, however, like very much to be able to sedate her at night. Unfortunately, my medical bag, in which I carry some opiates, as well as a few surgical instruments, for emergencies, was stolen shortly after our arrival here (or did I already mention this?). I have made complaint at the desk downstairs, receiving only blank protestations of ignorance for my pains. (Probably the hotel's employés have had a hand in the theft—it is a nation of scoundrels.)

As regards monetary value, the loss is trifling, but under the circumstances it is damned inconvenient.

Well, I shall simply have to keep a closer eye upon her, especially at night.

The second development of which I spoke—

Wait a moment, Charlotte is stirring.

No, she sleeps still.

The other thing of which I have to tell, William, involves less perhaps of present danger, but is to me even more heart-breaking.

I speak, quite simply, of the progressive disintegration of her mental condition, as revealed in her delusional writings.

I have stolen every occasion I could to read further in the book she keeps hidden from me. I have it now, on the bed-table beside me (its author sleeping an uneasy sleep, at my other elbow!). I have waded through perhaps three-quarters of this morass of phantasy. With every page she writes (or rather, disfigures), Charlotte is drawn more deeply into her fixed idea, premised upon the existence of this imaginary play-house. And what is more disturbing to me, is the increasingly diseased *character* of the conceits and images she employs, in the elaboration of her pathetic "history." Her mind roils, I now perceive, with the most frightful scenarios of violence and horror, which she projects onto the imaginary stage of her "theatre."

But her own words are, surely, the most eloquent evidence of her state of mind:

And now, with the later years of Antiquity, we enter upon that dark period of the Theatre's history, associated with its decadence and suppression.

I should begin by saying, that I cannot myself accede to the theory, now becoming fashionable, that the Theatre, even at the very *nadir* of its degeneracy, ever became a mere play-house of horrors, like the *Grand-Guignol* theatre lately opened in Paris.

Let me not be misunderstood. By this I mean simply to say, that it is inconceivable to me that some spark of the poet's original inspiration did not remain to animate even the debased productions of this period, with some measure of true artistry.

For endless horrors *were* acted there, to be sure—horrors so shockingly conceived, and so vividly pictured (by means of cunning machinery which included a kind of primitive kinematograph or phantasmagoric projector), that an Empire which had winked at the depraved excesses of a Nero and a Commodus, now sent a picked detachment of Prætorians to the remote colony in secret, charged with the utter extirpation of the Theatre from the face of the earth, by whatever means necessary.

By way of example, my poor darling here relates—or rather fabricates—some five or six synopses of mythological stories (none of which is in the least familiar to me), supposed to have been performed by her imaginary theatre. (These are in a kind of "free verse," as I believe the term is, with the occasional lapse into iambic regularity.)

Each tale is positively redolent with horror; I cannot bring myself to summarize here even the least appalling of them. They are the most eloquent—and most depressing—indices yet, of the retrogressive state of her mental health.

After these dreadful abstracts, she returns again to her theme of the fictitious theatre's extermination:

In this awful task the imperial powers succeeded, at least to all appearance: the Theatre was first driven underground (perhaps literally: see Halévy's essay, "Les Grottes d'Ovide"), before dying out altogether. (I do not count, of course, the feeble *simulacrum* of the Theatre which flourished for some years near Byzantium.)

This apparent extinction proved, however, to be but a transitional phase in the Theatre's *own* transformation or metamorphosis; one analogous to the state of the *pupa* before its emergence, in transfigured glory, from the *chrysalis*.

This period of rebirth, roughly coincident with the first stages of Western Europe's own Renascence, is characterized by a radical *erosion of distinctions:* the effacement, above all, of the dividing-line between Art and Life. In the Theatre, it became increasingly difficult to know, where *performance* ended, and *reality* began...

Whereas the Theatre had previously been content to generate mere (if astonishing) illusions—*representing* transformation by means of paint, pasteboard, rope and pulley, as well as coloured lantern-light, cast upon skins—it now stamped its changes indelibly upon bodies, through a diversity of new devices and techniques.

At the same time, there now appeared a decided attenuation, and ultimately *an utter dissolution*, of the boundary-line (the *membrane*, if I may so express it) separating player from spectator.

It becomes, indeed, a fair question to ask of the Theatre during this period: Had it an *audience* at all?

Were not all those who assembled beneath its roof in secret—those who stood, at the evening's commencement, upon the boards of the stage, as well as those who sprawled on the planks used as benches—equally subject to its laws? Were they not all, by the first light of dawn, equally likely to emerge from its doors in a transformed state, whether for good or ill?

Did not player and auditor now mingle their bodies without check or restraint—both together, and with the properties and implements of the Theatre—the better to effect more profound and irreversible changes?

There is much more, in the same vein.

Very obviously, a further period of confinement at Thornton House—probably a long one—will be necessary, upon our return to England. The roots of her illness are sunk more deeply than I had imagined. But the case is by no means hopeless. I have no doubt that with a more rigorous course of treatment she——

But she begins to stir, and murmurs my name, the poor darling. I must put the book away.

*

18 MAY (VERY LATE),

CONSTANTZA

When I wrote to you this morning, William, I spoke of the need to keep a close watch on Charlotte, for fear that, in her present condition, she might come to some harm.

My fears were, alas, too well justified: Charlotte's delusion has, this very night, led her into a highly dubious situation, to say the least.

Happily, my vigilance was rewarded, and I was able to lead her home without scathe either to body or honour. Furthermore, the worst of the crisis, I have reason to hope, may have passed...

But let me tell you what happened.

We went to bed, as has been our custom on this journey, at around nine o'clock. Bidding my wife good-night, I blew out the candle, and turned away, as if to sleep.

Then, after a quarter of an hour or so had passed, I counterfeited slumber by a very slow and regular breathing, while actually remaining wide awake, waiting to see if Charlotte would attempt another nocturnal expedition.

I had not long to wait. Not ten minutes after I had begun my feigned sleep, she slowly got out of bed and crossed to the door, frequently pausing as if to see if I stirred. Then I heard the creaking of the door, the sound of its closing again, and the soft patter of slippered feet scurrying away.

In an instant I was on my feet, struggling into my boots and jacket. I rushed from the room and hurried down the stairs and out of the hotel, where I looked wildly up and down the empty street. (My wife was much faster than I would have believed!)

Then I saw Charlotte, just vanishing into a doorway down the street, over which a wooden sign hung, in shape of a dragon.

I rushed to the spot, pushed open the door, and entered what proved to be a low, dingy tavern, in which some half-dozen grimy-faced men were drinking. Dully they stared at the strange foreigner who stood before them in striped pyjamas, panting and perspiring.

Ignoring them, I strode to the bartender (who wore a maddeningly knowing look on his wrinkled, seamed countenance), and demanded to know where my wife was.

At first, he affected not to understand English. Angrily I threw a few coins onto the bar, which he slid with a practised paw into the filthy folds of his apron. Then, touching his drink-reddened nose, he bid me follow him into the back of that loathsome den.

After leading me through a dark tangle of malodorous rooms and hallways, he pointed to a darkened doorway, the shadow of a smirk on his lips. With a last glare in his direction, I hastened down a pitch-black flight of stone steps, finally emerging into a dimly-lit cellar of vast size.

There I found Charlotte, on all-fours upon on a packed floor of earth, in her night-dress!

In astonishment and disgust, I cried out her name, at which she turned her head in surprise.

In one hand, she held a rusty trowel, with which she was engaged in an *excavation* of the cellar's earthen floor! All around her pathetically quadrupedal form gaped wide and deep holes, ringed about with untidy mounds of earth, as though they were the handiwork of a host of monstrous moles.

Roughly I lifted her to her feet, seized her by one soil-stained hand, and without saying a single word more, dragged her from that place. As we passed the barman, he directed a most hateful leer at my wife, who I thought *winked* in reply; but in this I was surely misled by the uncertain light.

Neither Charlotte nor I spoke a single word, until we were back in our bedroom.

Once there, I ordered her to wash her hands, then began to pace the room angrily, giving voice to my profound disappointment in her conduct in terms rather more violent, perhaps, than I should have wished, had I been less irate.

I believe that an unthinking out-burst even escaped my lips of which the essence, if not the exact phrasing, was: *I ought to have left her in the mad-house...*

At this she broke down completely: falling into my arms and deluging me with tears.

She had been "wrong, utterly wrong": this was the import of her sobbing cries as she buried her face in my breast, a kind of wild joy infusing her words.

"John," she said at length, looking up into my face, her lovely grey eyes wet with tears, "Oh John, will it be at all to my credit if I tell you that I realize now, how *very mistaken* I have been?"

Soothingly I stroked her disordered hair and wiped her shining cheeks. She was not to blame, I told her. The phantoms of the brain could seem exquisitely real, to one in her condition.

I am not sure, however, whether she heard me. *All this time*, she began to murmur as I clasped the poor child to my bosom once more. *All this time...* Here I felt her shake again with a fit of sobbing (which for a moment—only a moment!—I took for *laughter*).

"We have all the time in the world before us yet," I whispered, rather lamely I fear.

Then, desiring that she should betake herself to bed straightaway, after her late adventure (once more do I feel the loss of those opiates, very keenly!) I suggested that she might take a glass of wine. (I have bought one or two of the local vintages, which are by no means to be despised.)

With a childlike shyness, she replied that *she* would take a glass if *I* would. I laughed and told her to fetch the bottle and two glasses from the sideboard. To your *health*, I said to her as I lifted my glass, laying particular emphasis on the last word, at which she crimsoned, most charmingly, and looked at the floor.

She sleeps now, there on the bed, as I write this. The poor child is, no doubt, quite exhausted, after all of these night-time rambles.

For that matter, I can hardly keep my *own* eyes open; it must be very late indeed...

Hum—I am rather surprised to see that it is not yet midnight; astonishingly, the events of tonight have taken less than two hours to unfold.

Yet I am *very* tired, of a sudden.

My eyelids droop; the room begins to swim.

Indeed, I find that I can hardly hold the

*

Earlier, I likened that chapter of the Theatre's history coeval with the Renascence, to the transformation of an insectile *pupa* into its final form.

But (as it was given me to understand a mere three days ago) I realize that a far more just comparison would have been with the *larval* stage of such a creature. For I can see quite clearly now (it is indeed as though my head were flooded with a luminous radiance, so powerfully do I perceive the truth!) that the Theatre was then entering, into not the *ultimate*, but the *penultimate* phase of its being. That such a final, and unspeakably glorious, transmutation *has now occurred*, however, it is no longer possible for me to doubt.

It was previously believed that, for those wishing to become initiated into the Theatre's secrets, entering thereby into its eternal fellowship, it was necessary to act a novel transformation upon the stage of the original Theatre.

But this is no longer the case.

This is because it no longer makes sense to speak of the Theatre as being contained within a single building or fettered to a particular locality...

Rather, *the Theatre must now be understood as a vast, invisible net-work, distributed across the surface of this planet, a net-work whose members may never behold one another in the flesh, though all are bound inextricably together by an intricate web of unseen filaments...*

That the Theatre should have evolved into such a form, is surely not to be wondered at, in an age in which wire-borne whispers slither and race beneath the very seas, penetrating into the remotest corners of the globe...

(A vivid and exact map of the net-work, with its profusion of connective points *clearly indicated*, may easily be perceived by the initiate.)

Henceforth, I now understand, initiation into the Theatre's sublime mysteries may be achieved by the simple expedient of *acting a transformation at any of the net-work's countless nodes or cruxes, and*

subsequently recording the new episode in the Theatre's eternal Archive,
which has neither beginning nor end...

Let the following, then, be officially entered into record within
the Archive.

This transformation was acted upon 19 May, 1898, in Constantza,
Roumania:

THE RAPE OF CLIO

Who does not know Clio, a Goddess born,
Serene recorder of History?
One day as she sat, among her books,
A mortal dared interrupt her sacred labours.
To another mortal was she taken
In state of ignominious capture,
And shut up in a prison, a dungeon of light.
(Her books he gave unto the flames.)

Here would he touch her, with his mortal hands
And by other mortals suffer her to be touch'd.
Here would he watch her, with his staring eyes
And with droning tongue torment her sore
With words, words, endless flow of words.
But by a ruse she freed herself
And brought her captor to a distant shore,
Where 'twas ordained, her vengeance should unfold.

And now the hour of his reckoning has come.
First, she administers to him a sleeping-draught

Made from the juice of poppies crush'd.
Then, like a rainbow, she bends over his slumb'ring form
And touches him with fingers of silver,
Touches him in a thousand places,
Touches him all the night long,
While the knowing stars crawl in silence, far above.

At her Goddess-touch, shrivel away the fingers
That had filed her, one by one;
Then eyes and tongue fall away, ensanguined—
Ay, even those eyes that had stared and stared,
That tongue that would not be silent for an instant.
She touches too his loins, the seat of Priapus;
Then linger long her fingers at the place
Where Achilles' mother held her son

And lo! The rising cart of Phoebus
Now illumes a changéd thing.
What had been Man, has now become
One of the monstrous blind worms of the earth,
A mute and sexless creature.
Lamed and hobbled now, it can only crawl:
A being fit for tunnels, holes, and caves.
In dark earth shall it writhe and wawl—

But it stirs; it wakes.

For more Tales of the Weird titles
visit the British Library Shop (shop.bl.uk)

We welcome any suggestions, corrections or feedback you may have, and will
aim to respond to all items addressed to the following:

The Editor (Tales of the Weird), British Library Publishing,
The British Library, 96 Euston Road, London NW1 2DB

We also welcome enquiries through our Twitter account, @BL_Publishing.